For Cathy

THE
GLASSMAKER'S
WIFE

— A NOVEL —

LEE MARTIN

DZANC
BOOKS

2580 Craig Rd.
Ann Arbor, MI 48103
www.dzancbooks.org

First Edition: December 2022
Cover design by Matt Revert
Interior design by Michelle Dotter

ISBN: 9781950539482

Printed in the United States of America

10   9   8   7   6   5   4   3   2   1

Beauty is but a vain and doubtful good;
A shining gloss that vadeth suddenly;
A flower that dies when first it 'gins to bud;
A brittle glass that's broken presently:
A doubtful good, a gloss, a glass, a flower,
Lost, vaded, broken, dead within the hour.

—William Shakespeare, *The Passionate Pilgrim*

She Hath Done What She Could

HER NAME WAS ELIZABETH REED—BETSEY, to everyone who lived around Heathsville; Miss Betsey to Eveline Deal, the hired girl who adored her—but after the summer of 1844, she would be known as the glassmaker's wife, an odd match to Leonard Reed—the Mister, Eveline called him, the man who back in the winter told her he'd teach her his craft.

"If I had a daughter, Eveline, I'd want her to be just like you," he told her one day in January when she was glad for the warmth of the glasshouse. He showed her how to mix the sand and soda and lime. He put the crucible inside the furnace to cook. "I've been thinking I might like to teach you the art of glassmaking. A woman glassblower. What would you think of that?" He picked up an apothecary jar full of a white powder and gave it a shake. "Stay around until this batch is cooked, and I'll show you how to add enough antimony to take out the bubbles in the glass."

It was too much for her, this adoration. Not that she didn't want it—of course, she did; hadn't she watched with admiration as he made vases, tumblers, footed bowls, cream pitchers, sugar bowls, and wondered what it would be like?—but how would she feel if she had no knack for it and ended up disappointing the Mister? He stood before her now, not a handsome man, but instead a plain-faced sort who'd surely relied on his common sense and his hard work to get ahead in life. Somehow, he'd convinced Miss Betsey to marry him, but Eveline couldn't imagine how. He couldn't hold a candle to Miss Betsey's looks, and talk had it he was the one who insisted that she veil her bonnets so men wouldn't be able to see how beautiful she was. The veils, though—Eveline felt sure of this—only made her more desirable. Whenever Eveline saw Miss Betsey's face in shadow, she recalled from memory the curled eyelashes, the high cheekbones, the dainty nose, the full lips, the long white throat. Miss Betsey parted her hair in the middle and pulled it back into a chignon, which she held in place with an ivory comb. More than one man, Eveline imagined, hoped that he'd be fortunate enough to be in church, or a shop, or at a party, and see Betsey Reed remove her bonnet and turn her lovely face to him and smile and, oh Lord, then he'd find himself lost in the rapture.

The Mister was a rough-looking man with red hair wild in curls about his ears. Miss Betsey was always hard after him to cut those curls, but he didn't pay her any mind. He didn't have need of her opinion, Eveline heard him tell Miss Betsey one day. He was who he was, and at one point that had been good enough for her, and if it wasn't anymore, well, that would just have to be a bitter herb for her to chew on. There wasn't anything he could do about his prominent forehead that drew his eyes in and made him look apish—Eveline had seen newspaper cartoons of Irish immigrants (the Mister was of their number) that drew them like gorillas—or his nose with the large bump in it, or the fact that his left eye had a tendency to wander, turning out instead of following the right one when he adjusted his gaze to look on something. It gave one a most disconcerting feeling, Miss Betsey always said, but to Eveline, it was just the fact of the matter and nothing to concern her at all, for what she really noticed was the warmth of those blue eyes and the way they looked at her with what she could only describe as a fatherly love.

Her own father had gone away and taken up with a woman in Dark Bend, that swampy woodlands in the crook of the Embarras River south of St. Marie, where highway men and counterfeiters and horse thieves hid from the law. "Don't be a lowlife like him," her mother told her, and Eveline promised she wouldn't.

Since winter past, Eveline had earned money to give her mother by helping Miss Betsey with her chores: before and after school and all day long come summer. Oh, those long, dreamy days of summer. Eveline, whose own father had left her and her mother destitute—"Abandoned," her mother always said. "He just up and walked away."—liked being at the Reeds'. She liked being with the Mister in the glasshouse. She liked being with Miss Betsey in the house where they read letters from the lovelorn in *Godey's Lady's Book* when the chores were done, and Miss Betsey told her not to worry, she'd be pretty someday. She'd find her true love. Just wait and see.

"As pretty as you?" Eveline said.

"Yes, as pretty as me," said Miss Betsey.

Eveline knew she was lying. She wasn't a pretty girl at all—her face was too round, her eyes too pale, her nose too broad, not a girl any boy would take note of—but she couldn't help but be enchanted. She found herself dawdling with the evening chores just for the extra time it bought her at the Reeds', where she pretended that she remembered what it was to be a family.

But sometimes, Miss Betsey would say something that hurt her. Eveline wasn't but fifteen, and even though her mother told her not to be so sensitive, at times, though she wished otherwise, she couldn't help but take offense.

"You're a mooncalf," Miss Betsey said one morning as Eveline drew water from the cistern and let the rope slip from her hand and the bucket drop to the bottom. "Your head's in the clouds. You're dreaming of glory."

Eveline's cheeks burned with humiliation.

She was one of the Millerites, the believers who swore, come March, the Ascension would be at hand, and 1844 would be the last one lived on Earth. *The clouds at length are breaking*, she'd been singing just before she let go of the rope and knew the bucket was lost. *The dawn will soon appear.*

Sometimes Miss Betsey would snap at her because she scorched a shift she was ironing or she left the bread to bake too long, and Eveline would let herself hate her just a little, all along wishing that Miss Betsey would throw her arms around her neck and press her close and say she was sorry, oh, my precious girl, forgive me.

"Do your best," Eveline's mother told her when she brought her hurt home. "You can't expect to please everyone. Just do what you can and try not to take everything to heart."

She reminded Eveline of the story of Jesus, near the cross, and the woman who opened herself to scorn for wasting a precious ointment on his head. Jesus came to her defense. *She hath done what she could,* he said to those who complained. *She is come beforehand to anoint my body to the burying.* "There's a lesson for you in that," her mother told Eveline, who couldn't puzzle out exactly what she meant. All she knew was she wanted Miss Betsey to love her always and best.

If Betsey took a mind to, she could tell Eveline that it was all that Leonard lacked that first touched her heart. He was never a hale or beautiful man, not even when they were first starting out. Now they were nearing forty, and still she wanted to gather him into her arms and protect him from the people who gossiped about how they ever came together. If they'd seen him work with the glass, they'd understand exactly what she felt the first time she saw him at his craft—that he was a man who knew exactly the how-much and the what-for of everything that was fragile. Imagine a man with his lips to a clay blowpipe and on the other end a blob of melted glass heated up and glowing orange, just hanging there, waiting for the short puffs of air to inflate it, the twirling of the pipe to shape it. All of this had drawn her to him—that beautiful glass, and the delicate way he formed it. If he could do that, wouldn't a life with him always be gentle and beautiful and good?

But that winter of 1844, it turned out to be anything but. The trouble started in January when the Mister sold twenty acres of land to Tom McKinney, the man who owned forty acres to the south of them.

"What gives you the right?" Betsey asked one evening when the snow was falling outside, and they were sitting in rocking chairs close to the fire. "Without even a word to me? Is that how much I count to you?"

Leonard drew on his pipe and squinted at her through the curling smoke. The flame in the fireplace popped. He leaned forward and poked at the logs with a stoker. The applewood filled the cabin with the most delightful aroma, and had Betsey not been so distressed, she might have taken a moment, as she often did during the course of a day, to give thanks for her good fortune: a steady husband who provided for her, an established homestead not far from the broad road that ran from Palestine to Heathsville and then on down to Lawrenceville. Nothing to want for. Nothing to need. Why, then, did she sometimes find herself all at loose ends as if there were a hunger inside her she'd never be able to satisfy? Was she, as her mother always said, a filly who didn't know how to stay behind the gate? She was spirited. That's what Betsey decided. And now Leonard had sold twenty acres away from her, and she felt it well within her right to express her displeasure that she hadn't been consulted.

"Mrs. Reed." He tapped the stoker on the hearth. "It pains me to think you might not trust my judgment."

For more than a year, Leonard had been listening to stories of the Oregon Trail and the fertile land it could carry someone to if he had the gumption and the faith required to make it. All the way to the Pacific Ocean. All the way to the other side of the continent, he said. Imagine that.

Betsey let her hands drop into her lap. They were bound by the thread she'd been tatting. The thumb and forefinger of her right hand pinched the tortoiseshell shuttle from which the thread unwound. She'd been tying it into rings and chains with cow hitch knots as she tatted a lace table cover. She felt the thread dig into her skin, and she realized she was close to breaking it.

"I would think I'd have a right to a say in the matter." She slipped her left hand from the loop of thread. "After all, I *am* your wife." She paused a moment to let that word linger, and the only sound was the crackling of the logs in the fire and the creak of Leonard's rocking chair. "And surely you haven't forgotten how we came by this land."

Her father had made the farm a part of her dowry. It had been in her family long before she even had a glimpse of Leonard Reed. He'd come from his apprenticeship in Pittsburgh with the Bakewell, Page, and Bakewell glasshouse, and he'd set up shop in Heathsville. That's where Betsey had first seen him making glass. That's where she'd fallen in love with him, and then they were married—it seemed to happen just like that, in the tick of a heartbeat—and her father gave them the land, and Leonard was happy to move his glass furnaces there and become a gentleman farmer in the bargain. "Don't let that man do anything stupid with your land," her father told her, and then just days before the wedding he died, crushed in a pen by a mad bull. Betsey went to Leonard with that in her soul. She vowed she'd never let him disrespect her father's memory, and now look what had happened.

"Mrs. Reed, surely you know that you have absolutely no legal right in this matter." Leonard stood up from his rocking chair and knocked his pipe against the fireplace stones to empty it into the flames. "When you married me, you lost any right to control this property. That's the law, Mrs. Reed, and I'm afraid you have no choice but to abide by it."

"A body always has a choice." She kept her voice even. "Whether it be inside the law or out."

"The only rights you have, Mrs. Reed, are the ones I give you."

"We'll see about that," Betsey said.

The next morning, a Saturday, Miss Betsey told Eveline they were going to the village to shop for something special.

"Some pretty cloth," she said. "The winter's so dreary. It's time for a splash of color. I'm thinking something purple. For a new dress, Eveline. We'll sew it together. What do you think?"

Eveline was glad to see Miss Betsey's good mood. "I think that would be divine," she said, trying out that word, *divine*, a word she'd often heard Miss Betsey use. "I think you'd be very pretty in purple."

The snow had stopped, and they walked along the broad road with little trouble. Eveline carried the market basket. Miss Betsey hummed a merry tune. At one point, she reached out and took Eveline's hand, and they walked along like that the rest of the way to Heathsville. Though they each wore mittens, Eveline thought the feel of Miss Betsey's hand in hers . . . well, she thought it simply divine.

Inside Ethan Delz's Dry Goods, Miss Betsey looked over some fabrics and found a purple wool that she fancied.

"Aren't we lucky?" she said to Eveline, and Eveline agreed that they were.

Finally, Mr. Delz was free to help them.

"May I ask your impression?" Miss Betsey asked him. "Do you find this cloth flattering?" She draped a bit of the purple wool across her arm at the wrist to better observe it next to her bare hand. "To my skin tone, I mean. Do you, Mr. Delz? I'm thinking of making a dress. Is this color something you find attractive?"

"It's a good weave, Mrs. Reed." Ethan Delz wasn't a shy man. He was, to Eveline's estimation, quite wonderful. He was a graceful man with beautiful hands. His long fingers could sweep up a pencil, wield a pair of shears, hold a book, tip his hat, and sometimes Eveline dared imagine him fitting his hands to her waist and pulling her close. Now, he placed his hand on the fabric where it lay across Betsey's wrist, and

Eveline felt a pang of jealousy. Of course a man like Mr. Delz would have no interest in the likes of her. "The color charms you," he said, and Eveline took note of the way he held Miss Betsey's gaze.

Eveline wasn't a stupid girl. She'd seen the way that he and Miss Betsey had been exchanging flirtatious looks since Christmas: among the fiddle playing and dancing of a shivaree party, across the counter whenever she came into his store.

"It flatters you," he said before moving his hand from her wrist, to her hand, and her fingers, before finally lifting away. "Oh, yes. I'd say it flatters you very much."

∞

Evenings, Eveline helped Miss Betsey cut the pieces and stitch them together. Sometimes Miss Betsey did the work herself while Eveline finished her chores. Then, when the supper dishes had been scrubbed and put away in the step-back cupboard and there wasn't much else that required Eveline's attention, Betsey asked her to read the letters from the lovelorn that appeared in *Godey's Lady's Book*. They were stories of secret or furtive loves, loves unrequited. Listening to them as she sewed, Betsey felt her heart tear, caught up as she was in all those lives full of anguish and yearning. She could tell that Eveline felt similarly affected. She read in a hushed voice as if she were afraid that the Mister, who was generally out at his furnaces, might somehow hear her and take objection. From time to time at the end of a sentence, she took in a deep breath and held it before letting it out with a sigh. *Mmm, mmm, mmm,* she sometimes muttered. *My, oh my.*

One evening, she read a letter from an extremely lovelorn swain who signed himself, "A Very Bad Case."

"You should see my Mary," the letter began. "When she fixes her radiant orbs upon my face, I seem to be in a blaze of light; her ringlets are tightly twisted around my heart." Here, Eveline took a breath. She thought of the way Mr. Delz had touched the purple wool that day in his store. Keep reading, Miss Betsey said, and Eveline did. "Her complexion is, to me, more beautiful than the finest miniature; her tiny feet are pressing on my heart; her small white hand, were it to touch mine, would send thrills through me; her teeth are like rows of Orient pearls; and oh! to touch her lips 'twould be heaven—I dare not continue; my feelings now are too deep for utterance."

Eveline closed the *Godey's Lady's Book* and used it to fan her face. "It must be something to feel as deeply as that," she said. "Do you think these letters are from real people?" She let the book lie in her lap. She smoothed her hand over the front cover which had a drawing of a woman sitting in the cradle of a crescent moon among the clouds. Her gown rippled across her hips and legs. One shoulder was bare. Her long hair trailed down her back and curled around the moon. "Do you, Miss Betsey? Do you think people really have lives like that? You know what I mean, lives of longing?"

"I think there are many cases like that. Very bad cases." Betsey looked up from her sewing and let her gaze stray to the window, hearing, as she had, the door to the glasshouse banging shut. She knew Leonard was closing the smokehouse lock he kept on the door, and soon he'd be coming up to the house, snow dusting the crown of his slouch hat and his shoulders. "Very bad cases, indeed," she said.

Then Leonard was in the cabin, and he brought with him the smell of the coal from the furnaces and the unpleasant odor of the elements he used to put color into the glass, or to keep color out of it—some of those elements came all the way from China on ships—or to thin the pockets of air that sometimes got caught in the melted glass, and Betsey felt her heart shrivel. How nice it had been there by the fire with Eveline reading that letter, but that was all gone in an instant. He tromped in and the snow melted from his boots onto the plank floor. He stood by the fire and beat his hands together. The loud claps startled Betsey, and she stuck herself with a needle.

"Oh, look at you," she said to Leonard. "Just look."

He stopped with his hands held in the air, as if he'd been caught at something. "What?" he said. "What did I do?"

The nail of the pointer finger on his left hand was black from where he'd mashed it with a mallet. To Betsey, it was the ugliest thing she could imagine. She recoiled from the thought of his hands on her shoulders when he turned her to him in their bed. The pads of his fingers were callused; the skin on his palms was rough with thatched lines and scabbed with cuts and blistered with burns.

"That's your problem," she said. "You never know. You just blunder about, knocking into this or that and never seeing the mess you've made."

Leonard looked around him, turned from side to side, his eyes following the path he'd made into the cabin and to the fire. "That snow water?" he finally said, pointing now to the floor. "That's what's got you in a tizz?" He said to Eveline, "Will you please mop that up? Lord forbid that I track up Mrs. Reed's floor. You'd think I'd killed someone."

Eveline got busy with a rag. She got down on her knees and sopped up the water from the floor and wrung it out into a pan.

"It's not the water on the floor," Betsey said to Leonard. "You stupid, stupid man."

"What is it, then?"

"It's the way you treat me. The way you didn't even bother to talk to me about the acres you sold to Tom McKinney. Like I wasn't worth the bother. Do we really have to go over this all again?" Betsey stood, the purple wool clutched to her chest. "And do you want Eveline to hear our troubles? Really, Mr. Reed, is that what you want?"

He seemed to notice the purple wool for the first time. "Is that a new material, Mrs. Reed?"

His voice was softer now, and he glanced over his shoulder at Eveline, perhaps taking what Betsey had said to heart, perhaps imagining the stories the girl might tell once she was away from them. For an instant, Betsey felt her heart unclench, so contrite Leonard appeared to be, but there was still the fact of that land sold and the anger it brought up in her.

"I'm making a dress," she said.

"Are you now?" said Leonard. He came down with a coughing spell. He bent at the waist, and she heard the rattle in his chest. Finally, he squeaked out another few words. "Well . . . won't . . . that . . . be nice?"

Eveline was thinking of Mr. Delz and his beautiful hands. Ethan Delz and the way he stroked the purple wool with his fingers that day in his store. Ethan? Could she call him that? She imagined herself saying his name—*Why, Ethan, for you to take my hand would be divine. For you to kiss my lips. For you to hold me close. For you to* . . . . She dared not continue; her feelings now were too deep for utterance.

"Yes, it will be, Mr. Reed." Miss Betsey held the purple wool across the front of her, pressed the ball of her right foot into the floor, and made a dainty turn of her ankle. "It will be very, very nice."

Receive Your Sight

Spring came, and the promised day of the Ascension passed, leaving Eveline feeling all at loose ends. March went by as regular as clockwork, and folks who were supposed to know started looking at the scripture again and refiguring. Finally, word came from Exeter, New Hampshire: the Reverend Samuel S. Snow promised that Christ would come on October twenty-second.

Did Eveline wish it so? She did and she didn't. The preachers made it all sound so wonderful, going up to live forever in Heaven, but what about the living she'd never have a chance to do here on Earth?

Then, come summer, Leonard Reed sold a heifer cow to a man named Heinz Ernst, and Betsey took that as more evidence that Leonard was getting ready to sell the place entirely and move them farther west. There were opportunities in the territories, he told her. He'd talked about it all through the winter, and now summer was here, and Heinz Ernst was leading the cow, a red roan milking Shorthorn, out of the pasture.

He was passing the house when Betsey came out into the dooryard to shake something from an apron. She raised her arms, and the apron billowed up into the air. Heinz stopped to watch. Then Betsey brought her arms down hard, and the apron snapped until it was hanging straight down.

"Dat," Heinz told people later, "vas ven it happened."

Milk started leaking from the red roan's teats and didn't stop until Betsey tied her apron around her waist and went back into the cabin. By that time, the red roan's bag was empty, and from that day on, it never gave a drop of milk, which, according to Leonard Reed, wasn't his concern and as far as he considered it, the sale was a good faith sale, and that was that.

But Heinz claimed that Betsey had put a curse on that red roan—a witch's curse. For some time there'd been talk of Betsey and her odd ways. She'd put a spell on a banty hen once by holding it on the ground and using a stick to draw a line in the dirt a little ways in front of it. When she let go of that hen, it stayed where it was, its breast and beak on the ground as if all the life had left it, mesmerized by that line in the dirt. Finally, Betsey erased the line with the toe of her shoe, and the hen got to its feet and staggered away.

Just a little trick, Betsey told those who'd watched. Just something her father had taught her.

But it was enough to start people talking. Betsey Reed was a mysterious woman. She wore bonnets with black lace veils to shadow her face, and she was known to be able to tell your fortune by feeling the bumps on your head. It was said she came from Gypsy blood, and if that wasn't troubling enough, she wrote her letters with her left hand—a sure sign, some folks said, that she was in cahoots with the Devil. So whenever something out of the ordinary happened, more than one person's first inclination was to say it was on account of Betsey Reed.

A milk cow going dry was one thing, but the death of a child was something else altogether.

Not long after the incident with the cow, Heinz Ernst's young son, Jacob, died. He died not long after spending the day with the Reeds. Although Heinz Ernst had forbidden him to go there, Jacob slipped away across his father's fields because he liked Miss Betsey and the little tricks she showed him—how to find honeycomb in a hollow tree, how to catch a bird by first sprinkling salt on its tail feathers, how to dowse for water with a divining rod. Who knew what she might have done to cause his fever and the twitches and jerks and fits that kept coming until dawn when Jacob was dead.

Eveline, upon hearing the ugly gossip about Miss Betsey, came to her defense.

"It's horrible, Miss Betsey," she said. "It's just evil people spreading rumors. It makes my heart hurt for you."

"I'm used to the things people say about me." Miss Betsey put her arms around Eveline and gave her a hug.

All her life, people had been quick to story about her because she was the kind of woman who invited it. Her mother had been a healer, a stooped-over woman who scoured the woods and pastures for ginseng root, pokeweed, burdock, yarrow, goldenseal. She made poultices and potions and cured folks of their ailments. Some said she could witch you if she wanted, a rumor that took legs after a man she'd been doctoring for a catarrh in his lungs up and died. Then there was her father who taught her to hypnotize chickens, and once she began to grow into her womanhood and he saw what a beautiful girl she was, he insisted that she veil her face when she was out in public, a practice she continued even after she was married. She came from these oddities, but a witch? Ridiculous.

"Don't fret now," she told Eveline. "It's just talk."

So Eveline kept moving through the summer days though she felt agitated so much of the time over how things were threatening to change. Who knew where her father was and whether he was ever coming back? And now the Mister was talking about moving west, and there were those rumors about Miss Betsey. Who could say what might be waiting just down the road?

The promised date of the Ascension in March had come and gone and she was still there, still working for Miss Betsey, working all the day and into evening now that school was out; still making biscuits and churning butter and carding wool and carrying water in from the well; still scrubbing dishes and ironing clothes; still spending time with the Mister in the glasshouse learning what she could; still helping with the milking whenever he asked her to, as he did one day toward the end of June.

He was, he told her, about to make a trip to St. Louis to investigate some land opportunities, and he'd need to make sure the milking was done.

"Morning and evening," he said. "You know just how to do it, don't you, Eveline?"

"I do, sir," she said. "You know you can count on me."

They stood inside the glasshouse where the Mister was stoking the fire in the furnace.

"I know I can," he said. "You're a dependable girl." He took off his leather gloves and dropped them on a bench. He looked at Eveline and smiled. "It's a good thing we didn't lose you back in March." For a moment, she thought he was making fun of her and her belief in the Ascension. Then he said, "I wish I had your devotion. Mrs. Reed says I've got my sights set too much on the land. I envy the way you can hold faith in the great beyond."

Eveline never wanted to fall short of his high estimation of her. She assured him once again that she would make sure the milking got done.

He left a few days later, just after the Fourth of July. He left before first light that morning, intending to travel to St. Louis by coach. He'd be gone from home a week or more, and Eveline understood that she was to do the milking, which she did that morning. Then in the afternoon, Miss Betsey told her she could go home.

"I won't be needing you the rest of the day," she said.

"Ma'am?"

"I said shoo."

The locusts buzzed in the chestnut trees behind the granary. A cowbell around the neck of one of the Shorthorns clanged somewhere from the pasture. A trickle of sweat trailed down Eveline's nose.

"But the Mister said I was to milk twice a day," she said.

"I'll take care of the milking," said Miss Betsey. "Mercy! You and Mr. Reed must think I'm helpless."

Eveline shook her head. "No, ma'am. It's just that the Mister . . ."

She didn't know how to say it, that she loved how kind the Mister was to her, always polite when he asked her to fetch him something, treating her not like a hired girl at all, but more like—dare she think it?—a daughter. Sometimes he brought her rock candy from Mr. Delz's Dry Goods. Last Christmas, the Reeds gave her an embroidered handkerchief, and she could tell from the way the Mister looked at her, his eyes shining, that the gift had been his idea. A beautiful linen handkerchief embroidered with a border of red roses. *Take care not to lose it*, Miss Betsey told her. *It's hand-stitched. From a shop in St. Louis. You don't know how lucky you are.*

Maybe she didn't, but now she felt certain she shouldn't leave the milking to Miss Betsey.

So that evening, Eveline found herself, after supper, walking through the woods to the Reeds'.

When she got there, she saw the Shorthorn heifers come up from the pasture to the stable of their own accord. Their bags were heavy with milk, and they stretched their necks, noses in the air, as they bellowed from unease.

The door to the cabin was shut tight. Banty hens pecked at the ground in the dooryard. Eveline couldn't stand to hear the Shorthorns' bellowing any longer, so she went to the stable where she found the three-legged stool and the oaken bucket, and she went out into the feedlot to get to work.

That's where she was when she heard the door to the cabin creak open and then Miss Betsey saying to someone, "It's a sin is what it is. It's just a horrendous sin."

"It happens." Eveline heard a man's voice answer, and at first she couldn't name the speaker. She was on her stool, her cheek pressed into the haunch of one of the Shorthorns. She stopped her milking to listen. She was to the north side of the stable, out of view of the cabin, and she was afraid to move, afraid because she knew Miss Betsey wouldn't like it if she were to catch her eavesdropping. The man said, "Now here we are, and I can tell you I don't mind a bit. Do you?"

"No, I don't," said Miss Betsey in a honeyed voice, low and sweet. "I can't say I mind at all."

The man went on. "I was glad to get away from the store. Not a bad night for a walk."

Ethan Delz. Eveline recognized the voice now, and she knew it was Mr. Delz who'd come to call on Miss Betsey. Now the two of them were talking in cozy tones.

Miss Betsey said, "Can you believe Mr. Reed's run off to St. Louis and left me all by myself?"

"His loss," said Mr. Delz.

Eveline knew she should announce herself. Step out from behind the stable, toting the bucket of milk to store in crocks in the springhouse, as if she had no idea that Miss Betsey was entertaining company, but really it seemed too late for that now. Miss Betsey wouldn't take kindly to the fact that she'd disobeyed her about the milking, nor would Miss Betsey like that she'd been listening to her conversation with Mr. Delz. But what kept Eveline frozen more than anything else was the fact that she understood that Miss Betsey was being flirtatious, and Mr. Delz was playing along, and she wondered whether somewhere in that game things might get serious. Eveline waited, feeling like she was on the brink of knowing something, feeling like she did when she read the letters from the lovelorn in *Godey's Lady's Book*. A love affair.

In spite of her love of God and her belief in the Ascension, she couldn't get those letters from the lovelorn out of her head. *'Twould be heaven.* It was a shameful thing, but there it was, the truth—she was still tethered to the earth beneath her feet, unable to escape her own desires.

"Don't you have earth hunger like Mr. Reed?" Miss Betsey's voice was playful now. "Aren't you looking for the next good thing?"

"Oh, I imagine I've already found it."

Then there was nothing. No words at all. Only the warbling of the swallows as they swooped in graceful arcs toward the stable.

Eveline couldn't stand the quiet, couldn't bear not knowing what was happening in the dooryard. She got up from her stool and crept to the corner of the stable. She peeked out and, in the gloaming, the light fading, she wasn't sure what she was seeing. Had Miss Betsey just moved her hand from Mr. Delz's shoulder? Had he just straightened from leaning toward her? Had they been kissing? Eveline couldn't say for certain. No, she couldn't say at all, but as time went on, and her imagination had room to run, she began to feel certain that she knew exactly what had happened that night when she'd come to do the milking, and what was more, it filled her with a tremendous rage. She felt the fool because Miss Betsey told her she'd be pretty one day, and little by little, as she read the letters from the lovelorn in the *Godey's Lady's Book*, she'd let herself believe she might find herself in love with a man like Mr. Delz. But that hadn't been the truth of things at all. Men wanted women like Miss Betsey and not mooncalf girls like her. Eveline felt certain that Miss Betsey had known that all along, and she waited for the Mister to come home to see what she might tell him.

Mr. Reed, You Need to Trust Me

THE MISTER CAME BACK FROM St. Louis feeling puny—an upset in his stomach—and Eveline couldn't bring herself to tell him what she thought she knew about Miss Betsey and Mr. Delz.

"Did you keep the milking caught up?" the Mister asked her, and she told him yes, she had. "Good girl," he said. "I brought you something from St. Louis."

It was a comb for her hair—a comb of tortoiseshell with cameos carved from coral along the top.

"The woman's face in the cameos reminded me of you." They were in the glasshouse where he was mixing antimony with sulfur in a glass of water. He drank it down. In the proper amounts, the dose could soothe his membranes. "You wear the comb in your hair as an ornament," he said. "I imagine Mrs. Reed can show you how."

He was making beveled glass for a hand mirror that he wanted to give to Miss Betsey. He'd found the most elegant silver frame that needed a new glass.

"Do you think she'll like it?" he asked Eveline, showing her the ornate scrolled silver.

"Oh, I'm sure she will," Eveline said.

The Mister's eyes were filled with so much love for Miss Betsey that Eveline knew she'd never be able to tell him about the night Mr. Delz came to call.

Each morning, Miss Betsey sat at the table, admiring herself in the mirror the Mister had made her, and Eveline wondered if she might be considering how pleasing Mr. Delz would find her. Finally, Eveline couldn't bear to watch the way Miss Betsey held the mirror this way and that, taking in her face from every angle.

She recalled how after Mr. Delz left that evening, she finished the milking and brought the oaken bucket to the cabin. There were two teacups and saucers on the table, a parcel of paper tied up with a snatch of string, and a candle nearly burnt down to nothing. A little breeze was up through the door Eveline had left open, and the candle flame flickered and then went out.

"I've brought the milk," she said. "Have you crocks to pour it in so I can take them to the springhouse?"

Betsey said, "I told you I'd do the milking. Didn't I tell you that?"

Her voice had a bite to it, but Eveline didn't back down. "Those heifers were heavy with milk," she said. "Poor things. The Mister . . ."

Before Eveline could go on to remind Betsey that Mr. Reed had asked her to do the milking, Betsey said with a laugh and a wave of her hand. "The Mister, the Mister. Is that who's on your mind? The Mister. You'd think the two of you were sweet on each other."

To recall that now while Miss Betsey preened before her mirror was too much for Eveline. She said, "I saw you out there with Mr. Delz the other night."

Betsey lowered the hand mirror. She looked at Eveline for a good while. Then she said, "And what did you see?"

Eveline faltered and nearly lost her nerve. "I heard the two of you talking. It was nearly dark."

"Mr. Delz was kind enough to bring me a parcel of salt." So that had been the paper on the table beside the teacups and the candle. "He forgot to put it in my basket when I was in his shop this afternoon."

"You were talking about the Mister," Eveline said in a shaky voice. "You and Mr. Delz. I heard you."

"Oh, and what were we saying? Do tell me, Eveline."

"Sweet things. Things you shouldn't have said."

"Don't be silly, dear." Miss Betsey reached out and caught Eveline by the wrist. Eveline felt the sharp nails dig into her skin. Miss Betsey held her for what seemed like a very long time. Then she let her go. Eveline moved away from her to stand at the hearth. "We were talking about what I forgot, dear girl. We were talking about salt."

Dear girl! Said with such exaggeration to make it plain that Miss Betsey thought her anything but dear. *Stupid girl* was more like it. Stupid for trying to threaten Miss Betsey. Stupid for coming back to do the milking. Stupid for eavesdropping. Stupid for saying anything about what she'd heard. Eveline felt certain that Miss Betsey and Mr. Delz had been talking about much more than salt, but there were the fresh punctures on her wrist from those sharp fingernails, those dots of blood to warn her to keep what she'd heard and seen to herself.

Eveline knew she was too bold for her own good. "I could tell the Mister, you know."

That's when Miss Betsey hurled the hand mirror at her. It struck the stones of the hearth, and the glass shattered.

"Oh, now look at what you've caused me to do." Miss Betsey was up from the table, frantic now. "My beautiful mirror that Mr. Reed made for me. Quick, pick up the pieces and bury them lest I have bad luck." Eveline hesitated. "Now!" Miss Betsey stamped her foot, and Eveline got to work cleaning up the mess and taking the glass pieces outside to bury in the dirt behind the granary.

Miss Betsey's temper scared her. She never said another word to her about Mr. Delz, nor did she mention what she'd witnessed to the Mister.

Then the Mister took to his bed. He came down on a Thursday morning in August when the corn was firing for want of rain and the locusts were chirring in the woods. Not a breath of air in the house and flies making a nuisance of themselves. Not a day anyone would want to feel ill, particularly not on the morning he'd meant to blow the candlesticks he'd promised to his darling Betsey for their anniversary, which was quickly approaching. After breakfast, he'd gone out to the glasshouse, but he hadn't been there long before he was back, a horrible pain in his stomach.

"Run, fetch Mr. Logan," Betsey told Eveline. "Shoo. Don't dawdle. Can't you see the Mister is in need of doctoring?"

Eveline got as far as the door sill, where she turned back to watch Miss Betsey ease the Mister down onto the featherbed mattress.

"Lord, have mercy," he said to Betsey. "I'm all broke out with chills."

"I'll get you something." She laid the back of her hand to his forehead and then stroked his face. "Some sassafras tea to soothe you until Mr. Logan can get here. I've sent Eveline to fetch him."

It was a half mile through the woods to Mr. Logan's apothecary in Heathsville, and even though Eveline could see that the Mister was badly afflicted, she'd yet to venture out. Something told her that once she left, she'd never be able to come back to the way things had been.

Then Betsey turned and spotted her. "What did I tell you?" she clapped her hands together. "Ugly girl! Go!"

Eveline was running then, snaking down the deer path that trailed through the woods, sapling branches snapping at her face, the sting of Miss Betsey's words, *Ugly girl,* still hot in her cheeks. She *was* an ugly girl. But what did that matter? Come October, she'd be with the saints in Heaven, and where would Miss Betsey be? Left behind, that's where. Cast out. Gone to the fire. Still, for her to have said what she did. *Ugly girl.*

The smell of wood smoke tanged the air—fires in the fields where new settlers were clearing land and burning brush. Thunks of ax blows, the calls of *Watch it now. Here it comes. One more cut and we've got it.*

Then the crash of the tree and the earth trembling beneath Eveline's feet. What she wouldn't give to just keep running, to get as far away from Miss Betsey as she could, but the Mister was bad sick, and he needed Mr. Logan. So Eveline went on through the woods, the light of the clearing coming fast to her as she neared the broad road into Heathsville.

In the cabin, meantime, Betsey carried the tea to the Mister and begged him to drink it.

"Not sure I can choke it down," he told her.

"Try," she said. "Oh, won't you please try?" She held the cup to his lips. "Go on now. Mr. Reed, you need to trust me."

❦

Mr. Logan was mashing lavender with his pestle when Eveline Deal ran into the apothecary. She could smell the herb right off, and it was so wonderful she stood a minute, just breathing it in, along with the other dried herbs hanging from the rafters: sage, thyme, chamomile, horehound. A ribbon had come undone, and her hair fell over her shoulders. Her face was all a-sweat, and her breath was coming hard and fast.

"It's Mr. Reed," she finally said. "He's in trouble."

"Leonard Reed?" Mr. Logan let the pestle drop into the mortar. He had on a black wool waistcoat over a white linen shirt with no collar. A tall stalk of a man with narrow shoulders. A caved-in face, shaved clean, with deep lines from his nostrils down to the corners of his mouth. "What's wrong with Mr. Reed?"

"Sick." Eveline pressed her hand to her breastbone, trying to catch her breath. "Awful sick."

Mr. Logan dusted his hands and grabbed up a case by its brass handles. Eveline knew what was inside: glass bottles, most of them hand-blown by the Mister, glass bottles with squared corners and covered with fruitwood caps—tinctures of opium, cannabis, castor, camphor. All manner of cathartics, emetics, caustics, and laudanum. When folks were ill thereabouts, they eased themselves with teas and poultices and compresses and infusions and decoctions. When they were as bad off as Mr. Reed, they sent for James Logan.

"We'll take my buggy," he said to Eveline. "Step fast, girl."

❧

The door to the cabin stood free from its latch, and Mr. Logan stomped right in and set his case on the floor beside the Mister's bed.

Eveline lingered in the dooryard, scared to be inside the cabin where urgent doings were afoot.

Mr. Logan's voice was tight with worry. "Lord sakes, Betsey. How long's he been like this?"

"Since breakfast this morning," Miss Betsey said.

"Have you given him anything for it?"

"No, sir."

"Nothing at all? Not even a little sassafras tea?"

Miss Betsey was standing at the foot of the bed, her back to the door. Eveline saw her shake her head. "I tried, but he couldn't get it down."

The teacup sat on the plank table along with the breakfast dishes Eveline had yet to scrub. She could see the cup from where she stood. A porcelain cup with red roses painted on it and a gilt band around its rim. There'd once been a saucer to match it. Eveline remembered Miss Betsey sipping from the cup one day when she was trying to decide which bonnet to wear into town. Eveline said she preferred the green straw poke to the black coal scuttle. "The blocked crown on the black one hides your face, particularly with the veil, and makes you look . . ." She started to use the word "severe," but then caught herself, knowing it was nothing Miss Betsey would take to. Eveline searched for another word, but all that came to her—"heartless," "cold-blooded," "harsh"—

were no better, and in the silence that lingered uncomfortably long, Miss Betsey understood quite well what had first come to Eveline's mind and exactly what the girl thought of her. Then Eveline said, "It makes you look so alone."

"I feel that way so much of the time." Miss Betsey lifted the cup from its saucer. Eveline felt a shiver come over her, aware as she was that the missus was speaking to her from the heart. "Lonely," she said. "All alone in this world." Her hands started to tremble, and just like that she dropped the saucer and it broke into shards on the floor. "Oh, now look what you've made me do. Just look."

That's what Eveline was doing now, watching, unsure whether to go into the cabin or whether to stay where she was.

She came, then, to see a most curious thing. There at her feet, as if tossed by the wind, lay a scrap of paper that looked familiar, a paper like a piece of an old book leaf that had been considerably smoked. She remembered that morning, as she was carrying a pan of biscuits to the table, she saw Miss Betsey reach between two glass tea plates that sat in the step-back cupboard. She drew out a paper folded and tied with string. She set it on the cupboard and undid the knot. Then she took up a pinch of white powder between her fingers and dropped it into the Mister's morning coffee.

It took Leonard Reed four days to die. Betsey stayed by his bed, easing him as much as she could. He told her he still intended to make her that set of candlesticks and would just as soon as he was back on his feet.

"I know you will," she said. "Now you just need to rest."

She thought of how grand it had been the first time she'd seen him blow glass—those gentle puffs of air as he turned the pipe. Now toward the end—those four days of his misery—his breath shortened until finally there was one puff more and then nothing.

By nightfall of the fifth day, the coroner had assembled a jury for an inquest into the cause of his death.

Eveline wore her best dress to the inquest. When it came her time to speak, she looked Miss Betsey straight in the eye, wishing she could say, *Who's ugly now?*

But what she really said was, "I saw her go to the cupboard and take a paper from between the tea plates. I saw her put some white powder in the Mister's coffee. Then later I found the scrap of paper in the dooryard. Someone had tried to burn it."

Did she think Mrs. Reed had tried to dispose of that paper by lighting it afire?

"I can't say," said Eveline. "I really can't. I've told you all I know."

"Wasn't nothing but salt," Betsey said when she was allowed to speak in her defense. "Mr. Reed always took a pinch of salt in his coffee."

But Mr. Logan's testimony focused on the scorched paper Eveline had found in the dooryard. "That paper? Yes, that's the sort of paper I wrap arsenic in. Do I remember Betsey Reed coming in to buy any? I do not, but I can tell you this: I feel certain that she did, perhaps under the cover of some sort of disguise. When I left the cabin that night, I knew there wasn't much I could do for the poor man. To my mind, he died from arsenic poisoning."

After a short deliberation, the coroner and his jury decided there was enough evidence to arrest Betsey Reed and charge her with murder.

"All because of her," Betsey said when the verdict was made known. She pointed at Eveline. "All because of what she said."

"I told the truth," said Eveline, but her voice was barely a whisper, and in the midst of all the stir and clamor no one took note of it. They'd heard her say what they'd wanted her to say, and nothing much mattered after that.

Except to Eveline, who lay that night, trembling in her bed, unaccustomed to her word counting for so much. She'd told what she'd seen. Now she wished she could take back her words. She wished she'd never come forward. *I'm just a girl,* she wanted to tell the jury. *I'm just a mooncalf.*

She lay awake long into the night, wishing that she could go to Miss Betsey and tell her she forgave her for calling her an ugly girl, wishing she could tell her she loved her still.

What Hath God Wrought!

EVELINE LOVED JESUS BECAUSE SHE believed he loved her first, loved her when no one else did. No one save her mother, and she didn't count because mothers were supposed to love their children. Mothers didn't have any choice. She'd told Eveline not to be a lowlife like her father, so she testified in front of the coroner's jury the way a stand-up sort of person would do. She said exactly what she'd seen.

A scrap of paper. White powder. The Mister's coffee.

"I can hardly believe it," Tom McKinney said to Eveline the evening after the inquest. He lived across the pasture down a grassy lane. A man just now twenty. A bachelor man whose mother died birthing him. He carried the things of his and his father's that needed mending to Eveline's mother and paid her for the favor. Sometimes, like tonight, he stayed to supper. "Betsey Reed killed her husband. And it was your word that put her in the jailhouse."

"The world's getting stranger and stranger." Eveline's mother laid out the log-plank table: tin plates and cups and spoons carved from walnut wood. "People sending words over those telegraph wires. Something unnatural about that."

"That Morse fella," Tom said. "Know the first message he sent? 'What hath God wrought!' Comes right out of the Bible. Do you think they'll hang Betsey Reed?"

"I don't want to hear any more talk about that woman," said

Eveline's mother. Dessie Deal could have a sharp edge to her when the circumstances required. "If anyone had the right to kill her man, it was me, and you can see I resisted the temptation."

Tom laughed at that. "I imagine Mr. Deal is grateful."

"If there's anything to be thankful for up there in Dark Bend," said Eveline. "He'll be sorry when the Ascension comes."

"Do you really believe that story?" Tom asked.

"Yes, I believe it," said Eveline. "I believe it with all my heart."

Her mother moved away from the table and went to the cooking fire to see how supper was coming.

"Stew's about ready to eat," she said. "Same with the pone. Better fetch a crock of butter from the springhouse."

"We'll go for it," said Tom. "Eveline and me."

They walked out past the smokehouse and the vegetable patch, where there were still tomatoes on the vines and green pumpkins and white long-necked squash. Eveline opened the low door to the little house built from sandstone over the spring and stepped inside. The cool air pleased her. She started to dip her hands down into the cold water running through the trough where they kept their milk and butter, but then Tom took her by her shoulders and pulled her to him. He bent his head, drawing her closer until she understood that he meant to kiss her on the mouth.

She tried to squirm away, but he held onto her. She couldn't believe that he'd want her, just a girl and nothing to look at. "Let go, Tom." She beat her fists against his chest. The coarse material of his linsey-woolsey shirt scraped the sides of her hands. "It can't be me you want."

He let her go. "Why can't it be?"

"I'm naught but a girl, Tom McKinney."

"Coming on sixteen. Lots of girls have jumped the broomstick by then."

She took up the crock of butter from the trough, the slick stone cold on her hands. Outside, the storm crows were making their mournful cries, calling for rain. The air was wonderfully cool in the springhouse, and had she been alone she might have lingered a while. But she wasn't alone. A man had tried to kiss her, and she was antsy to leave. She couldn't think about what Tom had done. It was too twisty of a thing to think on.

"You know what it cost me to testify about what I saw?" she finally said.

"You just told the truth. Where's the wrong in that?"

"It cost me the money I was making being Miss Betsey's hired girl. Now what will Mother and I do?"

She didn't tell him the rest. Her testimony had cost her the company of the one who'd always made her feel like she might have a chance for happiness in this world. Miss Betsey and those wonderful days of reading *Godey's Lady's Book* opened up the land of romance and made Eveline feel that she had a right to it, that one day a gentleman would come to court her, and then her life would never be the same.

Now, without Miss Betsey, that world seemed distant and closed to the likes of Eveline.

Tom reached for her again. She made a quick step toward the daylight beyond the door of the springhouse. "Tie the knot with me," he called after her, "and I'll take care of you and your mother both."

A part of her wished she'd let him kiss her just to see what that would have been like, but another part of her saw no use in it. October was coming. October twenty-second. Nothing of earthly desires would matter then. Going up, going up. She was going up.

"Come on," she called over her shoulder, already running toward the cabin. "Just see if you can catch me."

All through supper, Tom talked big about his plans for his place. His acreage, he called it, all puffed up like a turkey spreading his tail feathers.

"I'm a hard worker," he said. "Everyone knows that. You know I bought twenty acres from Leonard Reed."

"Miss Betsey didn't care for that," Eveline said. "She thought the Mister had slighted her."

Tom swiped a piece of pone through the leavings of his stew. "Guess she was the sort to carry a grudge."

Eveline's mother said, "That woman always did think folks should bow to her. That's what happens when a pretty person starts to notice herself. She takes a notion she's a huckleberry above a persimmon." Dessie laid down her spoon and crossed her arms over her big stomach. "Tell me I'm lying," she said and narrowed her eyes at Eveline.

It was true, there was that fire and grit in Miss Betsey, but Eveline hated to admit as much because there was so much more to Betsey Reed. As spiteful as she could be, she could also be loving and tender. "Let's put a curl in your hair," she said to Eveline one afternoon. "Would you like that? Just to see?" Yes, Eveline said, she'd like that very much, and in a whipstitch she was gazing at herself in a looking glass, admiring the ringlets Miss Betsey had given her, cupping her palm beneath one to feel what a delicate and airy thing it was. So pretty. And then there was the morning Eveline caught Miss Betsey in the dooryard, head tipped back, looking up into the clouds. "What if you're right?" she said. "Eveline, what if there's a Heaven, and you're soon to go there?" Eveline took her hand, and Miss Betsey let her hold it. "You could come, too," Eveline said. "All you have to do is believe." Miss Betsey tightened her grip. "It's a lovely thought," she said. "A beautiful dream." Then she let go of Eveline's hand, and Eveline wanted to reach for her again and never let her go.

She told none of that to her mother or to Tom. It was a secret, how much she loved Miss Betsey.

"It's the truth," she said. "She had a way of making me feel as ugly as sin."

"I wouldn't say you're ugly," Tom said.

He pushed the wedge of stew-soaked pone into his mouth and chewed.

Would you say I'm pretty? Eveline wanted to ask, but she didn't have the sand to do it. She feared what his answer might be—*no, I wouldn't say that*—or worse yet, she could imagine him not saying a word, just sitting there working his jaw muscles on that pone until it became clear exactly what he thought.

Then Eveline's mother said, "You see what happens to prideful people like Betsey Reed? They find the trouble they deserve. Least you don't have to worry about that, Eveline. You've always been a good girl, and if Betsey Reed couldn't see that, then God help her."

Tom pushed his chair back from the table. "Might be too late for that. I fear God would have his hands full with the likes of her."

"But God saves us," Eveline said. "God can forgive us. All we have to do is ask."

Tom studied her for a good long while. "I've always admired those who can believe that," he finally said. "Me? I'm more of a mind that most folks are too concerned with the here and now to give much thought to the hereafter. Folks heading west. All those supporters of Polk for President shouting, 'Fifty-four Forty or Fight.' Who knows how much more of that land out west will fall our way? Just see if we don't go to war with Mexico." He tipped his head toward Eveline, a gentle bow the way a horse might nuzzle someone he loved with a slight touch of his nose. "I don't have that kind of earth hunger. I'm content to make a good home here. Maybe you're right about the Ascension being near to hand, but, if you'll forgive me, maybe you're wrong. Maybe the real reward is right here in front of you."

Eveline couldn't believe he'd been so bold, right there in front of her mother.

"Tom, give our good wishes to your father," Dessie said, rising up from the table. "Maybe next time, you should bring him along. I'll soon have that mending done for you."

He plucked up his wool felt hat from where it hung on a peg by the door. "I'm always obliged to you, Dessie." He lifted his hat toward Eveline. "Think on it," he said, and then he was gone.

She helped her mother scour the plates and spoons with sand, and finally Dessie said, "He's sweet on you."

"He's older than me," said Eveline, "by almost four years."

"A good man," said Dessie.

Eveline stamped her foot on the puncheon floor. "Don't you believe we're going up come October? Aren't you sewing an Ascension gown for yourself?"

Dessie nodded. "Aye. But what if it never comes?" She looked around the one-room cabin with the sleeping loft above and the greased paper at the window, the wooden bowls and spoons, the tin plates, the pile of trousers and shirts waiting for the needle. "What if all we have is right here? What if we have to make our own way to glory?"

"I can't believe you'd be a doubter."

"Now, Eveline, I didn't say that. I guess I'm just being practical. What if October twenty-second comes and we still have a life to live? Maybe you won't turn up your nose at Tom McKinney then."

"The Mister was a good man, too," Eveline said. "And look what happened to him."

"Do you really think Betsey poisoned him?"

"I'll take the butter crock back to the springhouse," Eveline said.

Outside, it was darkening. She stepped into the dooryard while her mother lit candles inside. Up the lane, Eveline saw the flares of pine torches passing along the road toward Heathsville. The night was still and the men's voices carried down the lane. She heard, *white poison, devil woman, witch,* and she knew they were on their way to see what they might do about Betsey Reed. Men who couldn't tolerate the notion that a woman—a woman like her—could kill a man and get away with it.

Did Eveline really think Miss Betsey had poisoned the Mister? The evening star hung overhead. Eveline closed her eyes and prayed on that star, prayed to God that no one would ever ask her that question, for if they did, she'd have to tell the truth.

Accused

BETSEY CLOSED THE BOOK OF verse she was reading. She sat in a cane-bottomed rocking chair inside her cell on the second floor of Constable John Wynn's house in Heathsville. She could hear the men's angry voices below her. She knew why they'd come.

John Wynn, said, "Betsey, blow out your candle," and she did. "Sounds like those boys are near to bust. Probably been drinking corn whiskey to give them nerve." He was a big-bellied man with curly black hair and mutton-chop sideburns, a solid man Betsey had always held in high regard. "I'd be quiet if I was you," he said. "Don't rile them up even more." He reached for his revolver, a five-shot Colt. "I'll go downstairs and do what I can."

Heinz Ernst was one of the men in the mob, and he was the one who met John Wynn at the door. Betsey recognized his voice when she heard it. That accent from the Old World.

"You know vy ve're here, John Vynn."

"Heinz," John Wynn said. "You and these other boys should go home. Sleep it off."

"You tink ve're drunk?"

"I can smell it on you."

Betsey could smell the smoke from the pine torches the men carried. She heard the flames crackling, the men coughing and hacking up phlegm. The hobnails from their brogan heels scratched across the planks of the porch. John Wynn's home was a two-story wood frame house with a porch out front and a vegetable garden along the side. Glass windows with lace curtains because John Wynn was a recently married man, and his wife had applied her homey touch.

"Not too drunk to hang a vitch," said Heinz Ernst.

"There'll come a trial," John Wynn said, "and you'll have to kill me right here right now to keep that from happening."

"Get out the vay, John Vynn," Heinz Ernst said. "Ve mean to have her."

The mob pushed forward. John Wynn staggered back over the doorsill. He pointed his revolver at Heinz Ernst and for a moment the mob fell quiet.

Then a voice from somewhere in the rear rang out. "Just a minute here. Boys, don't be fools. I've come to say what I know."

The men parted, and Betsey, her heart leaping, recognized the voice of Ethan Delz.

"I've been away," he said. Betsey could picture him in his traveling clothes—a frockcoat and a broad-brimmed hat. She knew he'd driven a wagon the eighteen miles to Lawrenceville to take on goods for his store and had spent more than a week there, visiting his parents. "I heard about Leonard Reed."

"Vat business is it of yours?" asked Heinz Ernst.

"It's plenty my business," said Ethan. "I understand Mrs. Reed has been charged primarily on the evidence of Eveline Deal concerning a scrap of paper and the accusation that Mrs. Reed put white arsenic into Leonard's coffee."

John Wynn answered. "James Logan says that paper was like the paper he used to wrap arsenic, and he feels certain that Mrs. Reed made purchase of some just prior to Mr. Reed's death. That, plus what the Deal girl said, was enough to put Mrs. Reed under arrest."

For a long time, no one said a word. Then Ethan said, "It's the same paper I use in my dry goods." Betsey wished she could see his face. Such a fine face he had, lean and pleasing, with a squared jaw, high cheek bones, blue eyes, delicate lashes, and a perfect Greek nose, straight from bridge to tip. "Before I left for Lawrenceville," he said, "I sold her a large-cent worth of salt." The men in the mob lowered their pine torches, and their faces twisted in the shadows. "That's what I came to say. That's what I'd have said to the coroner's jury if I'd been there. Leonard Reed always liked his coffee with salt."

A Peck of Salt

EVELINE HEARD THE STORY OF what Ethan Delz had said the next day when she went by the schoolmaster's house to return a book he'd let her borrow. *The Ingenious Gentleman Don Quixote of La Mancha.* She'd spent the summer reading whenever she could—at first light, as she dawdled in the woods on her way to the Reeds; in the afternoons, when the Mister was in the field and Miss Betsey had gone to town with her market basket, her veiled bonnet's ribbons tied in a bow beneath her chin; after supper, until her mother told her to put out the candle and lie down to sleep. What a tale it was, what a book about dreams and what a body might do to follow them.

"A perfect book for you," the schoolmaster said when he lent it to her. "A girl like you with her head in the clouds."

The schoolmaster knew she was a Millerite. He, himself, was not. His name was Brookhart. Lemuel Brookhart. A tall, lanky man whose figure was made from the sharp angles of arms and legs and fingers. A man with a knob of an Adam's apple that slid up and down his long throat when he spoke. A man who smelled of chalk dust and India ink and lampblack. A bald man with fringes of ginger hair over his ears. He'd taken a special interest in Eveline. She was smart, he told her, too smart to fall for all that second-coming, Ascension balderdash. "If you want to turn your back on the here and now," he told her, "at least do it through a book."

"Dear Eveline," Miss Betsey said when she caught her reading behind the granary one afternoon. "Off on one of your flights of fancy?"

"It's just a story," Eveline said.

"I love a good story, too," said Miss Betsey.

Now, at the schoolmaster's, Mr. Brookhart took the book from her and said, "Tell me, Eveline. How did you like this story of deception?"

"Deception, sir?"

Mr. Brookhart tipped his head down as if he were looking at her along the length of his nose, the way he always looked at a pupil when he thought the child was falling short of his expectations.

"How we deceive ourselves into believing we know exactly who we are."

Eveline stood inside his parlor and listened to the steady ticking of the regulator clock that hung on the wall beside the fireplace. The pendulum swung back and forth without a hitch, and in its presence she felt small and somehow less than the girl she'd convinced herself she was, the one who would rise, pure of heart with the rest of the saints on Ascension day. The girl who had done her duty and told the coroner's jury exactly what she'd seen that day at the Reeds'.

"I'm just me," she said to Mr. Brookhart, and then she handed him the book.

He held it in his big hands, his long fingers curling around its spine. "Have you heard about what Mr. Delz did last night?"

"No, sir. I haven't."

"He stopped a lynch mob from hanging Betsey Reed." Mr. Brookhart opened the book and smoothed a page with his hand. "Seems he'd heard what you told the coroner's jury about the paper and the white powder. Said he sold salt in a paper like that. Sold some to Betsey Reed, in fact." He glanced down at the book, turning a few pages until he found one that interested him. His eyes scanned the print. Then he said, "Ah, yes. Here it is. The line I was looking for." He read it in his teacher's voice. "'It is a true saying, that a man must eat a peck of salt with his friend, before he know him.'" He closed the book with a sudden squeeze of his hands and the noise in the house was sharp and startling to Eveline. "It seems that your story is now under suspicion," he said. "Are you sure you saw what you think you did? Or could it be you were only dreaming?"

She'd seen the scrap of paper, the white powder. She'd seen Miss Betsey put a pinch into the Mister's coffee.

"I told what I saw," she said to Mr. Brookhart.

He said, "Eveline, they'll hang Betsey Reed if a jury finds her guilty. You need to be sure."

She did her best to keep her chin level, her voice even. She couldn't let Mr. Brookhart know that she felt herself slipping into a dark woods of brambles and tangles, unable to see her way out.

"I'm sure," she said. "Now, please excuse me. I have to get along home."

Mr. Brookhart followed her to the front door. She went down the stone walkway to the road. There, she turned back and saw him watching her.

"I told the coroner's jury everything there was to tell," she said, and then she made herself walk away without hurrying, as if she were merely out for a stroll—la-di-dah—not a care in the world.

She didn't know how to say a word about the other things that had taken place at the Reeds' house that summer.

For Now We See Through a Glass

BETSEY SLEPT ACROSS THE HALL from where John Wynn and his wife lay down each night. She slept in a cell inside her room. The cell had a straw tick mattress, a stool, a pitcher and a basin, a chamber pot. Once John Wynn took her candle away, she had the darkness and the dream world she slipped into, trying to forget, at least for a time, that she was in jail, accused of poisoning her husband to death.

She dreamed about him. One night, he showed her some mother of pearl buttons with streaks in them—shadows—from the irregularities inside the mollusks' shells. That's what made each button unique, more precious, he told her. Those bumps and shadows and streaks. In another dream she was with him in the glasshouse, and he was telling her that it was the flaws in the glass that he cherished most. A few seeds in the stem of a wine glass, for example, from where the inconstancy of his breath through the blowpipe left air bubbles, or straw lines on the glass once it cooled. Inevitable flaws, each one of them a mark, one that people would recognize even long past the time when he was gone and they couldn't say exactly who had blown that glass, only that someone had, and he'd left those flaws as a sign of his time on earth.

Betsey woke, wondering why she hadn't been able to treasure Leonard's flaws—not the ones on his skin, not his wild hair, not that lazy eye, but the imperfections that their years together had created from their friction: her impatience, his sometimes chilly reserve. It had been deceit, finally, that had broken them. That was it, pure and simple. The deceit of his selling those twenty acres to Tom McKinney as if what she thought didn't matter a speck in the world. *The only rights you have, Mrs. Reed,* Leonard had told her, *are the ones I give you.* She hadn't been able to overlook that, the way he believed he owned her along with the land.

He'd worn hobnail boots in the winter when the ice was on, glad for the extra traction that the heads of the nails in the soles provided. She dreamed about him taking careful steps through the icy dooryard, coming up at day's end from the glasshouse. She watched, her heart in her throat, for fear he'd fall. She opened the door and grabbed onto his arm. *Thank heavens,* she said. *You made it.* She woke, imagining that she'd actually touched him. As much as he'd angered her, he'd always been her husband, the first man to love her, and now, to her great sadness, he was gone, and she was alone in the world and accused of being a murderess.

ಌ

One night, she sat reading by candlelight, waiting for the sound of John Wynn's footsteps on the stairs.

In time, he opened the door to her room and told her she should put out her candle.

"It's time to go to sleep," he said.

For some reason, she said to him, "I loved my husband. I tell you I did. On my word."

John Wynn wrapped his fingers around an iron bar of her cell and bowed his head, kept it down a good long while. When he finally looked at her again, he did so with what Betsey could only call sadness in his eyes. His voice, when he spoke, was hushed.

"Court don't care about love. They'll put you on trial, Betsey."

"And if they find me guilty?"

"I wouldn't be surprised if they hung you."

"Wouldn't that make a sight?" said Betsey. "A woman hung from her neck."

"It's something I've never seen. Don't expect anyone else has either. But that don't mean it won't happen." He slapped his palm against the bar. "If you've got any other notion of how your man died—anything else we ought to know—I expect it'd be the time for you to say it."

"Leonard was sick ever since he came back from St. Louis in July. Why don't you ask Eveline Deal about that?"

John Wynn nodded. "All right, then. I will."

He waited until Betsey blew out the candle. Then he bade her goodnight.

❧

It was indeed the case, Eveline said when John Wynn came to her mother's cabin the next evening to ask about the general health of Leonard Reed in the months leading up to his death. The Mister had come home from St. Louis a little puny.

"He had a distress in his stomach." Eveline was hoeing weeds from the garden patch. She stopped a moment and wiped sweat from her forehead with her apron hem. "But nothing that seemed out of the ordinary."

"Was he sick a lot after he got home?"

"Not all of the time. No, I wouldn't say that."

"How was he doctoring his stomach?"

"He had a powder he took."

"A cathartic?"

"I don't know. Just a powder he had in his glasshouse." Eveline halted for a moment, and John Wynn noted the stricken look on her face before she glanced down. When she lifted her head, she was smiling. "He showed me a trick once."

"A trick? What kind of trick?"

"We were in the glasshouse. He was showing me how to mix a batch of soda and lime and sand, and he said that he could eat glass and not hurt himself a bit. 'But there's a trick to it,' he said, and he asked me if I wanted to learn it."

"Eat glass? Sounds like risky business to me."

No, Eveline said, it wasn't risky at all. Not the way the Mister did it. "He ground some up. Mashed it with a mortar and pestle until it was nearly powder. Then he took a pinch and put it in his mouth. 'Just like that,' he said, and he opened his mouth to show me it was gone. It was just sand and soda and lime, he said. Nothing to hurt you at all."

"Did you believe him?"

Eveline looked down at her feet. She bumped the edge of the hoe's blade against her shoe.

"It's true," she finally said. "I've done it myself."

She went on to say how the Mister had taken another pinch of the ground glass that day and held it to her lips. He asked her didn't she want to try it, too. "He said, 'Don't you trust me? Do you really think I'd do anything to harm you?' I told him, no, no, I didn't think that. I knew he wasn't a man like my daddy, not a man to hurt me at all. 'Good,' he said, 'then open your mouth.' And I did."

"And you ate the glass?" John Wynn said.

Eveline nodded. "He told me the trick. He told me not to chew. 'Just swallow it,' he said. 'Just trust me. I do it all the time, and now you can, too.' So I swallowed the glass, and I walked out of that glasshouse, and I thought, *here I am, the same girl I've always been*, but I wasn't. I was someone else after that."

"That's crazy talk," John Wynn said. "Who were you if you weren't Eveline Deal?"

"I was someone I didn't know."

After John Wynn was gone, Eveline told her mother she meant to walk into Heathsville to fetch some things from Ethan Delz's dry goods store; they were low on sugar and coffee and flour, and maybe there'd be a few cents left for a piece of chocolate. Eveline's mother loved chocolate. "But don't you spend too much," she said, and Eveline told her not to worry.

In town, she lingered on the street outside the jail, a wicker basket dangling from her arm by its handle. She looked up at the window. A breeze lifted the curtains away from it, and candlelight flickered inside. Eveline heard a woman's voice singing, and she knew it was Miss Betsey. She was singing the song she'd heard Eveline singing at the cistern on the morning that the Mister took sick. *The clouds at length are breaking.*

Eveline wondered whether Miss Betsey was afraid. She wondered whether she had a comb and brush to take to her hair. Did she have *Godey's Lady's Book* to read? Did she remember all the afternoons she'd spent listening to Eveline read the letters from the lovelorn? Eveline wanted to call up to the open window, wanted her voice to reach Miss Betsey's ears, but what would she say? She didn't know. She only knew this desperate desire to say something so there'd no longer be this silence between them. She stood there so long, looking up at the window, that she missed the moment when the dusk turned to night.

She moved on down the street. A cur dog came toward her, barking, and she shooed him away by swishing the skirt of her dress and stamping her foot. Ahead of her, a man stumbled out of a doorway and lifted a bottle to his lips.

She moved to the other side of the street and stuck to the shadows. A piano was playing somewhere nearby, and a man was singing "Tippecanoe and Tyler Too," the old campaign song from the last election that carried the Whig candidate, William Henry Harrison and his running mate, John Tyler, to the presidency. That all seemed a long way past now. Come fall, there'd be another election. Harrison had died in office after catching pneumonia at his inauguration, and the new President, Tyler, had just withdrawn, leaving the choice now between James Polk and Henry Clay. Polk was the favorite because he favored western expansion, the earth hunger that Eveline felt certain had fallen upon the Mister like a fever.

"Shut up that old stuff," a man shouted, and the piano stopped and another man—Eveline assumed it was the man who'd been singing—said, "Sir, your sentiments offend me."

She walked into Ethan Delz's store. It was almost time for him to close his door, and she was his only customer.

"Well, well," he said. "If it isn't Eveline Deal." He was behind the fabric counter, his arms crossed over his chest, black sleeve garters tight on his biceps. "Come for some white satin for your Ascension gown?"

She knew he was poking fun at her. Her cheeks burned, and she had to look away from him. Then she met his gaze again, and she managed the word "sugar." Then "coffee." Then "flour."

"How much of each?" he asked, and she told him.

While he wrapped the sugar and flour in papers like the one that Eveline had found in the dooryard the day the Mister took sick, she kept her head bowed, sneaking glances, enchanted with his long fingers and the way they wrapped the papers and tied them off with string from a spool on the counter.

She remembered that night in July when she'd come upon Ethan Delz and Miss Betsey. The light faded, and the swallows became invisible. The Shorthorns bellowed as she peeked around the corner of the stable. She closed her eyes and saw what she'd imagined ever since that night—Miss Betsey's arm coming down to her side, Mr. Delz's back straightening. The tender leave-taking of lovers.

Hadn't it been so?

Now, in Ethan Delz's dry goods store, Eveline heard him asking her if that would be all.

"A square of chocolate," she said.

"A little something sweet?"

She nodded.

"So Eveline Deal has a sweet tooth."

She could tell he thought there was something delicious in what he assumed to be true—that a Millerite could fancy chocolate—and she kept quiet, leaving him to imagine other pleasures she might like to enjoy.

He winked at her, and she didn't know what to feel. Was he telling her he knew she'd seen him that night at Miss Betsey's? Was he saying he was that kind of man?

"A square of chocolate for Miss Eveline Deal," he said. "A sweet to hold on her tongue."

Was he telling her to keep quiet, to not breathe a word of what he imagined she knew about him and Miss Betsey?

Eveline took her parcels up in her basket and hurried out of the store. She passed the hotel, the tavern, James Logan's apothecary, the soap factory, the livery stable, the distillery, and the granary. Then toward the end of the street, she turned back to the west, aware now that she was headed to the home of the schoolmaster, Lemuel Brookhart.

"I've come to ask you," she said once she stood in the dooryard of his meager home and looked up the steps to where he waited, slope-shouldered, candlelight behind him, to hear why she'd come to call. "Please, Mr. Brookhart, will you carry me home in your buggy?"

He leaned out of the doorway, peering into the darkness, stretching his long neck first in one direction and then in the other. He'd loosened the top button of his shirt and undone his waistcoat.

"It's late," he said. "Too late for you to be out."

"I'm not afraid," she said.

"What is it, then?"

She looked above her to the dark sky. "There's no moon tonight."

"What's caused you to be in the village at this hour?" He stepped out into the dooryard. "Is your mother with you?"

"No, sir. She's waiting for me at home." She lifted her basket. "I came for some things from the dry goods store."

"Now something's left you unsettled."

How difficult it was to hide that she was afraid—of what, she couldn't exactly say. Ethan Delz had spooked her, and she'd rather not step into the dark woods alone.

She didn't know how to explain that to Mr. Brookhart, so she said, "I want to be home."

"All right, then. Home you shall be." He turned and went back up the steps to the open door. "Stay there." He looked back at her before going into his house and shutting the door. "I'll be round with my horse and buggy."

She stood in the dooryard, listening to the starlings as they wheeled down to roost in the branches of the chinkapin trees. The rattles and whirrs and whistles and twicks unnerved her even more, and she prayed that Mr. Brookhart would hurry. She had no way of knowing that at that very moment, John Wynn was telling Miss Betsey the story that Eveline had told him about the Mister showing her the trick to eating glass. Could she imagine that Mr. Reed would do such a thing, he asked Betsey. Eat glass?

Betsey couldn't find her voice. The thought of Leonard and the girl alone in the glasshouse, his fingers dipping into her open mouth, sent a shiver through her. What would she have done if he'd asked her as much? But of course, he hadn't asked her. He'd chosen Eveline. Betsey's throat tightened against the thought of that ground glass.

"My husband ate glass?" she finally said.

"So it seems," said John Wynn, "and it might have been what killed him."

There'd need to be an autopsy. They'd need to disinter Mr. Reed's body.

"Would be a shame to disturb him now that he's at his rest," Betsey said, but John Wynn insisted in a way that told her she had no say in the matter.

"He might be carrying the truth of his death," he said.

Then he came into the cell, and he made certain that he had all the matches. He took the candle, and the room went dark.

In the schoolmaster's doorway, Eveline felt the night tremble with the starlings' calls. She heard the horse's shoes on the hard-packed dirt and the creak of the traces. She turned to see Mr. Brookhart sitting on the buggy's seat, and she was glad for the sight of him.

Then she saw the sky to the east brighten, and for just a moment, she thought this was the Ascension. She thought that Christ had come and now, *now,* she would rise to Heaven.

"Look," she said to Mr. Brookhart, pointing to the glowing sky. "Oh, look!"

Mr. Brookhart said, "Have mercy. There's something on fire."

She heard a faint call, a voice caught up in the noise of the birds. She couldn't make out who was calling or why. She didn't know it was Ethan Delz, come out from his store and running now, running up the street to the jail, calling out again and again, *Betsey! Betsey! Oh, Lord!*

❧

By the time Mr. Brookhart and Eveline arrived, flames were licking from the second-story window, the window that she'd gazed up at earlier, listening to Miss Betsey singing. Eveline knew she was inside that burning room. Ladders were up against the wall facing the street, and a bucket brigade was in place. The men hollered, and their muscles strained as they passed the oaken buckets full of water on up the line.

"It's burning fast," Mr. Brookhart said. He had to fight the reins to keep his horse from bolting. "Pray the water holds out and the men are quick and sure." He handed the reins to Eveline and jumped down from the buggy. "Hold firm," he said. "I'm going to do what I can."

Eveline held tight to the reins while the horse, a chestnut Morgan, arched his neck against the bit and pranced inside the traces.

John Wynn's wife, Caroline, was on the street, her long hair, the color of ripe wheat, already let down for the night. It hung in a thick braid to the small of her back. "John," she was calling, looking all about. "John Wynn."

"Here," he said. "I'm here."

Just then, Ethan Delz came running past the buggy.

The man atop the ladder shouted, "Lord God." Through the flames at the window, Eveline saw a shadowy form retreat, and she knew it was Miss Betsey. The man said, "She's still in there. Betsey Reed."

Ethan Delz didn't hesitate. He ran into the jail even though the men, once they saw what was afoot, shouted for him to stop.

"He doesn't know where I keep the key to the cell," John Wynn said, and with that he ran into the burning building, too.

Eveline thought, then, of the fires kept blazing in the Mister's furnaces and how hot they were when she stood close to them, watching him take up a gather on the end of his blowpipe. His face became even redder than normal. The gather glowed orange at the end of the pipe, and his breath began to shape it. Eveline stood still, amazed. No matter how many times she saw a wineglass, a candlestick, a vase appear, she was astonished. A man's breath, the delicate turn of the pipe, sand and soda and lime becoming something she could hold in her hand.

A charred shutter dropped from the wall and fell to the street, nearly missing Caroline Wynn, who had edged closer to the fire.

"We've got a purchase on it," the man atop the ladder said, and for the first time, Eveline realized it was Tom McKinney. "Keep 'em coming, boys," Tom shouted as empty buckets came down the ladder and then went back up full. "We're gaining ground."

What passed through Eveline's heart, then, was hard for her to describe. She could only say that it was a similar feeling to what she got when she watched the Mister at work in the glasshouse—a tingle inside her, a feeling of amazement that something so beautiful could come from such common things. Only now she was feeling it for Tom

McKinney, who was remarkable atop that ladder. At some point, he'd peeled off his shirt, and she could see the muscles of his broad back, his sturdy shoulders. She could see the sweat that gave his chest a golden sheen. This was a man. *Her* man, if she wanted him, and suddenly she did. At that moment, she envied Caroline Wynn for what she stood to lose when her husband ran to danger. Eveline wanted to have the right—a wife's right—to feel that dread for Tom.

Smoke curled from the window now, and she heard him cough. He waved his arm, trying to clear the air. The fire was smoldering, Eveline knew, and she also knew that Tom, if he had a choice, would be down from that ladder and not taking in the smoke, but he stayed because he needed a few more buckets to make sure the fire was out, and he said, "A thimble or two more, boys," and she thought that the most wonderful thing to say. In the days to follow, people would repeat those words in the tavern and then raise a glass to the courage of Tom McKinney.

Eveline was so caught up in the rapture she felt for him that she almost missed the sight of Ethan Delz carrying Miss Betsey from the building. One of his arms was under her knees, and the other had her around the waist. Her head fell back, and Eveline could see wisps of smoke rising from her clothes and the char upon her face, and she felt her heart sink for fear that Miss Betsey was dead.

John Wynn came outside, coughing from deep in his lungs. Mr. Brookhart and some of the other men gathered around him, holding him upright. When he finally had his breath, he said, "That fire started in her cell, and it didn't start by itself. I can tell you that."

Mr. Brookhart said, "Did she try to burn her way out?"

Said John Wynn, "I don't understand it. She had no matches, nor anything else that would start a fire."

Ethan Delz had laid Miss Betsey on the ground. He was kneeling beside her, and his sobs were enough to let Eveline know that what she suspected about the two of them was true.

Autopsia Cadaverum

THE WORD SPREAD THROUGH HEATHSVILLE. A fire at John Wynn's. A fire started by Betsey Reed in spite of the fact that she had no matches. A witch's fire, some said, and the story of how she'd made a milk cow go dry got told again and again. And don't forget the boy, Jacob Ernst, who died after being in Betsey's care. Looked like she wouldn't go to trial now for the death of her husband. Looked like she'd pass over herself. When they carried her away after the fire, it looked like she hadn't a breath left in her body. Not a breath. Mercy sakes alive.

Little by little, though, in the home of James Logan, she came back to life.

When she woke, it was near to dawn. A watery light lurked behind the window shade. She was in a bed that was strange to her, and on a table beside it rested a pitcher and a glass and a pair of rimless spectacles, left atop a black-covered Bible.

James Logan was dozing in a rocking chair on the other side of the table. Betsey tried to call to him, but her throat was parched. She managed a croak, and that was enough to wake him. He reached over and took up the spectacles, curling the wire sidepieces over his ears.

"Awake, are you?" He picked up the pitcher and poured a glass of water. "Drink this," he said, and held the glass to her lips.

She managed to drink it all down, and when she was done, she said, "Last night."

Mr. Logan stopped her before she could go on. "Tell it to John Wynn. He's the one you owe an explanation."

She could see that someone had removed her dress and petticoats and chemise and slipped a night dress over her head. She picked at the embroidered daisies at the end of the billowy sleeves.

"Mrs. Logan saw to getting you into bed last night." Mr. Logan put the glass back on the table. "Then I gave you a little tincture of opium to help you sleep. You were talking out of your head."

She could remember saying something about Leonard.

"'Dead is dead,' you kept saying." Mr. Logan went to the window and raised the shade. "I guess no one would argue with that, Mrs. Reed."

She remembered the fire and the thought that if she perished, there'd no longer be a need to raise Leonard's body and subject it to the humiliation of autopsy. Such were her crazed thoughts then. Now she felt mortified over what she'd done, putting others at risk. At the same time, she felt thankful that she was still alive to feel this shame.

"Will they raise him up?" she said. "Leonard?"

Mr. Logan's back was still turned to her. He nodded his head. "The gravediggers will be at it this morning. The undertaker is on his way to Lawrenceville to fetch a surgeon."

A knock came on the door. It opened slowly, and Mrs. Logan's round face poked through. She had on a frilly linen cap, and her gray curls spilled out from beneath it. "It's John Wynn who's come," she said in a whisper.

"Bring him up," said Mr. Logan. Then to Betsey, he said, "He's going to want to know how you set that fire."

❧

She wouldn't tell. Not even when John Wynn pressed her. Did she somehow have a match? Or a piece of flint to strike against the iron bedstead? She wouldn't say a word.

"You owe me an answer." He stood beside the bed, his slouch hat in his hands. He still smelled of smoke, and Betsey understood he'd been up all night. "You practically burned my wife and me out of our home. It'll take days to repair the damage. Lucky thing the bucket brigade was able to contain the blaze."

Still she wouldn't answer. Of course she'd had a match, a single match she'd kept hidden in the hem of her petticoat, a match struck and touched to the curtains at the window. And why? She didn't know. Something about the fact that Leonard and the girl, Eveline Deal, had kept secret what they'd done in the glasshouse. Something about that had thrown her into despair, and she'd thought, better now by her own choice rather than waiting for a jury's decision, a judge's sentence, a trip to the gallows, for she was certain that's what awaited her.

Perhaps the men on the coroner's jury hadn't known they'd long been waiting for a chance to sit in judgment of her. For years, they'd watched her come and go with the air of a woman entitled by her beauty, that lift of her head, that cool glance behind the veils of her bonnets, everything about her that said she walked on better ground than anyone else. When Eveline and James Logan testified, the opportunity was there for the jury to believe what they hadn't even known they wanted to believe: Betsey Reed had killed her husband. She knew, just before she struck the match, that more of the same sort of judgment was waiting for her.

"Do you know what folks are saying, Betsey?" John Wynn stood there, looking down on her. "They say you're a witch. They say that's how you started that fire. The same way you dried up that milk cow, the same way you . . ."

"I did *not* put a spell on Jacob Ernst." She said this in a low voice, but with great insistence. "I'm not a witch. Good Lord! Can't you feel my grief? I'm a woman who's lost her husband."

"Aye." John Wynn put his hat back on his head. "And the surgeon will have something to say about how your man died."

❧

The surgeon, a Dr. Kirkwood, arrived the next day, and a place for the autopsy was made in a storeroom at the rear of James Logan's apothecary shop.

Betsey was looking out the window when the undertaker's wagon brought the pine box that held Leonard's body from the graveyard. She watched the undertaker and Mr. Logan and John Wynn and Dr. Kirkwood carry the box inside. She heard their boots scuffling about on the floor below her and then the groan and creak of the nails being prized up from the coffin's lid.

She tried to stop listening after that, choosing to sing an old hymn she could remember singing in church when she was a little girl—"Blest Be the Tie That Binds"—but still she heard a dull sound, and she imagined it was Leonard's body being laid onto the table. She sang louder: *When we asunder part.*

Then there was only the murmur of voices from below her, and the distant whisk of boots moving over the floor, and the delicate chime of medical instruments as they tapped what she imagined was the rim of a bowl.

She could hardly bear it. When John Wynn came to give her the news, she was sitting in the rocking chair by the bed, her hands pressed to her ears.

"Betsey, the doctor has finished." She was rocking in the chair, and he had to take its arms to hold it still. Then he took her hands, and she let him draw them away from her head. "I've come to tell you what he found."

John Wynn explained how Dr. Kirkwood had looked for any sign of glass in Leonard's stomach and intestines and had found none. He went on, then, to perform a test for arsenic. John Wynn took the time to explain how the test was done, and though Betsey could barely follow it all, she had the notion, from his low, patient voice, that he wanted her to know all this so she wouldn't imagine it was some sort of magic they'd concocted against her, but instead conclusions drawn from an exact scientific procedure.

The test, John Wynn said, was one developed by a Dr. James Marsh in England in 1836.

"A very accurate and scientific instrument," John Wynn said.

It involved adding human tissue to a glass vessel containing zinc and either hydrochloric or sulfuric acid. Dr. Kirkwood used the latter. He took tissue samples from Mr. Reed's stomach and intestines and put them into the vessel. He then applied a flame to the bowl which became stained with a silvery-black film.

"Do you know what that film was, Betsey?"

"I suppose you're about to tell me."

John Wynn nodded. "Arsenic," he said.

Don't You Want to Believe?

Now there was evidence. Word spread through Heathsville, and the next day Tom McKinney carried the word of the autopsy to Eveline. He told her the doctor would testify at Betsey Reed's trial, which was to commence in November when the Circuit Court would next be in session.

"You were right in what you told them," Tom said. "Everyone will know that now."

They were in the garden behind her mother's cabin where Eveline was picking pole beans. She worked her way down the row, snapping off the beans, one, two, three, four at a time, and dropping them into the basket at her feet. Summer was passing. Already some of the vines were turning a paler green; a few leaves were drying and curling at the ends. It hadn't been long ago when Eveline had pushed the seeds into the ground and watched them sprout and vine. She and her mother had stripped sassafras saplings of their leaves and set them in the ground, leaning them to a point and lashing the tops together with string. All summer, the vines had been lush and green, but now the killing frost wasn't far off; sometimes it came in the middle of October. As she picked the beans, Eveline felt the days dwindling and she knew that winter would soon be upon them.

"November will be too late," she said.

Tom reached over her shoulder and snapped off a bean. "Not the

Ascension? Oh, Eveline, not that again."

"Yes, that." She turned to face him. "Looks to me, Tom McKinney, that you'd want to be a part of it. Don't you want to believe?"

"I just can't cotton." He held the bean out to her, and she snatched it from his hand and dropped it into the basket. "Honestly, Eveline. I wish you'd put that thought out of your head."

She thought of how she'd watched him at the top of that ladder, bare to the waist, fighting the fire at John Wynn's. What had happened to her thoughts of the Ascension then? Gone up in smoke. Gone up to leave her firmly planted on the ground, thrilled with the danger of the evening and the marvelous sight of Tom's broad back and muscled shoulders, arms, and chest. Afterward, she'd been ashamed of how easily she'd turned her thoughts from God and His glory. She'd spent the days thereafter rededicating herself to her faith. Now Tom was turning his nose up at it, trying to tell her what she could and couldn't believe.

"Are you wanting to be left behind?" she asked him.

"I'm wanting you to say you'll marry me."

The sun was behind him, and Eveline raised her hand to shade her eyes. "And what would be the good of that?"

She lifted her shoulders and let them fall as if she were saying she was sorry. Then she picked up the basket and started walking toward the cabin.

"Eveline, don't say things like that," he called after her, but she didn't stop or turn around. She just kept walking.

❧

Which is what she should have done later that day when she was on her way through the woods to the Reeds' place. She wanted to go into the glasshouse to see what had happened to the Mister's things—to the sand and soda and lime, to the oxides of lead, aluminum, and magnesium, to the sulfur compounds and the calcium salts, and most of all to the stibnite, the shiny gray mineral from which the Mister got the antimony that he used for getting bubbles out of the glass. She loved the shine of the stibnite before it turned black from exposure to the air, and she had a fond memory of one day when the Mister made a paste by crushing some stibnite to powder and then mixing it with tallow.

"Close your eyes," he told her, and, when she hesitated, he added, "Go on. It's all right."

She did as he said. It was warm in the glasshouse, the furnaces burning, and when she closed her eyes, she could see flames behind her lids.

Then the Mister touched her. She didn't know with what. She only knew she felt something tracing the bottom of her eyelids, just the slightest tickle, and she smelled the tallow. The Mister told her to keep her eyes closed, and then she felt the air stirring and she could see little changes of light through her lids, and she knew he was leaning close, fanning her face with his hands.

After a time, he told her to open her eyes. She saw, then, that he was using a fine-bristled brush made of horsehair to paint the paste around her eyes. He licked the bristles to get a finer point.

"Look up," he told her, and she did.

She felt the tickle of the horsehair along the bottom rims of her eyes. When he was finished, he brought her a looking glass.

What she saw astounded her.

"You see how pretty you are?" the Mister said.

She looked and looked, disbelieving. Was it really her?

"How?" she said.

"Your eyes are so lovely. The liner makes them stand out. Women have been doing this since before Christ."

Eveline knew she'd have to stop at the creek on her way home through the woods to wash the paint away, lest her mother call her a strumpet, but for now she was content to look at herself in the glass and to think of herself as pretty.

On this day near to autumn, she thought of that moment in the glasshouse and considered it a gift, another gift the Mister had given her. She wanted to see if she could mash up that stibnite, find some fat to mix it with—maybe there was bacon grease left in Miss Betsey's kitchen—and then paint her eyes again. She'd have the whole place to herself. She could read Miss Betsey's *Godey's Lady's Books*, try on one of her veiled bonnets, maybe even slip into that dress of purple wool. She'd do all that until the shame started to come over her, as she knew it would. Then she'd slip back into her gingham dress, her apron. She'd run back into the woods and kneel down and ask God to forgive her. She'd pray, as she did again and again, to be a better girl, one who didn't put any faith in things like eye paint and *Godey's Lady's Books* and veiled bonnets and dresses of purple wool and the love of someone like Tom McKinney—all things trying to trap her in this world and keep her from glory.

She was thinking all that when she heard someone call her name. She was on the deer path that she always took through the woods, and she stopped to look behind her. The sun splintered through the leaves of the hickories and the sweet gums. The air was still, and Eveline had thought herself all alone.

Now a man was calling her name.

"Eveline." She heard a rustling in the brush off to her right. "Eveline Deal."

She felt her heart sink when she saw her father step from behind a blackberry thicket. A thorn snagged his shirt, and as he stopped to pull it free, she thought about running, but something held her there, something she couldn't even know to call by name. Something, she would think later, about what it took to hold people together, what it meant to love someone even when you didn't want to, what it was to believe that what once was could very well be again.

Her father said he meant to come home. He'd been gone long enough. "Life in the Bend ain't no life. I miss you and your ma. I miss having a home."

Eveline eyed him. A blue jay was jeering overhead in an oak tree. *Jaay-jaay, Jaay-jaay.* The noise put her on edge.

"What about that woman, the one that hooked you and took you away?"

"Sweet drop," her father said. "It's time you had your pa with you again."

Eveline knew all of this meant that something had happened in Dark Bend to send him running home. Maybe some scoundrel had threatened to cut his throat. Maybe his fancy woman had gone off with someone else. Whatever the reason, there he was, Moses Deal, come back from the river.

"Don't you love your pa?" he said.

He looked like he'd had a time of it. His beard was down to the hollow of his throat. One of his eyes was blacked and nearly closed. His trousers were kept up on his bony hips by a length of rope.

"You talked to Mama?"

He shook his head. "I was hoping you'd sorta grease the wheels."

So that was what he wanted—her favor to win his way back home.

"You left us in a mess." She crossed her arms over her chest and tilted her head back just enough to point her chin at him. She wouldn't give in, at least not without letting him know how she felt. "Mama takes in sewing. We couldn't even get a crop in this year. That's what you left us. I had to go to work for the Reeds, and I guess you've probably heard how that ended up."

He nodded. "Betsey Reed killed her man, and you're in the thick of it. Word made it up to the Bend." He shook his head. "I'd hardly think it of her, but I suppose they know what they know. Are you sure of your word?"

Eveline almost laughed at the thought of her father, rapscallion that he was, calling her to account for her testimony.

"They've got proof," she said. "Evidence. Scientific evidence. Miss Betsey poisoned the Mister."

"Scientific evidence, you say?"

"They dug up the Mister. They cut him open and did a test. Arsenic. That's what he had in him. That's how he died."

For a good while, her father didn't speak. The blue jay gave one more call and then flew away. "Women poisoning their men," her father finally said. "What a state of affairs."

"You sure you want to come home?"

He gave her a puzzled look and then she saw as his face relaxed that he understood what she was suggesting. "Oh, your ma? I doubt she's the kind."

"Never know." Eveline stepped closer to him, then, so close that she could reach out and touch a finger to his swollen eye. "What happened to you up at Dark Bend?"

Her father winced, and she let her hand fall back to her side. "Well, now, daughter, that's a story best left for another time."

She raised her hand again, let it hang in the space between them, her finger pointed, inches from that hurt eye.

He took a step back.

She followed. "Tell me," she said.

Her father took his time. He told his story. "Back in July, Heinz Ernst started coming up to Dark Bend. He knew some fellas up there, and he started talking big about how he was going to come into some money soon and then he'd be set. Well, I told him if he did to come and see me on account of I had a business venture going and I was always looking for investors."

"What kind of business?" Eveline asked.

"Doesn't matter." He waved his hand in the air. "It's all done now." He touched a finger to his swollen eye and winced. "Done and gone, and it cost me some flesh. Let's just say you can't always trust those fellas up at Dark Bend, fellas like Heinz Ernst and his friends. One day, I said to him, 'See here, I don't think you're coming into money at all. I think you're just talking.' That's when he showed me some silver. He said there was more to be had, and have it he would just as soon as he did the deed. 'What deed is that?' I asked him. He said someone had hired him. 'Hired you?' I said. 'Hired you to do what?' He just grinned. Wouldn't say a word. Just grinned like the cat who fell in the milk. So I threw it up in his face, called him a liar. He didn't take kindly to that. No sir, he didn't. We tussled some and he ended up knocking me a good one."

"Did you ever figure out what he'd been hired to do?" Eveline said.

"He never said, daughter, and after he hit me, I never asked him again. I've got my suspicions though, just like you do, I bet. Suspicions about Heinz Ernst and what he might have had to do with Leonard Reed's death. Surely you knew Betsey had reason to want him gone."

It was as if her father had seen straight through to her heart, which was thumping inside her chest now, and she couldn't bear to be in that place any longer for fear of what she might come to say—Miss Betsey and Ethan Delz were looking for a way to be husband and wife.

She took a few steps back from her father, and he said, "I can see you don't want to believe it."

She turned and started running up the path.

"Now, daughter, don't go off like that." He called after her, his voice sharp in her ears. "Eveline, you come back here."

She wasn't listening anymore. She had no call to answer to him. She was running as fast as she could now, running over the deer trail, dirt packed hard, running to the glasshouse where the Mister had always made her feel loved and safe.

The Hocus-Pocus

MR. AUGUSTUS FRENCH WOULD SOON become governor of Illinois. His friend, Usher Linder, was a personal friend of Abraham Lincoln, and had once been state attorney general. Two men of considerable sway. Two men who had already made their reputations. No dirty pettifoggers. No sir, not those two. What was this case of Betsey Reed's to them?

It was Mr. French who first caught wind of her arrest and, after reading the testimony presented to the coroner's jury, decided to engage the assistance of his friend, Mr. Linder, to come to her defense.

"The evidence is dubious," Mr. French said one evening at his home in Palestine, to which he'd invited Mr. Linder for supper. He explained to Mr. Linder the testimony of Eveline Deal at the coroner's inquest and the apothecary who said that although he couldn't recall selling arsenic to Betsey Reed, he felt certain he had.

Mr. Linder cut to the chase, as he often did. He was a direct man, sometimes brittle, rougher around the edges than the more genteel Mr. French. Mr. Linder was a tall, lanky man, and the knobs of his wrists were in plain sight below the sleeves of his coat, and even more so as he leaned forward and tapped his long finger on the table. He said, "Goddamn it. Something about all this sticks in my gullet."

"Mine too," said Mr. French, and the two men sat long into the night, discussing the case while sipping the bourbon whisky that

Linder favored from his native Kentucky. "Will you help me?" Mr. French finally asked, and Linder said yes, by God, he would.

"There's one thing you should know first," Mr. French said. Then he told Linder about the autopsy and the presence of arsenic in Leonard Reed's stomach.

"Do you have an idea about how to turn that testimony on its ear?" Linder wanted to know.

"That's what we'll have to do together," Mr. French said.

A rooster was crowing; dawn was breaking.

"All right, then." Linder drew the jug toward him. "Let's get started. Let's figure out how to work the hocus-pocus."

⁓

It was the first of many such conversations during the month of September. Finally, when they had their plan in mind, they filed a request for a change of venue to Lawrence County, where they felt certain Betsey would face a fairer jury, one made up of men who didn't have the history with her that everyone in Crawford County did. No rumors or gossip about her witchy ways. No reason to believe that she might have murdered her husband.

The Crawford County Court granted the change of venue, so it came to pass that on October eighteenth, Betsey traveled to Lawrenceville under the guard of John Wynn, to be confined in the basement of the Lawrence County courthouse and held for trial on the first day of the next term.

She had no way of knowing what Moses Deal had told Eveline about Heinz Ernst that day in the woods, nor did she know that once Eveline got to the glasshouse, she found the smokehouse lock gone and the door standing wide open. She could only find one piece of stibnite left high on a shelf, blackened now from exposure to the air. Everything else—all the chemicals and the soda and the lime and the sand—was gone, taken by whom, Eveline didn't know, but someone had been in the glasshouse to clear it of any sign of the work that the Mister had done there. Even the furnaces were gone, as were the blowpipes and the glassware the Mister had made. Now the building was just a low-ceilinged shed with vent pipes poking through the roof. No sign at all that he'd ever been alive. No sign of the time she'd spent there with him. It was nearly too much for her to stand.

"God have mercy," she said aloud.

She knew she had to hold on to something, and God was there for her. No matter how horrible people were, no matter how imperfect she was, no matter how evil the world could be, there was God, and there was the Ascension coming, and in spite of how much she might have wished to marry Tom McKinney and have a family with him and the years and years it would take to make a life, she was going up. She was going up to a kingdom where there was no evil, only love, love forever, eternal joy, amen.

Still, she couldn't let the stibnite go. She put it in her apron pocket and slipped out of the glasshouse. She prayed her father would go back to Dark Bend and leave her and her mother to the Ascension in October. She knew her father was lost and had been for some time. Nothing she could do about that. Not a thing in this world.

A Brittle Glass That's Broken Presently

ON THE EVENING OF OCTOBER eighteenth, the sheriff, a man named Fyffe, brought a visitor to Betsey's cell. It was the first time she looked upon the face of the Reverend Seed, a man of slight stature but possessed of a deep, rich voice.

"Elizabeth Reed," he said, "I've been praying for you."

He was long-armed and slouch-shouldered. His hair was thin on his scalp, its few wisps the color of old harness leather. He carried a Bible in his right hand. The Bible reached nearly to his knee, as if the heft of it was stretching his already long arm. Betsey studied him in the light cast by Sheriff Fyffe's candle. Deep lines etched his face from his nostrils to the corners of his lips which he pressed together in a tight line. A pair of small round spectacles perched about midway down his long nose. He stared at her over the tops of the lenses, and Betsey had to force herself not to look away, as shaken as she was by the sadness and the kindness in those brown eyes, a look that said he was disappointed in her but he wasn't going anywhere; they were going to see this through together.

"Didn't know I needed praying over." She sat on the rope bed inside her cell. The small window let the last of the daylight through its bars. It fell across her hands in stripes. "They won't let me have a candle, not after what happened in the Heathsville jail. If you really want to be a help, maybe you could bring me a little light. How am I supposed to read after dark?"

She was reading a collection of poems attributed to W. Shakespeare. One in particular had struck her, a poem about the uselessness of beauty. How quickly it vanished. *A brittle glass that's broken presently.* And so she feared it would be with her own pleasant features. Look where they'd gotten her. Accused of murder.

The Reverend Seed nodded to the sheriff, and Fyffe, a portly man with a red bulb of a nose, fit the key to the lock of her cell. The door swung back, and the Reverend Seed stepped inside. Three steps carried him to her. She looked up at him, and for a good while she breathed in his scent of freshly ironed linen. She wanted to look away from those eyes, but at the same time, she wanted to have them hold her in their gaze forever. If it came to what everyone said it would—if it came to her hanging—she wanted the Reverend Seed's eyes to be the last eyes she looked into before the gallows trap gave way.

He touched the Bible to her forehead. "The light you need is in here, Elizabeth." His voice was the sound of a grandfather clock chiming, a rumble of distant thunder, a door latch springing open. "And in here." He touched the corner of the Bible to her chest, just below the vee of her collarbone. Then he said, "Thy word is a lamp unto my feet, and a light unto my path."

She knew the scripture from Psalms, but she didn't tell the Reverend Seed that. She wasn't sure, just then, that she could have found her voice even if she wanted to. Her life had unfolded along such a strange trail of twists and snags. She felt a pulsing in her neck. Who knew that the Reverend Seed was waiting for her, offering to save her soul if she would only give him the chance?

"I want you to pray with me." His voice was a whisper now: a rustling of leaves, steam rising from heated water, a stirring of hummingbird wings. "Will you do that, Betsey?"

She didn't say a word. She closed her eyes and bowed her head.

The next morning when Mrs. Fyffe, the sheriff's wife, brought her breakfast, Betsey asked her for a comb and a looking glass.

"I know I must be a fright." She snagged at her hair, tangled over her shoulders. It irked her to have to ask for something as ordinary as a comb, but she was under careful watch after the fire in her cell in Heathsville. She still refused to offer any explanation for how it started. Let them guess, she decided. Let them imagine. Let them think her a witch and the teeth of a comb necessary to some incantation that would free her—if indeed that's what they thought. She didn't mind if they were afraid. "I haven't combed my hair since leaving Heathsville," she said.

The sheriff's wife was called Floss, a round woman with loose flesh under her chin and a white pinafore apron stretched tight across her ample bosom. She walked on her toes, mincing steps that gave her the look of a fat robin redbreast hopping about.

"Why, Missus," she said, "I hardly imagine you could ever look a fright."

She left Betsey to her breakfast—corn mush with molasses, fried fatback, and poached pears—and went off to see if Mr. Fyffe would allow her to bring the looking glass and the comb.

The cell was spare—the rope bed and the stool, a short-legged table and a chamber pot—only the barest needs met with nothing left over for comfort. The walls were made from stone. Last night, for whatever reason—maybe a mouse had scurried across the window ledge—flakes of that stone had fallen on Betsey's head while she slept. She could still feel them in her hair.

Soon, Floss was back with a comb and a square of glass that she polished with her apron. She held the glass up so Betsey could see.

"Lord-a-mercy." Betsey plucked at her hair with her fingers. "Would you just look?"

She started in with the comb, trying to work its teeth through her tangled hair, but it was too much for her. The fire in her scalp nearly brought her to tears.

Finally, Floss laid the glass down on the bed and told Betsey to sit on the stool. "I'll help you, Missus," she said, and then she started in, as gently as she could, working at those snarls until she could comb the hair without a snag. "I can't let you have any ribbons," she said. "You'll just have to leave it hang down, but that's not a bad thing, is it Missus? Your hair's a glory."

"Thank you." Betsey picked up the glass and studied her face, a face she recognized but also one that seemed a stranger to her now. Here she was, far from home, waiting in this jail for her trial and whatever awaited her beyond it. Here she was, having to rely on the favor of others. "Thank you for your kindness," she said.

Betsey was trying to hand the glass back to Floss when she heard some kind of ruckus on the courthouse lawn outside her cell. Through the window above the bed, Betsey could see two men—at least she could see their boots—who were standing near the window. She could hear their angry voices.

"My folks just want to get home," one of the men said.

The other man answered—Betsey recognized the voice as belonging to Mr. Fyffe—and, when he did, it was with an authority that made it clear his word wasn't to be doubted or corrected.

"I've set up shotgun barricades," he said. "No one's coming in if they've got the sickness."

"But my folks have been on that steamer ever since Memphis. Where are they to go if they can't come home?"

"Anywhere but here," Mr. Fyffe said.

The glass slipped from Betsey's hand and struck the corner of the iron bedstead before falling to the floor, shattered.

"Oh, I'm so sorry," she said. "I'm just so clumsy sometimes."

Floss grabbed her by the shoulders. "Quick," she said. "Stand up."

Betsey let her pull her to her feet. "Turn around three times," Floss said. "Counterclockwise. That'll spin the bad luck back where it came from."

"Bad luck?" Betsey was still distracted by the voices outside the window. "What are they talking about?" she asked Floss.

"Spin, spin," Floss said, as she turned Betsey around. "No one can be too careful now. Not with the death at our door."

"The death?" said Betsey.

"Aye, Missus. The cholera has come."

The Twenty-Second Lasts All Day

It was a glorious October, sunny and warm. The pumpkins were fat and orange on the vines. Crows called to one another from the treetops. Squirrels scrabbled about, gnawing at hickory nut husks. Spider webs glistened with dew.

Tom McKinney and his father were busy cutting cornstalks and gathering them into shocks. The dry leaves scraped together in the wind that came from the south and smelled of summer. Shafts of sunlight splintered through the grove of trees around the Deal cabin, and Eveline and her mother took stools out into the dooryard so they could sit in the air, sewing the last of the lace on their Ascension gowns.

"Don't drag them in the dirt," her mother said.

"I won't, Mama," said Eveline. She sat on her stool, her gown gathered on her lap, and she closed her eyes a moment and tilted her head so she could feel the sun warm her face. Here she was, and here was her mother, on the verge of Heaven's reward.

It seemed as if the killing frost might never come, and though it was tempting to think that this might be paradise on earth, Eveline knew that all this would pass and the only thing to trust was God's promise of life everlasting.

"It won't be long now," her mother said. "Are you scared?"

Eveline said she wasn't, but, truth be told, maybe she was, at least a little. Lifted up. She could hardly imagine the rising, the ground below her shrinking until it was no more. She'd burst through the clouds, but to what she couldn't say. A city of gold? A land of angels? She tried to dream it, but every time she did, she felt her nerves all on edge because of all she didn't know.

But there were other things that frightened her more. The Asiatic cholera, for instance. Word had come from Lawrenceville. The cholera was a horrible way to die—the dysentery, the purging, the swollen flesh blackening, the body actually falling to pieces sometimes. In Heaven, though, there'd be no need for fear, no need to worry ever again about suffering, no thought of Miss Betsey and what waited for her at her trial. A trial that would never happen, Eveline kept telling herself. Choices had been made; lives were going to change, particularly Eveline's. She had no cause to worry about having to testify at the trial, nor any thought of what her testimony to the coroner's jury had wrought, because in four days' time—hallelujah—she was going up.

"I'm not scared," her mother said. "I'm ready. Lord knows this life has been a misery."

Many of the Millerites, their eyes on Heaven, had been giving away their possessions, joyfully releasing themselves from the burden of ownership, but Eveline's mother was too embarrassed to take part in that charity, too embarrassed by their meager and shabby belongings. She told Eveline she couldn't imagine they'd have a thing that anyone would want.

What was there among their things worth cabbaging onto? The rough-hewn table and bench? The straw tick mattress? The worn quilts? Better to just latch the door and walk away. There was a spot south of Heathsville, off the broad road in a field, where the land rolled to a hillock atop of which stood a tall oak tree. It was agreed that all the brothers and sisters would gather atop the hill on the night of the twenty-first and wait together. When the clock struck midnight and the sky split open, as it surely would, the path to Heaven would be clear and easy. No use taking a chance on being overlooked. A number of folks were sleeping out there in the field now, wanting to take no chance on a miscalculation. When the trumpet called, they wanted to make sure they could answer.

Her father had come back, but unless he believed, he'd have to be left behind. She had no way of knowing that he was moving from one abandoned cabin to another now, scavenging foodstuffs left behind, sleeping in beds still made up with quilts, drinking cool water brought up from cisterns, biding his time. She didn't know that the shadow she barely sensed passing by her window as she slept belonged to him, as did the stir of air she felt toward dawn and the rustling noise she heard in the garden, a sound she convinced herself must be rabbits or quail. She didn't know he was watching.

And so it was, on the morning of October twenty-first, that he saw her behind the granary at the Reeds'. He watched from inside the log house, where he'd taken to sleeping. She flailed away at the ground with a mattock, moving from spot to spot, digging.

Finally, she stooped down and brought something up from the earth. A crock, it appeared to Moses Deal. She dusted the dirt from it, lifted the lid, and looked inside. Then, apparently satisfied, she put the lid back on the crock and carried it away.

That evening, Tom McKinney came to again ask his question, or rather to put it in the form of a statement this time, a command.

"Eveline, you're going to forget all this nonsense and agree to be my bride. I mean it. We're going to get on with the business of living our lives in the here and now."

"Don't tell me what to do, Tom McKinney." Eveline was paring potatoes for her and her mother's supper, while her mother was in the springhouse, fetching a crock of milk. Eveline pointed her knife at Tom. "You know you can't marry me without my father's bond."

Tom nodded. "Yes, and your father says he'll give it."

So her father had made himself known to Tom, and they'd discussed a possible marriage. Men thought they had a right to everything. Even the Mister who had sold those twenty acres of land, even he had seen no need to consult Miss Betsey even though that ground had been in her family for years. And now Eveline's father had conspired with Tom to marry her away. Her father wasn't even a part of her life now, but in the eyes of the law he still had rights to her.

"You hush about my father," she said to Tom. "I don't want my mama to know he's lurking about."

"He says he'll sign a marriage bond. He wants you and me to be happy. I don't know what happened to him up in Dark Bend, but I can see he's a different man now. He's ready to do right by you and your mama if you'll only give him the chance."

Eveline let her arm drop to her side, overcome by a sudden sadness. She recalled how her father had looked that day in the woods—broken down and about to give up hope. She'd turned away from him once she heard his story, but she'd been unable to forget the way he'd stood there with his blackened eye, his long beard, the hank of rope he used to hold up his britches. He was, after all, her father, and she found it impossible to completely dismiss him.

"Did he say that to you?" she asked Tom, her voice catching a bit on the lump that had settled in her throat.

"He did," said Tom.

"Where did you see him?" She heard her mother's singing as she came up the path from the springhouse. "Quick, tell me before Mama's back."

"Over at the Reeds'. He sleeps some nights there."

The door to the cabin opened, and Eveline's mother walked in, the crock of milk held before her.

"Mama, look who's here," Eveline said with a bright tone. "It's Tom."

Her mother set the crock on the table. "Tom, we're not long for this old world."

"So they say, Missus Deal."

"Have you come to say goodbye to Eveline?"

It struck Eveline then that there were things she wanted to say to him, things she couldn't say now in front of her mother. That was all right. She wasn't even sure she had words for these things. She only felt them inside her, these stirrings. She thought of the way her life might have been if not for the Ascension. She thought of days and days with Tom McKinney. She wondered whether he had things he wanted to say to her, too, but of course she knew that he didn't feel the dwindling hours the way she did. To him, this was like any other night and the ones he was sure would follow.

"Will you stay to supper?" Eveline's mother asked.

For a good while, Tom didn't speak. He stared at Eveline, and she heard what he wanted to say in the way he looked at her. *I'll always love you, Eveline. One day, you'll admit that you love me, too. You'll see that there can be a world of happiness right here beneath our feet. Joy isn't the province of Heaven alone.*

But what he actually said was, "No, I won't be staying."

Then he walked out of the cabin, leaving Eveline and her mother to what they both thought would be their last night on Earth.

After they finished supper, Eveline's mother lay down on her bed, and soon she was asleep.

Eveline was restless, filled with a great excitement but also needled with the feeling of unfinished business. She slipped out of the cabin and walked into the woods, not admitting to herself where she was going until she found herself on the deer path that led to the Reeds', wondering whether she'd find her father there.

She hurried over the path as she'd done so many times. So many steps without a thought that her life was dwindling. Now she felt it with a certainty she couldn't escape, this impending release from the cares of the world. She was going to that place where time would be no more. She looked all around her, taking in the red leaves on the sumacs, the yellow on the hickories, smelling the sharp scent of the cedars, listening to the rill of the creek she was about to cross. Her life had been made up of moments like this—ordinary moments of grace—and now that they were almost gone, she knew how precious each of them had been.

The air got cooler in the woods; the sun was sinking in the west. Eveline quickened her pace, and finally, up ahead, she saw the tree line give way to prairie grass—turkey-foot and foxtail, shimmery in the last of the golden light—and she stepped into the clearing and saw a wisp of smoke rising from the chimney at the Reeds' log house.

A covey of quail lifted up, just inches in front of her, and for a moment the air was astir with the frantic clicking of their wings.

Eveline closed her eyes and said, "Oh, my." She felt her heart pounding in her chest.

"That's just the way, isn't it?" She opened her eyes and saw her father coming toward her through the grass. "You think you know exactly what's what. Then something comes along to surprise you."

He'd cut his beard and shaved his face clean. Somewhere, he'd found a pair of trousers that fit him and a set of black braces to hold them up. He had on a clean white shirt, and he'd combed his hair as best he could. His hurt eye was open now. He looked like a man with prospects, a man folks could count on. He looked, Eveline realized, like a father, and for a moment she found herself remembering what it'd been like before he'd gone away to Dark Bend. He'd been a diligent man, one of purpose and backbone. A landowner, an upright citizen. She didn't know what had happened to change him or what had happened now to change him again. She only knew he took up with that woman and ran away to Dark Bend from which he'd now returned.

"Like this morning," he said to Eveline. "I saw you dig something up from behind the granary over there. A most curious thing to see."

"Not so curious," she said. "It was just pieces of glass from Miss Betsey's hand mirror that she broke back in the summer. She said I was to bury them or else she'd have bad luck. She's superstitious that way."

"What need do you have for them now?"

"The Mister made that glass. I just wanted to look on them one more time."

"Leonard Reed must have meant something to you."

"He did. He was like a father to me."

She knew she'd hurt her father with what she'd said. When he reached for her hand, she let him take it.

"Come along, daughter," he said. "You might as well know what I found."

❧

The log house was much the way it'd been on the day the Mister took sick: the tea plates still in the step-back cupboard, thread spindles poking out from a sewing basket, a stack of *Godey's Lady's Books* on the hearth. Eveline had sat there so many afternoons reading letters from the lovelorn to Miss Betsey. It felt odd to be in the house now with only her father. He let go of her hand and moved to a humpback trunk at the foot of the bed. The hinges creaked when he lifted the lid.

"I was looking for another quilt," he said. "As warm as the days are, the nights cool off quick." He reached into the trunk. "That's when I found this."

The gloaming was full upon them now; soon the dark would come, and Eveline would have to hurry back to her mother. They'd put on their Ascension robes and make their way to the hillock in the field south of town where all the believers would be gathered.

But first there was this: her father turning to her, a *Godey's Lady's Book* in his hand. He opened it and took a scrap of paper that had been pressed between its pages.

"You better read this," he said.

She went to him and took the paper. In the dim light, she thought she saw her name, but when she moved closer to the hearth and could see better by the light of the fire, she saw that what she'd first thought was "Eveline," was instead, "Everything." Only the word was misspelled: *Everytink you have I can take.*

That was the whole of the message, at least all that was left, or perhaps all that ever was. It was hard to tell since the paper had been ripped. One thing was very clear to Eveline, though. Heinz Ernst had written it, and, what was more, she knew what those words meant. She knew the story of his son Jacob, and how Heinz Ernst blamed Miss Betsey for his death. This was a message that promised revenge.

Eveline let her arm fall to her side. She bowed her head.

"There are other papers pressed between these pages." Her father held the *Godey's Lady's Book* a little closer, inviting her to look for herself. "Daughter," he said, "you remember what I said about Heinz Ernst and the killing of Leonard Reed?"

She could hear the joyous shouts, the banging of pots and pans, an occasional musket blast: all the noise of the believers moving along the broad road. She had to be going. She had to be with her mother.

"I came to tell you goodbye," she said, "and here you are giving me this and filling my head with wicked thoughts. Oh, Papa, won't you come with us?"

He shook his head. "I'm not in God's grace. Surely, you can see that." He nodded toward the open door. "And even if I was, I'm not so sure I'd want to be part of a glitter show like this."

She tried to give him the paper, but he wouldn't take it. "I'll have no use of it," she said. "Not after the Rapture."

"You keep it," he said. "Just in case. You know where the other ones are." He lifted the lid of the trunk and put the *Godey's Lady's Book* back inside. He closed the lid and patted it. "Right here, inside that book."

"Papa?"

"Go on," he said. "I know you have to. Just remember, there's more than one way to spin a story. Make sure you spin it the right way. Sometimes we don't have to say everything. Sometimes we just have to say enough."

~~~

Her mother was frantic when she returned. "Eveline," she said, "I feared you'd gone on without me."

"No, Mama. I wouldn't dream of doing that." It was full dark now, the hours dwindling. The candlelight made a shadow of Eveline and cast it on the wall as she took off her dress and slipped her Ascension gown over her head. "Are you ready, Mama? Should we go?"

"I woke up and you weren't here."

"I went for a walk, Mama."

"With Tom?"

"Tom McKinney doesn't own me."

"Did you see your father?"

Eveline wondered for a moment if she'd heard her mother right. "So you know he's back?"

"I saw him snooping around a few times. He's cleaned himself up some. Guess that woman got tired of him, or maybe the other way around. What did he want from you?"

"I think he's hoping he might come back home to us."

For a good while, her mother didn't say anything. There was only the distant sound of banjo music coming from the believers still moving along the broad road, that and the noise of crickets, and the call of an owl.

"That's just like him." When her mother finally spoke, her voice was hoarse and distant, all stripped down until it was nearly nothing. "Day late and a dollar short."

❧

So it was that Eveline and her mother closed the door to their cabin for what they assumed would be the last time and set off up the road. The night air had cooled, and Eveline wished they'd taken time to throw on shawls over their Ascension gowns.

"Are you cold, Mama?"

"No, no, I'm not a bit cold. I feel all lit up inside."

Eveline hurried to keep up with her. A waxing gibbous moon hung high overhead. The full moon, a hunter's moon, was still five days off, but there was enough light to see the way into Heathsville easy enough.

Just outside the village, they caught up with two women, also in Ascension gowns—the spinster sisters, Ferne and Edna Mobley. Ferne was tall and straight with worry lines on her forehead. Edna was round and squat and had a merry laugh, even though she always seemed to be "down in the back," "down in the mouth," "down in the heart." She was bent over a hickory stick, hobbling up the road.

"Lands. Who is it?" she said.

"It's just us," Eveline's mother called out. "Dessie and Eveline Deal."

"Oh, Dessie," Edna said. "Isn't it wonderful? It makes me feel like singing, but Sister says I shouldn't."

"There are people about," Ferne said. She wore a white bonnet on her head. "People who think we're fools. Better not to call attention to ourselves."

"Oh, shaw." Eveline's mother waved her hand in the air, offering a quick dismissal of Ferne's concerns. "I wasn't born in the woods to be scared by an owl. What should we sing, Edna?"

"I've always been partial to 'Rock of Ages.'"

"So it is, then."

Eveline listened to her mother's and Edna's voices rising in the night as they walked into Heathsville.

Although the hour was late—past eleven now—the main street through the village was lined with people.

"Lord, have mercy," Ferne said.

Edna and Eveline's mother kept singing.

The men sat upon hitching rails, on their horses, on the wooden boardwalk in front of the shops. Eveline saw more than one jug being passed around. Some of the men held pine-knot torches, and she knew that they'd congregated at this late hour because tonight was the night when the believers were gathering on the hillock south of the village. Eveline took note of how the men fell quiet, how they studied her and her mother and the Mobley sisters. She could only describe the looks on their faces as hate-scarred. She imagined that some of the men had been a part of the mob that had come to John Wynn's jail, hoping to lynch Miss Betsey—men with anger thwarted, pent-up now and simmering on this night when the Millerites believed that the glory would soon be full upon them.

Her mother and Edna kept singing. They sang as they walked past James Logan's apothecary and Ethan Delz's dry goods store. If they registered the silence around them, they gave no sign of discomfort.

Then at the corner of the street where the hotel sat, someone called out, "Shet your mouth, or I'll fix your flint."

Someone threw a tomato and it struck Edna on the back of her Ascension gown, staining the white satin with red pulp. The force of the throw nearly knocked her down. She teetered but held to her hickory stick.

The men were laughing now, a great uproar that spread up and down the street.

Edna straightened. She pulled herself upright and brandished her hickory stick at the crowd. "You're all no-account," she said. "Every last one of you. You're a sin to Moses."

Ferne slipped an arm around her waist and spoke to her in a low voice. "Come along now, Sister. They're not worth your time."

∼⦾∼

Eveline saw the campfires burning in the meadow long before they reached it. The singing was louder there. Groups of believers stood around the fires, some with quilts draped over their shoulders, and they sang. The words came one on top of the other, so Eveline couldn't make them out. But the sound was lovely. The music made by those fervent voices.

Ferne helped Edna onto an empty stool that they found in front of a tent.

"That's my husband's stool," a dark-haired woman said. She was wearing a man's slouch hat. "But you can rest a spell if you're a mind to."

"Someone in town hit her with a tomato," said Ferne. "There were lots of men there. Lots of angry men."

The dark-haired woman nodded. "We soon won't have to tolerate the likes of them."

Edna said, "They can't dampen my spirit, especially not tonight."

"That's right," said the dark-haired woman. "Good for you."

Eveline edged closer to the fire, intent on warming herself. The encounter with the men in town had spooked her. The dark-haired woman's husband was there, a short man with his hair parted on the side and combed over his ears. He was plucking the strings of a banjo, not really making a song, just plucking from time to time. Eveline knew he was married to the dark-haired woman because he nodded toward her and said, "We gave away everything we had exceptin' the clothes we've got on, this banjo, and that stool."

He stopped plucking the banjo. He studied Eveline a good long while, long enough for her to start to feel uncomfortable with the way he was looking at her.

Finally, he said, "Ain't you Eveline Deal? The one who worked for Betsey Reed?" He didn't wait for an answer, and Eveline was glad for that. "Now there's a woman who's lost her soul," he said. "It's a good thing that you're shed of her."

"Amen," said Eveline, and then she retreated from the fire, slipping back into the shadows.

Her mother was talking to the dark-haired woman who said, as Eveline joined them, that she and her husband had been in the meadow all that week—"Why take a chance?"—and from time to time some of the rabblerousers from town came to torment them.

"You know how they are," the woman said.

"Weren't you scared?" Eveline's mother asked.

The woman pushed her slouch hat back onto the crown of her head. "Sister, I just pray for them. I surely do."

A voice rang out from somewhere in the meadow—a man's loud voice. "It's nearly midnight," he said.

The singing stopped, and the night got so still Eveline felt a shiver go up her neck. Something was about to happen. For a time, there was only the sound of the logs popping in the fires. Eveline gazed up into the sky and watched a skein of clouds pass over the moon. The night got darker then, and people started to murmur. Then as the moon came out from under the clouds, and the sky brightened, someone said, "Could it be now?" And that started people to praying. They got down on their knees in the meadow and they prayed for the Ascension.

But the sky didn't open. The believers sat on the ground and waited.

"No one worry," Edna Mobley said. "The twenty-second lasts all day."

That sent a ripple of laughter through the meadow. Soon Eveline could hear the line being repeated. *The twenty-second lasts all day.*

Someone found quilts for her and her mother and the Mobley sisters, and they huddled together and soon, in spite of her efforts to stay awake, she was asleep.

She woke to the sound of her father's voice.

"Dessie, it's me. It's Moses."

"I know who you are," her mother said.

Eveline was full awake now, her heart full of hope. "Papa," she said, "have you come to join us?"

"I've come to warn you," he said. "I was in town and I didn't like the talk I heard. Those men . . ." He shook his head. "They're coming out here, and they'll be looking to make trouble. I'd be thinking about leaving if I was you."

Eveline said, "But it's the twenty-second."

And Edna, who was dozing on her stool, murmured, "The twenty-second lasts all day."

"If you ask me," Eveline's mother said, "you're the one who's good at leaving."

"Dessie, I . . ."

"Don't even try to explain. You're in a holy place. Don't dirty it with your lies. And I don't want to hear a word about that woman. Not a word, do you understand?"

"I do, Dessie. I've come back to ask you to forgive me. I'm asking for us to be a family again."

A ground fog settled over the meadow, casting a veil over the fires. People milled about, their watery figures vanishing and then reappearing in the fog. Eveline heard their voices, and sometimes, because she couldn't match a voice with a body, it was like the words came from nowhere.

"Moses, it's not me you should be asking to forgive you," her mother said. "It's God."

"What makes you think I haven't?"

Somewhere downhill from them, a commotion broke out—angry voices, shouts. Eveline felt an urgent moment was at hand.

"Mama, listen to him," she said. "Please."

Her mother took her time. She gathered a breath, and Eveline thought she would speak. Then she let out the breath and sat there staring at the fire. Finally, she said, "Moses, you stay here. You stay right here for now. You stay with us and wait."

Without a word, he sat cross-legged on the ground beside her, and Eveline couldn't help herself. No matter how much he'd hurt her by leaving and taking up with that woman in Dark Bend, he was her father, and now he'd asked for their forgiveness. She reached across her mother and took his hand, pleased when she felt his fingers cling to hers. None of them said anything. They sat there in the fog, and soon Eveline could hear the angry voices getting closer.

"What in the world?" she said.

And then the fog split open, and like that the men were upon them.

Vibrio Cholerae

IT TOOK ONLY A FEW days for the townspeople of Lawrenceville to get the word—despite Sheriff Fyffe's best efforts to keep it out, the cholera had come—and then people began to take flight, convinced that it traveled to them by air in the miasma they breathed in this town on the Embarrass River. The unnaturally warm October days were more humid than most and the air was filled with the stink of rotting vegetation and dead fish and wet corn. *There's not a breath to be found*, people were heard to say in the days just before the news broke. *Not a breath.*

So many houses had the shades drawn and black crepe tied around the doorknobs. Fresh graves dotted the hillside at the City Cemetery. Newly built coffins stacked up at the cabinet-maker's shop. The shotgun barricades were keeping people from entering the city, but they could do nothing to stop folks from leaving if they were of a mind to, and many of them were. They packed their trunks and left by steamer, stagecoach, or in their own wagons and buggies. They went to where they had family living—north was the preferred direction—hoping for cooler days, cleaner air.

The streets around the courthouse square were empty most of the time. The shopkeepers came outside to sit on benches and stools and kegs, aprons tied around them, their black sleeve garters taking on an air of mourning. Sometimes they swept their section of the plank walkways in front of their stores to give the appearance of business as usual, but nothing could have been further from the truth. Nothing was happening in Lawrenceville.

Nothing except people taking sick with the cholera.

One of them was Floss Fyffe, the wife of the sheriff.

Betsey knew that something was amiss when the sheriff started bringing her meals. She could tell from his stooped shoulders and the distant look in his eyes that something was troubling him. Then one morning she saw the doctor hitch his buggy to the rail outside and come inside the courthouse with his black bag.

When the sheriff brought her dinner, she noticed the way he glowered at her with disdain.

"There you are," he said. "Healthy as a horse."

She laid down her fork and waited to see if he'd say more. When he didn't, she asked, "Is it something about Floss?"

"Here I am cooking food for you," he said, "and toting it to you on a tray."

"Is it the cholera?"

She saw him wince. His eyes squeezed shut and he turned away from her. He stepped outside the cell and shut the door behind him. Then he looked at her, and his voice shook when he said, "She's a good woman, my Floss."

"I know she is," said Betsey.

Good-humored, good-hearted Floss who brought her a comb and looking glass, who combed the snarls from her hair and told her she was pretty. Why should Floss suffer so?

That's the question that Betsey asked the Reverend Seed that evening when he came to visit. They sat in the glow of the candlelight, she on her bed, and he on the stool beside it, his Bible open on his lap.

"You say all the answers are in that book," Betsey said. "Does it tell you somewhere why God doesn't look out for good people?"

"Oh, but he does," Reverend Seed said. "He rewards them in

Heaven." He thumbed through the pages of his Bible until he found the scripture he was looking for. Then he held the Bible closer to the candle, so he could better read the words. "'Fear none of those things which thou shalt suffer: behold, the devil shall cast *some* of you into prison, that ye may be tried; and ye shall have tribulation ten days: be thou faithful unto death, and I will give thee a crown of life.'"

Betsey had heard it before, this story of faith and the trials that tested a soul and the eternal life that awaited those who were steadfast, but she'd never been able to understand how that could make it more acceptable that a good person like Floss should have to suffer, or for that matter her own husband. Even someone as unbelieving as he, why should he have to die the way he did long before it should have been his time? And the boy, Jacob Ernst. Dead before he'd had the chance to live. How to make sense of that?

"Is Mrs. Fyffe one of the faithful ones?"

"She is. She loves God with all her heart. Yes, I believe it to be so."

"Is she going to die?"

He closed the Bible and rubbed his hand over its cover. "Yes," he finally said, "I believe that, too."

For a good while, Betsey didn't speak. She was thinking about what might be ahead of her. She closed her eyes and tried to imagine that moment when life would be no more. If they found her guilty and took her to the gallows, her time on Earth would dwindle down, as it was now for Floss, and the last second would pass, and she would be gone. But where would she go? That was the question that haunted her. What happened to the dead once they crossed over?

"Are you sure there's a Heaven?" she asked Reverend Seed. "How do we really know?"

"All you have to do," he said, "is believe."

She wanted to, but something always stood in her way. Whatever that something might be—a hardening of her heart, common sense, or plain old stubbornness—it was a weight that was hard to move.

"What about all those Millerites?" she said. "They thought they were going to their reward, but here it is, October twenty-third, and we're all still here."

"It made for a good story, didn't it?"

Betsey recalled how desperately Eveline wanted to believe that she was going up. "Isn't your own Bible a good story, too?"

This time, he didn't need to open the Bible. The scripture he needed he'd committed to memory: "'But of that day and hour knoweth no *man*, no, not the angels of heaven, but my Father only.'"

Betsey heard footsteps and Sheriff Fyffe's voice calling with a great urgency. "Reverend, Reverend. Oh, mercy."

"So we're to wait?" Betsey said

"Yes, wait and believe."

"Reverend, I'd like to talk to Eveline Deal."

She wanted to tell the girl that she forgave her for what she'd said to the coroner's jury.

"She can't come into town while the cholera is here."

Sheriff Fyffe was at the cell door. "Reverend, come quick. Oh, mercy, my Floss, she's going."

The Great Disappointment

BAKER CEMETERY SAT ATOP A hill at the end of a lane just off the broad road into Heathsville, not far at all from the meadow where the believers had gathered only two nights past and where the men from town had come upon Eveline and her mother and father and the Mobley sisters with a vengeance.

Eveline smelled the whiskey on them and the smoke from their pine knot torches. One of the men touched his torch to the dry turkey-foot grass, and a fire started near her feet. She held up the hem of her Ascension gown and jumped back from the low flames.

"Mercy sakes," said Fern Mobley. She strained her long neck like a horse fighting the bit.

"You men," said Edna. "You there. What do you think you're doing?"

"We come to see Jesus," the man who'd started the fire said. Eveline didn't know him. He had a black beard and hair down over his ears. "Ain't that why you're here?"

Eveline's father was putting out the fire by slapping at it with his coat and stomping it with his boots.

Some of the men carried ax handles. One of them, Eveline saw, was Heinz Ernst.

"Mr. Ernst," she said, "I'd think you'd be ashamed to be here pestering good people."

He squinted his eyes and shaded them with his hand. "Hoo says I should be ashamed? Hoo are you, girl, to talk dat vay to me?"

"I'm Eveline Deal," she said.

"Eveline Deal," he said, stepping closer. "The hired girl to dat vitch."

"She's not a witch." Eveline was sure of that much. "She didn't have anything to do with your son. Jacob got sick. That's all. He got sick and then he died."

That's when Heinz Ernst grabbed her by her arm. "You don't have any right to say dese tinks."

He shook her, then pulled her down until she was kneeling in the grass.

"You're hurting me," she said. "My arm. You're hurting my arm."

No matter how hard she tried, she couldn't shake loose from him.

"You leave her alone," her mother said. "You wicked man. You let go of my daughter."

Then, in an instant, she was free. She got to her feet and saw her father standing over Heinz Ernst who was now sprawled on the ground.

"Get up," her father said. "Get up, and I'll hit you again."

He turned away for just a moment. He looked toward Eveline and her mother.

"You see to her, Dessie," he said.

Eveline felt her mother's arms gather her in, and she thought, all right then, we'll be a family, realizing, as she thought it, that she was giving up on God, knowing he wasn't coming, knowing she wasn't going up, not on that night, or the one after, and maybe not at all. All right then. She'd start paying more attention to the world around her. She'd start with her mother and father. They'd come back together, and life would go on.

Her father started to turn back to Heinz Ernst who was now on his feet, but Eveline said, "Papa," and he took a few steps toward her.

That's when Heinz Ernst swung his ax handle. He hit Eveline's father in the back of the head and the sound was like an overripe watermelon cracking open.

"Papa," she cried again.

"Lord have mercy," Ferne said.

"You've killed him," said Edna. "That's what you've done, sure as I'm sitting here."

Heinz Ernst and the other men were running, then, slipping back into the fog as if they'd never come.

But they had. By the time Eveline got to her father, she knew he was dead, and, what's more, she knew the story that he'd alluded to, the one in which Heinz Ernst murdered the Mister—hadn't that been what her father suggested?—was hers and hers alone now. If she told it, though, she'd look a fool. How in the world could Heinz Ernst poison the Mister? But if she didn't tell it, what would happen to Miss Betsey? Would they really hang a woman like everyone said they should?

All Eveline knew for sure that night was that her father was dead and there was no God to save them from that. No God to save Eveline from what she'd now have to face, the trial of Betsey Reed.

❧

But first there was the burying. Her father's pine coffin rode in a horse-drawn wagon up the lane to Baker Cemetery. The wagon wheels rolled over hickory nuts dropped from the trees along the lane, and the husks popped and cracked. Crows had come to roost in the high branches, and their raucous calls seemed to Eveline to be a most indignant noise, one that stirred her so she heard herself say to her mother, "They should hang Heinz Ernst. I'd gladly cut the rope and spring the trap."

"Eveline," her mother said in an urgent whisper. "You shouldn't say something like that. It's not Christian."

They were waiting by the open grave in the sunlight. The preacher had his Bible open, and a few mourners, the Mobley sisters among them, waited for the men—James Wynn; Tom McKinney and his father; the schoolmaster, Lemuel Brookhart—to hoist the coffin to their shoulders and carry it to the grave.

"I don't care about Christian anymore," Eveline said to her mother. She made no attempt to lower her voice. She was glad for the preacher and the others to hear her. "God and his Heaven aren't nothing but a hoax."

She was mad. Mad over the stories she'd believed. Mad because of the fool her faith had made her. And for what? The skies hadn't opened. Jesus hadn't come. No one had gone up. All there was that night was the darkness and the sound of Heinz Ernst's ax handle cracking her father's skull.

Now she was left to face the fact. There was no God, at least not a merciful one. There were only dark hearts, and now hers was one of them.

"Eveline Deal," her mother said, and she stomped her foot on the dusty ground. "I said hush."

So they buried Moses Deal, not far from where the Mister had been returned to his grave. Just a row over and a smidge to the east.

John Wynn came to pay his respects to Eveline and her mother. He held his hat in his hands. His hair was slicked back, and beads of sweat dotted his forehead.

"There's no question who did this," he said. "I've got witnesses galore."

"It was Heinz Ernst," said Ferne Mobley, who had her arm around Dessie's shoulders.

"That German man." Edna nodded. "You know the one I mean."

"I do," said John Wynn. "I just have to find him."

Eveline said, "You know where he's gone?"

"Where do the rotten ones always go?" John Wynn took a blue bandana from his coat pocket and wiped his forehead. "Dark Bend. Last refuge for thieves and counterfeiters and murderers." It must have dawned on him, then, that the deceased, Moses Deal, had lived there for a time. "No disrespect intended." John Wynn bowed his head. "Begging your pardon," he said to Eveline and her mother.

Such a strange day it was, the day she said goodbye to her father, the day of what would come to be known as the Great Disappointment, the day when no one ascended and Millerites who'd given away their belongings were left to wander aimlessly, not quite sure what to do, or else, like Eveline, they gave up their faith altogether and hardened their hearts.

"Sometimes people are in trouble," she said to John Wynn, "and they don't have anywhere to go."

John Wynn put his hat on his head. "It can be a cruel world," he said. "I'd tame it if I could."

He nodded to the ladies, turned, and went to fetch his horse from the hitching post.

Tom McKinney had been lingering near the grave. He came to stand beside Eveline now. "Eveline?" he said, but before he could go on, she interrupted him.

"Who's that man?" She pointed beyond John Wynn to a figure half hidden in the grove of hickory trees. "There," she said. "Who do you expect that is?"

Tom lifted his arm and shaded his eyes. "It's Mr. Delz," he said.

John Wynn swung up into the saddle and nudged his horse into a sidestep which brought him near to Eveline. "Betsey Reed has been asking to see you," he said.

Eveline felt her heart beat faster. "Me? Miss Betsey?" She wanted to go to her right away. She wanted to tell her she was sorry for inviting the coroner's jury to believe that she'd killed the Mister. "When can we go?" she asked John Wynn.

There was the cholera, he reminded her. No one could get into Lawrenceville, and who knew when Betsey's trial would be able to commence?

"I'd go if I could," Eveline said. "I hope she knows that."

When she looked back to the grove of hickory trees, Ethan Delz was gone. She wasn't alarmed. She could see very clearly what she'd have to do.

⚬⚬⚬

Tom and his father accompanied Eveline and her mother back to their cabin.

"A woman ought not be alone too much at a time like this," Daniel McKinney said. He was a hale man with a broad chest. His face and neck were reddened by the days he'd spent working in the sun. No, he said, a woman needed folks around her when death came. Murder, it was, at the hands of that German, Heinz Ernst. "He's a man who takes to his whiskey," Daniel McKinney said. "He's been talking crazy for a long time."

"Crazy? How?" Eveline asked.

Tom said, "Going around since last summer saying he was going to be a rich man."

"Said he'd never have to work another day," said Daniel.

Tom shook his head. "How would he do that, we wanted to know. He said that was his cabbage to chew, and he wouldn't chew it twice. We'd just have to wait and see."

"And now this." Daniel stuffed his bandana back into his pocket. "Murder, and Heinz Ernst the one who done it."

"That's right," said Tom. "And still stuck with the little end of the horn."

Something stirred just then inside the log house and inside Eveline as well. It may have just been the sun dipping down below the tree line in the west that caused the light to fade, and shadows to slide across the room, and for a chill to go down her neck, or it may have been, she thought, the cold knowledge of something about to be made plain, something that, even though it was unexpected, would seem familiar to her once it arrived.

"Mother, don't fuss so," she said. "Mother, sit down."

He mother had been moving slowly around the house, touching the things that were hers, all the things she'd thought she was leaving behind that night when she and Eveline left to join those who swore they were going up.

Now here they were, back in the house where she'd given birth to Eveline and lost four others to summer's complaint. Not one of them more than two years old, and now their father laid to rest among them. What could she do but handle the comb and brush, the sewing basket, the spinning wheel, the butter churn? What could she do but remind herself that she was still upon the earth and with a life to live.

It set Eveline's nerves on edge. She put her arm around her mother's shoulders and nudged her toward her rocking chair, the one by the fireplace, which, of course, was cold. Once her mother was settled, the rockers creaking, Eveline turned back to Tom and his father and said, "And still stuck with the short end of the horn?" She let the repeated words linger in the air between them. "There's something you're not saying."

"Eveline?" Tom scratched his head and gave her a puzzled look. "What are you getting at?"

"I'm not sure, really, but I hear it. I hear it all around the words you've said. It's there, but I can't quite snatch it. Maybe you don't even know it yourselves." She reached for the reticule that she'd set on the table when they came into the house, the drawstring bag she'd carried to her father's funeral and burying. "I want to show you something. Maybe this will help."

She pulled out the scrap of paper that her father had given her the night of the Ascension, the paper he'd found inside a trunk at the Reeds' house, the paper that said, *Everytink you have I can take.*

Tom took it from her, and, after he'd read it, he showed it to his father.

"Every-*tink*," his father said.

"What is it?" Eveline's mother asked.

It was the first time she'd spoken since they'd come inside, and her voice caught all of them off guard.

"Tom?" Eveline said.

He bowed his head a moment. "Oh, my word." Then he lifted his face to her, and Eveline could see the panic in his eyes. "Oh, my holy word."

For a good while his was the only voice inside the house. He could barely rein it in. His words bolted as if tied up too long, and now, finally let loose, they ran wild.

"One night," he said. "This was back in the summer. It must have been in June sometime because I'd been shocking wheat. I'd been at it all afternoon and on into the evening when the light was starting to fade, and I finally gave it up and started back to the house. That's when I run across Heinz Ernst coming from the woods between my field and the Reeds' house. He was in a hurry, I could tell that, but I shouted for him to stop, and he did. 'Where have you been?' I asked him, and he told me he'd been to see Leonard Reed. 'The man you claimed cheated you on that milk cow?' I said. 'The man married to the woman you say put a spell on your boy?' 'Ach,' he said, and something came up from his throat and he spit it on the ground. 'Why would you be paying a visit to them?' I asked him, and he said it was business.

"That's when I noticed he was toting something wrapped in a piece of muslin. I wanted to know what it was. I said, 'You sure it belongs to you?' 'Ja,' he said. Then he squatted and laid the muslin on the ground and unwrapped it. He took his time like there was something alive inside. I squatted down beside him. The moon had come up by now. The harvest moon, sitting full and bright in the sky, and as he unwrapped that muslin, the moonlight caught something—some sort of shine—and I saw that it was a bit of glass, and then as he unwrapped it more, I saw that it was a vase, a crystal vase, and I said to him, 'Did

Mr. Reed blow that piece?" and he said, 'Ja.' I wanted to know what he'd paid for it, and he told me nothing. It was a gift, a peace offering on account of the trouble between Heinz and the Reeds. 'Just sometink my missus will like,' Heinz said, and his voice was soft. 'Just sometink pretty for her.'

"There we were in the moonlight, that crystal vase on the ground between us, and Heinz Ernst had become all alive to me in a way he hadn't been before. Do you see what I'm saying? He was more than the man I'd always known. He was someone new, someone who could wrap that muslin around that vase with such care, someone who seemed embarrassed because I'd made him show it to me, and I was embarrassed, too, and it was like neither of us knew what to say next. So I let him get back to his feet and take up the vase and go back to the walking he'd been doing when I'd stopped him, and I stayed squatting down, listening to the sound of his boots whisking through the wheat stubble. I didn't think anything about his story at the time, but now that you've shown me that paper, Eveline, I wonder whether Leonard Reed had actually made Heinz a gift of that vase, or whether Heinz had stolen it, and if that's the case, then what else might be true. Eveline, didn't Leonard Reed keep a smokehouse lock on his glasshouse?"

She nodded. "He did."

"Is there any way that Heinz might have busted in?"

Now it was Eveline's voice that was too loud and bright. "Now that's just nonsense," she said. "Don't you think I'd known it if he'd broken into the glasshouse? I was inside it practically every day. Really, Tom."

Then she asked him the question that she'd been mulling over ever since she saw Ethan Delz in the woods at the cemetery.

"Did you ever hear Heinz Ernst make a threat to the Mister?"

It was Tom's father who answered. "Who hasn't that old German threatened? He's had it out for almost everyone at one time or another."

Eveline wouldn't let it go as easy as that. "Tom?" she said.

And Tom told her yes, there'd been a time when Heinz had sworn he'd get even with the Reeds. "He was pretty corned up when he said it, and coming, as it did, just after his boy died, I didn't make anything of it. I thought it was just talk."

❧

Eveline went to see Ethan Delz late that afternoon. She found him in his store near to closing time, and she lingered, pretending to admire the hair ribbons while he finished with a customer, a stumpy old man who was insisting that the flour he was about to buy was a tad shy of the pound he was promised.

"But Mr. Shank, you can see the scale for yourself."

"That scale's crooked," said Mr. Shank. Eveline seemed to recall him being acquainted with her father.

"Do you want the flour or not?"

"I want all of what's coming to me."

"And that's what you'll get. Now, take it or leave it."

Ethan Delz was angry now that his ethics were in question. He held the flour scoop above the scale, waiting.

Mr. Shank leaned over and spit a stream of tobacco juice on the floor. Ethan Delz let the scoop clatter onto the counter. "That's just your kind." He pointed his finger at Mr. Shank. "That's just your dirty kind."

"And that's your kind," said Mr. Shank. "A scoundrel and a cheat."

Eveline kept her head down, not wanting to be caught watching. But then Ethan Delz called her name.

"Eveline, come here," he said. "Take a look at this scale. What does it say that flour weighs out at?"

She didn't want to get involved, but how could she avoid it now? She walked to the counter and looked at the scale. "A pound," she said.

"Exactly," said Ethan Delz. "You see, Mr. Shank?"

"Call it what you will." Mr. Shank pulled out a leather coin purse to settle his bill. "I call it a cheat, but you've got the upper hand. You always know how to get what you want out of a man, don't you, Delz? Now, hurry it up. I got to get back to Dark Bend."

So that was it. Yes, an acquaintance of her father's. A man he knew from Dark Bend.

"Excuse me, sir," she said. "But perhaps you knew my father, Moses Deal?"

"Moses Deal?" Mr. Shank studied her. "Are you his girl?"

"I am."

Mr. Shank reached out and took her hand. "Honey, I feel a sadness for you."

"The constable's looking for the man who killed him," Eveline said.

"Well he shouldn't have to look too far," said Mr. Shank. "Only one place to go when a man's in trouble, and that's where I'm about to go right now."

Of course, Eveline thought. Where else would Heinz Ernst go but Dark Bend? The place was so full of danger, the law was reluctant to go there for fear of never getting out alive.

"Did you know my father well?" she asked.

Mr. Shank gathered up his parcels and started toward the door. "A dead man keeps his secrets," he said, and then he was gone.

"A crazy man." Ethan Delz hurried to the door to lock it. "All those folks are crazy up there in Dark Bend."

Eveline was well aware that Ethan Delz was suggesting that her father had been one of those desperate, dangerous sorts. She said, "Sounds like you speak from experience."

Ethan Delz pulled the shade down over the door glass. "I've been around a time or two," he said. He finally turned back to her. "What can I do for you, Eveline?"

She took a breath and slowly let it out, aware that she was about to venture into dangerous territory. She told herself to go slow, to work up to what she had to say and to ask what she wanted to know, but when it came time to speak, she lost all sense of care and got right to the point.

"I know about you and Miss Betsey," she said.

"Oh, you do, do you?" He showed no sign of alarm. He slipped the door key into the pocket of his waistcoat and patted it with his hand. "And what do you think you know?"

"I saw you back in the summer when the Mister was gone. I was there to do the milking, only you didn't know that. I heard you saying things to Miss Betsey, things a man hadn't ought to say to a married woman. And then . . ."

She stopped, unable to go on.

"And then?" Ethan Delz rocked up on the balls of his feet, thumbs hooked into the pockets of his waistcoat like he was somebody and she was no one at all. "Yes, Eveline? Go on. Or maybe you're not sure what you saw?"

"I'm sure of this," she said, and she showed him the scrap of paper on which Heinz Ernst had penned his threat.

Ethan Delz read the paper. Then he said, "Why are you showing me this? It's nothing I know about."

"Oh, but I think you do. I think you know exactly what this is."

He took a step toward her, the scrap of paper held out like an offering. She reached for it, but he snatched it back.

"Tell me," he said.

She'd meant to coax the confession out of him, but now he'd made it so she had no choice but to accuse.

"If we followed Mr. Shank up to Dark Bend," she said, "we'd find Heinz Ernst hiding there, a murderer. Isn't that right, Mr. Delz? Not just the killer of my father, but a man you hired to murder the Mister."

Ethan Delz gave her a hard look. His eyes narrowed just a moment. Then he laughed. He tossed back his head, and he laughed, and she felt her legs go weak.

"That's what you make of this?" He waved the scrap of paper about. "Murder for hire?"

"You wanted the Mister dead so you could have Miss Betsey. You couldn't kill him yourself, so you paid Heinz Ernst to do it. How did he get the poison to him? That's what I can't figure out."

Ethan Delz reached toward the pocket of his waistcoat and then caught himself and lowered his arm. It was enough, though, to make Eveline understand. It came to her just as clear as could be.

"You got him a key," she said. "He was in the glasshouse."

She reached for the paper again. This time Ethan Delz knocked her arm away. She felt his hand on her shoulder, pushing. She stumbled backward, thinking she might fall. Then the counter edge caught her lower back, and she watched as he began to rip the scrap of paper, tearing it into smaller and smaller pieces. He held the last pieces in his palm, and he blew them into her face.

"You've been dreaming, Eveline," he said. "Wake up. It's nothing. Just so much fairy dust. I believe you understand me."

She knew he was telling her to go home and forget what she thought she knew. She knew nothing. That's what he was telling her, and she should stop imagining that she did.

He turned to the door and unlocked it.

"You're dreaming," he said again, and he waited until, defeated, she stepped out into the night.

Oh, what a mess she'd made of things. She could barely stand to think of her missteps as she tramped along the trail through the woods from the broad road to the log house where her mother waited. Then she remembered the *Godey's Lady's Book* in the trunk at the Reeds' and the notes it held, all notes written by Heinz Ernst, her father had implied. Hadn't Ethan Delz stopped to consider that she might have more than that scrap of paper he tore to bits? Was he waiting for her to call his bluff?

The moon was full, shining down through the branches of the trees made thin by leaves that had already fallen to the ground. Just ahead of her she could see candlelight at the house.

As she got closer, she could see that the candle was being carried by Tom, who had come out to wait for her.

"Your mother's been worried sick about you," he said, and she felt a pang of guilt.

"Thank you for coming back to check on her."

"The constable's got her worried. John Wynn was here looking for you."

Eveline felt her heart pounding. "Has he found Heinz Ernst?"

"No, it's nothing about that," Tom said. "It's a lawyer, a Mr. French. He's going to defend Betsey, and he means to talk to you."

She felt herself grow distant from her body as if she were a spirit passing over and pausing for a moment to watch the girl below her, the one who was stunned by where her life had taken her.

"He wants to hear your story." Tom's voice was bringing her back to herself. She felt the girl she might have been move on. Just a stir of air, and she was out of her reach forever. "Eveline, what will you tell him?"

A skein of clouds passed over the moon, and then, as if someone— Miss Betsey, Eveline imagined—had been listening to her thoughts, Tom's candle went out.

"That's odd," he said. "I didn't feel a bit of wind."

Eveline didn't say anything. She took his arm, and, without another word, they turned and went into the house.

Come morning, she'd pay a visit to the Reeds', and there she'd open the trunk at the foot of the bed, and she'd take all those notes that Heinz Ernst had written, and then she'd wait until she was sure what she wanted to do.

No One Would Be the Wiser

ONE DAY IN JANUARY, MR. Fyffe brought a gentleman to call on Betsey, a soft-spoken man who introduced himself as Augustus French. The cholera had run its course, and people were now free to come and go. Betsey's trial had been set for the spring term.

Mr. French was a somber man in a frock coat, his face sagging into his shirt collar and his cravat forming a barrel-shaped knot upon which he seemed to rest his weak chin. He sat down on the stool beside Betsey's bed. Just a few moments prior to hearing footsteps descending the stairs, she'd been scraping at mortar between the stones at the head of the bed with her fingernail, taking note of how easily the mortar flaked and crumbled.

Mr. French sat with his back straight, his hands splayed out, palms down, on top of his legs. "Mrs. Reed," he said, "I'm preparing your defense."

"Defense?" She could still feel the powder of the mortar on her fingertips, and she took a great pleasure from the secret that she held, that she had swallowed a bit of that mortar, just two bits the size of a pea. If Eveline Deal could swallow glass. . . "And how will I pay you?" Betsey said to Mr. French.

"You're not to worry about that, Mrs. Reed. Proving your innocence will be compensation enough."

"How do you know I'm innocent, Mr. French?"

"Actually, Mrs. Reed, that leads me to the first question that I have for you."

Was it true, he wanted to know, that she had an—he paused, searching, she knew, for the proper word, and in that hesitation she felt fairly certain that she knew what he was going to ask. "An acquaintanceship." Yes, that was how he'd chosen to characterize it. "A friendship," he said, "with a man named Ethan Delz?"

Betsey drew her fingers back into her palms and sat, fists clenched in her lap. "Ethan Delz is a shop owner in my village."

"I know that, Mrs. Reed." Mr. French's voice had a sudden bite to it, and Betsey, surprised to hear it, snapped up her head. "If you want me to help you, you'll tell me the truth. Mrs. Reed, was Ethan Delz your paramour?"

She bowed her head, and for a moment she sat there in silence. Snow was coming down outside—a hard sleety snow that she could hear striking the barred glass in the high window at the foot of the bed. Then she relaxed her hands. She looked at the empty palms where her fingernails had left their marks. She knew Mr. French had gathered the facts, ones she couldn't deny. Someone had been telling him stories. Eveline Deal, she assumed.

"Yes," she told Mr. French. "Ethan and I . . . yes."

"All right, then," said Mr. French. "Now that's one thing we know. One thing that you and I have agreed upon. Let's see if there might be others."

He started, then, to lay out a story unlike any she could have imagined. A tale of deceit and murder for hire, a story that established reason that there were people who wouldn't mind a whit if Leonard Reed ended up dead.

"You know a Heinz Ernst, don't you?" Mr. French asked.

Yes, Betsey agreed. Of course.

"His boy, Jacob . . ."

Betsey couldn't stand to hear him say that she'd had a part in his dying. "I never," she said, and this time it was Mr. French who interrupted her.

"Of course you didn't." He even leaned toward her now and placed a hand on her shoulder. "I'm not trying to make things difficult for you," he said. "I'm only trying to sort through the facts, and another fact is Heinz Ernst held a grudge against you, and for all we know, against your husband as well."

"I suppose that's right."

Mr. French lifted his hand from her shoulder. He stood up and paced about the cell, his hands clasped behind his back. Betsey still felt his assuring touch, and she felt sure that his intention was to prove her innocence and to save her from the gallows. She knew she'd have to tell him everything.

"Ethan," she said, and then stopped. Mr. French turned on his heel to look at her. "It's not easy for a woman, for a divorced woman. Surely you know that, Mr. French."

"Go on," he said.

"So Ethan said the smart thing to do was to kill him. Mister Reed, I mean. He said it could be done with arsenic, and no one would be the wiser."

"And were you the one to do it?"

"I said I couldn't. No matter our troubles. Leonard was my husband."

Her voice was trembling now, and she could feel the tears coming to her eyes. She wiped them away with her fingertips, and then Mr. French was standing before her, offering his handkerchief. She took it and dabbed at her eyes, then sat for a while, gathering herself, the handkerchief—such good-quality linen—balled up in her fist.

"Did you purchase arsenic from the apothecary, James Logan?"

"I did not."

"Did you deliberately put poison into your husband's coffee?"

"I did not."

"But you and Ethan Delz discussed the killing of Mr. Reed. Will you admit that?"

It took her a while, but finally she nodded her head.

Mr. French said, "And you did not tell him no?"

"No, sir. I did not."

Mr. French was pacing again. Betsey knew he was working it all over in his mind, as he must have done a number of times since he'd first got the notion that she and Ethan had plotted Leonard's death. What more could she tell him that she hadn't already said? Yes, Ethan had been the one to propose that she put the arsenic into Leonard's coffee, but she'd refused. Ethan's suggestion should have been enough to sour him for her, but Leonard had sold that land, had treated her as if she had no rights to what her father had sweated and died for, and the days and nights with Leonard were interminable, and Ethan, who had sold her the purple wool for her dress, who had come to her with such tenderness, who had said, *Now look here, Betsey, here's this new life you can have.* Ethan who also said, *If you can't do it there are other ways, ways you don't need to know about,* and she couldn't stop herself from dreaming a life with him.

"Heinz Ernst despised me," she said. "It was me he blamed for his son, not Leonard."

"And yet, if enough money were on the table . . ."

Mr. French waited for Betsey to catch on to his suspicion, which she finally did. "Are you saying that Ethan and I paid Heinz Ernst to kill my husband?"

"Did you, Mrs. Reed?"

"The autopsy showed arsenic in my husband's body. He died from poisoning. Now how in the world would Heinz Ernst have been able to manage that?"

Mr. French turned toward Betsey now. "He's killed one man, this Heinz Ernst. Who's to say he hasn't killed two?"

"Another killing?"

"Moses Deal, back in late October. There were witnesses but the constable, John Wynn, hasn't been able to find Ernst."

"Oh, my." Betsey raised the handkerchief to her mouth. "Not Eveline's father."

"I ask you again, Mrs. Reed. Did you and Ethan Delz hire Heinz Ernst to kill your husband?"

"And I ask you again, Mr. French. How in the world would Heinz Ernst have been able to work that sort of magic with poison, unless he has the magic powers he accused me of using to kill his son?"

"Who had access to your husband's glasshouse?"

"I rarely stepped into it. That was where Leonard worked. He kept a smokehouse lock on the door."

"Anyone else?"

Betsey felt her stomach turn and she thought of those two pea-sized bits of mortar that she'd swallowed. She didn't want to say the next thing, but she knew she had to. "The hired girl, Eveline Deal. She worked with him there sometimes."

"Exactly. Mrs. Reed, did you know that Eveline Deal had a key to the lock?"

Of course Betsey knew that. She grew impatient with Mr. French. "What does all of this have to do with Heinz Ernst and your theory that he somehow poisoned my husband?"

"Mrs. Reed, that's exactly what I intend to find out."

Winter

JOHN WYNN HAD LOOKED FOR Heinz Ernst throughout the autumn. He'd chased after rumors, but always they turned to wisps of smoke and dissipated into the air. He even ventured a trip to Dark Bend, in spite of his fear, but still there was no sign.

Now winter had set in for good. The snows came, and the wind, and the drifts peaked above the split rail fences and the broad road became impassable.

Time to hunker down and wait, no matter if you were the hunter or the prey. Time to let winter have its way.

In her cell, Betsey read from the Bible the Reverend Seed had left for her. She read the scriptures about what God promised in the afterlife: grace, redemption, forgiveness of all sins.

"It sounds like a fairy tale," she said to the Reverend one day sat the end of January when he came to call, as he often did that winter. "Some beautiful story that someone made up to ease a child's nightmares," she said. "Surely it can't be true."

"Oh, but it can." He sat on the stool inside her cell, his hands folded in his lap. "It is. Betsey, don't you want it to be so?"

It was cold inside the cell. She pulled her shawl more tightly around her. This was her life now, this waiting and thinking and the long silence that mostly made up her days. Sometimes she imagined herself writing a letter from the lovelorn to *Godey's Lady's Book*. What would she say? That her love waited until she could be free, that she spent the days pining for him, that he'd promised her everything could be simple, and now look at the mess she was in. Or would she say she missed her husband, missed the life she'd had with him, no matter how much it frustrated and angered her at the time. Sometimes she closed her eyes and saw him coming up from the glasshouse in the snow, calling for her—"Betsey, Betsey!"—excited to tell her about a new piece he'd blown that day. Sometimes she heard the sounds of their time together—the ticking of the mantel clock, the popping of embers in the fire, the whisper of pages being turned as they both sat reading. Nothing to think on at all, unless you were in a cell, awaiting trial, not sure whether you'd live to see another winter.

"Betsey?" the Reverend Seed said again.

She wouldn't look at him. She kept her eyes on his hands, still folded in his lap. "If I'm to die," she said, and he interrupted her before she could go on.

"If you die, you won't be the first or the last. We'll all die, Betsey, but, if we believe, we'll live again with God in Heaven. Nothing will be able to hurt us then. Nothing at all."

Finally, she lifted her head to look at him. His face was so kind. He took off his spectacles to polish them with his handkerchief, and she could see the light in his eyes. He believed; without a grain of doubt, he believed. What must that be like? To live with that ease and comfort, convinced that no matter what hard times found you, a heavenly home awaited where there would be no more suffering.

Outside, it was snowing. The Reverend Seed had brought the smell of it in on his clothes, that sharp scent of wet snow on wool. She'd seen the cold in his cheeks, and she thought awhile of snow falling on the cedar trees in the woods beyond her old house and the way it would dust the backs of the Shorthorn cows. What had happened to them? What had happened to the glasshouse and all its beautiful vases, pitchers, glasses, candlesticks? Oh, to be able to walk by herself in the snow, or to sit by the fire with Eveline and listen to her read the letters from the lovelorn. Oh, to be able to do all that and to be happy for it, to wish for nothing more.

"My attorney came to see me," she said. "Mr. Augustus French. But that's been some weeks ago. Why do you think he hasn't come again?"

"It's a wicked winter, Betsey. Not fit for travel hereabouts. It'll be spring before your trial."

Betsey felt her heart sink and lift all at once. A few months to wait for justice, or a few more months until her hanging.

Purgatory

It was March before Eveline came. On a raw day, she rode in the closed coach of a brougham with Augustus French and Usher Linder to Lawrenceville. The snow had melted from the road, but the ground was still frozen. The ruts jostled her, and she barely said a word, listening instead to Mr. French and Mr. Linder, who were intent on discussing the whereabouts of Heinz Ernst.

· "I tell you," Mr. Linder said. "If we don't find Ernst—if we can't connect him to the poisoning—well . . ." Here he paused and looked out the window. Eveline knew what he'd kept himself from saying. If they couldn't find Heinz Ernst, there wasn't much of a chance for Miss Betsey. "We're passing through Purgatory," Mr. Linder finally said.

The marsh stretched out to the east, all the way to the Wabash River that ran down to Vincennes. They'd left the prairie now and were in the swampland. Eveline could see the muddy water standing in some places, the weak sunlight making it shimmer as it rippled between the trunks of the trees. The swamp grass was still brown, the foxtail, and the smart weed, and the yellow nutsedge. A green scum laced through the water. Eveline could smell it, the stink of sulfur. When the grasses rotted in the water, they put off a gas—Eveline recalled with a tender pang how her father had told her this—and if lightning happened to strike, it looked like the swamp was on fire. The first settlers called it Purgatory, a place of suffering and torment. A place of waiting.

"Not much to be done with this sort of land," Mr. French said.

Mr. Linder agreed. "Not much at all."

Eveline could feel their nerves on edge, for it was soon to be the date of Miss Betsey's trial—it was set for April—and still no one knew how to find Heinz Ernst.

∽♱⁓

At the courthouse, Mr. French and Eveline followed Mr. Fyffe to Miss Betsey's cell.

Mr. Linder had other business to attend to.

Eveline kept her head down, watching her feet as she went down the stairs to the basement. Mr. Fyffe led the way with Mr. French behind him.

"Is she of good health?" Mr. French asked.

"That she is," said Mr. Fyffe

"And her spirit?"

"I can't say what's inside a body. I'd guess, though, it's a might puny."

Eveline watched Mr. French's boots. The leather had a good shine to it. Then Mr. French stopped, and Eveline heard the key that Mr. Fyffe was putting into the lock.

"Hello, Mrs. Reed," Mr. French said, and then Eveline lifted her head, and for the first time since the night of the fire at John Wynn's, she saw Miss Betsey, and her heart went out to her.

Betsey was sitting on her stool, huddled in the far corner of the cell, her back curved, her head down. She had a frayed shawl around her shoulders, and her hair, which had always been her glory, had grown wild about her face. But it was her eyes, more than anything, when she finally lifted her head to see who had come to visit her, that knocked the life out of Eveline. It was an empty stare, no light at all in Miss Betsey's eyes—eyes that had once shone with excitement, with anger, with mischief. Now they were as gray as old dishwater. Whatever she'd been through in the months she'd been in jail had broken her. She seemed like an old woman to Eveline, a woman who'd already started to think about the end of things.

"Honey," she said when she saw Eveline. "Oh, honey. You've come."

Mr. French stepped into the cell, and Eveline came after him. She had yet to speak. She didn't know that she'd be able to. She felt all loose in her bones to see Miss Betsey in such a state.

"Eveline." Miss Betsey took her hands. "Sit down right here with me. Sit down and let me look at you."

They sat on the bed, and while Mr. French paced the cell, his hands clasped behind his back, Miss Betsey studied Eveline. She reached up a hand and laid her palm against Eveline's cheek.

"My, my," she said. "You're turning into a pretty girl."

Eveline felt the heat come into her face. What must Miss Betsey be seeing? Eveline wondered what had made her so precious. Was it Miss Betsey's fading youth that made her touch Eveline's face with such tenderness? She recalled how they had sat by the fire while she read the letters from the lovelorn in *Godey's Lady's Book*, and Miss Betsey sighed, and said, "My, oh my." Just the two of them, sharing that imagining.

"I want you to say the truth," Miss Betsey said to her now. "I want you to tell them all how much I loved my husband."

Mr. French was quick to interject. "The prosecution will have her testimony from the coroner's jury. What's been said can't be unsaid."

"She was a girl then." Miss Betsey looked directly into Eveline's eyes as she spoke, and it felt to Eveline as if she weren't there, as if Miss Betsey and Mr. French were talking about her outside her hearing. "Girls sometimes make foolish mistakes. But she's a woman now. I can see it in her, all the misery she's lived through. It's made her see things differently."

Mr. French said, "Eveline, on the morning of Leonard Reed's sickness, did you see Mrs. Reed put a pinch of something in his coffee?"

There it was, a fact she couldn't change. She nodded her head in agreement, and she saw just the slightest wince at the corners of Miss Betsey's eyes.

"And did you find a scorched paper in the dooryard?"

She nodded again.

"And you'd begun to suspect, hadn't you, that Mrs. Reed had begun an inappropriate relationship with Mr. Ethan Delz?"

Miss Betsey drew her hand away from Eveline's face. Eveline couldn't look at her any longer. She bowed her head.

"Eveline?" Mr. French said. "You will answer my question."

"He came to see her once when the Mister was away." Eveline knew what she knew. She could no more deny that than Miss Betsey could slip between the bars of her cell and be free. "We read letters from the lovelorn out of *Godey's Lady's Book*. The Mister sold part of their land, and she didn't take kindly to that. She sewed a dress from purple wool that Mr. Delz had sold her. I thought she wanted to look pretty for him."

By this point, Eveline had steeled herself. A recitation of the facts, nothing more than that.

"You see," said Mr. French, "where the facts take us, Mrs. Reed?"

"I loved my husband," Betsey said in a soft voice. "I don't want to die."

"I don't want that either," said Mr. French, "and if I can presume to speak for Eveline, nor does she."

Now it was Eveline who took Miss Betsey's hand. She squeezed it hard, hoping that Miss Betsey would know she was saying how much she'd always loved her, how desperately she wanted to save her, how sorry she was she'd caused her harm.

"My colleague, Mr. Linder, is upstairs now," Mr. French said. "He's arranging a warrant for the arrest of Heinz Ernst. There are facts connected to him that make up a different story, aren't there, Eveline?"

Eveline nodded again. She squeezed Miss Betsey's hand with even more fervor, telling her to hold on.

"If you know something," Miss Betsey said, "won't you please tell it? I know you're still a godly person even though the day for your Ascension has come and gone."

Eveline said, "My father is dead, and so is the place in my heart where I once held God."

"I know you don't mean it. You know he still loves you so."

Eveline's face softened, then, and when she began to speak it was in the sweet voice of the girl who'd first come to work for Miss Betsey. Eveline told her about Tom seeing Heinz Ernst making his way home with a vase that the Mister had blown.

"He'd been in the glasshouse," she said. "Heinz Ernst. Who knows how many times he'd been there? He must have had a key. And for what purpose? Oh, Miss Betsey, did you let Ethan Delz have a key so he could give it to Heinz Ernst?"

"I never did that," Miss Betsey said.

Eveline went on to tell her about the note that her father found in a *Godey's Lady's Book*, the note that Heinz Ernst had obviously written, the one Ethan Delz had torn to pieces.

"A threatening note," Mr. French said. "You knew about that note, didn't you, Mrs. Reed? You'd hidden it away."

She took a long time to answer. She bowed her head. Finally, she said, "Yes, I knew."

"Why haven't you said anything about it?" Mr. French wanted to know.

Miss Betsey raised her head, and when she spoke her voice was barely a whisper. "I didn't want you to know about Mr. Delz. I didn't want that shame."

"Or could it be," Mr. French said as kindly as he could, "that you were trying to protect Mr. Delz. Perhaps your love for him hasn't gone cold."

"I don't have a notion in the world about love," she said. "I don't even know what it is."

Eveline felt her heart break. To think that someone would sink so low they'd give up on love. All she could think to say was, "Oh, Miss Betsey."

Mr. French was more to the point. "The court doesn't care about love," he said. "It only cares about facts. The fact is, Mrs. Reed, I fear for you if we can't find Heinz Ernst and make him talk."

State of Illinois, Lawrence County
To the Sheriff of Crawford County, Greeting

WE COMMAND YOU to attach Heinz Ernst if he shall be found in your county, and him safely keep so that you may have his body before the Circuit Court of said county forthwith to testify, and the truth to speak in the case of Elizabeth Reed. Have you then this writ, to make return thereon in what manner you execute the same.

WITNESS, E.Z Ryan, Clerk of said Circuit Court, at Lawrenceville, this 12th day of March in the year of our lord, one thousand eight hundred and forty-five.

The Day Is at Hand

AND SO BETSEY WAITED FOR word that Heinz Ernst had been found. Each morning, when Mr. Fyffe brought her breakfast, she asked had he any news.

"None worth telling," he usually said.

Daybreak came earlier those April days. She heard birdsong outside her cell while she waited for the dawn. Months had passed since she'd breathed fresh air, and she felt as if she were fading to nothing. Her skin was pale and she could feel her rib bones. She was nothing like the woman who'd hungered for Ethan Delz, nothing at all. She felt that other woman somewhere in the shadows around her, that woman who'd been so angry with her husband, who'd been snappish with Eveline, who'd been brazen enough to imagine a life with Ethan, who'd listened to his plan to poison Mr. Reed. And yet here she was in jail, awaiting her trial, which had been slated to commence on the twenty-first of April.

One morning, Mr. Fyffe bent to put her tray on the table, and when he straightened, he did so only halfway, frozen by something that had caught his ear.

"Hear that?" he said.

Betsey listened. Finally she heard a series of sharp reports coming from somewhere in the distance.

"They're building the gallows," Mr. Fyffe said. "Usually, they wait until the verdict comes down. Looks to me like they're sure what it'll be."

The noise of the hammers was still echoing later that morning when the Reverend Seed came to pay another visit.

"It's getting closer," she said.

"What is, Mrs. Reed?"

"Whatever the end of this will be."

The Reverend Seed opened his Bible and read from it. "'The night is far spent, the day is at hand: let us therefore cast off the works of darkness, and let us put on the armour of light.'"

When he was finished, Betsey listened to the hammers. Then, without warning, they stopped, and she felt her heart come into her throat. A fierce silence filled the cell.

"It's so still," she said. "It's like everything just stopped."

Maybe that's how it was, she thought. Maybe everything just stopped, and there was nothing more after that. Maybe it was just the darkness and no memory at all of love.

She didn't want to believe that. She turned her face to the wall and sobbed. As much as she'd always bristled at Eveline's certainty of her salvation, she was shaken now to see the girl's faith gone.

The Reverend Seed came to her and lightly laid his hand on her shoulder. She felt his fingers tremble.

"My child," he said, "my child. Won't you let me help you?"

And she told him yes. "Yes," she said. "Oh, yes."

Dark Bend

FINALLY EVELINE DECIDED. SHE WENT to Tom one April morning and said she wanted him to carry her to Dark Bend. Although she still rebuffed him as a suitor, she'd come to rely on his good heart, which he gladly gave her. "If John Wynn can't find Heinz Ernst," she told him, "I will."

It was a good day for travel. Sun shining, the ground not too muddy, a pleasant breeze. A horse and wagon ought to be able to make the trip to the bend in the river with little strain.

"It's not the trip up there that worries me," Tom said. "It's the one coming back. I've heard some folks go to Dark Bend and never get out alive."

Her father had got out only to die on the verge of reclaiming his life. Now Miss Betsey was about to come to trial, and Eveline was determined to find Heinz Ernst, so someone would make him say what he knew about the death of the Mister.

"If you won't take me," she told Tom, "I'll go by myself."

"Walk it, will you?"

Eveline nodded. "If I have to."

They were standing in Tom's barn lot, where he'd been checking on his cows. It was calving season, and he had three heifers close to time.

"I guess Pa can handle things here," he said. "I can't very well let you go off and get yourself killed, now can I?"

He turned from her, then, and went to fetch one of his draft horses and the buckboard.

Eveline knew she was asking too much of him, and too much of herself as well. Dark Bend wasn't for the faint of heart. Constables had tried to make arrests there over the years, only to disappear and then turn up dead for their efforts. A skeleton found years later in a well; a corpse shoved in a fodder shock. How in the world, Eveline wondered, did her father ever make it out of there, and what history of deceits and betrayals had he left behind?

She feared she'd soon find out, for here came Tom with the horse and the wagon. He carried a Colt revolver, something she never even knew he owned. The sight of it told her what they were about to do was real.

"Ready?" he said.

Eveline had grown taller since last summer. She felt herself settling into her woman's body. She could feel the strength in her arms and legs, a strength that had come upon her gradually after her father's death.

"I'm ready," she said.

The horse faced west, the direction of the bend in the river, the Dark Bend, where who knew what might be waiting for them.

"Then I guess we ought to go," said Tom, and so they did.

Pecan, hickory, oak. The masts of trees rose up around them as they moved through their shadows. Eveline and Tom were north of the river now and moving more deeply into the heavily timbered bottomlands, where squatters plopped down and built a shack, or a wattle and daub hut. Some even dug into the riverbank and called that mud hut home. Eveline could see the wisps of smoke from cooking fires rising up ahead, the air heavy with the smoke.

The trail was narrowing, and finally the draft horse could pull the buckboard no farther. Tom pulled back on the reins and brought the horse to a halt.

"If we're going in," he said, "it'll have to be on foot."

The swampy woodlands made the construction of roads impossible. The criminals of Dark Bend held together in a mutual defense society. Suddenly Eveline was overwhelmed with the thought of what she'd come to do. Even if she were to find Heinz Ernst, how in the world did she ever think she'd be able to convince him to return and to tell what he knew?

She knew Tom was waiting for her to decide. For a moment, she felt like the foolish girl he surely thought her to be, and yet here he was willing to risk his life for her. By the same token, she knew if she said the word, he'd back the horse and wagon out until they could get it turned around and pointed in the direction of home.

Perhaps she would have done just that if not for the fact that she heard a voice call out from somewhere ahead of them.

"She tinks that's hers? Gott damn! No, I don't tink it is."

Eveline looked at Tom, searching for some sign that he'd heard the same thing. He had the revolver in his hand. He lifted his eyebrows, questioning. She nodded her head, and then, without a word, the two of them got down from the wagon.

The smell of the muddy river water was all around them. Eveline could hear crows calling overhead. A hog grunted and squealed as it crossed the trail and thrashed on into the brush. The trail was so narrow now that Eveline had to follow Tom. She grabbed onto one of his braces for fear that she might fall too far behind. She hoped he was right when he assured her the draft horse wouldn't spook. He'd be right there waiting for them when they came back out.

A little ways up the trail, a woman came walking toward them. She was wearing men's trousers, held up with leather braces, and brogans caked with mud. She carried a flintlock rifle, and when she saw Tom with the revolver in his hand, she stopped in the middle of the trail. She raised her rifle and drew a bead on him.

"You best stop right there," she said, and Tom came to a halt.

Eveline bumped up against him. Then she stepped around to his left, so she could get a better look at the woman.

She was rail-thin, with hair the color of stovepipe in need of a good blacking. It hung loose over her shoulders, and a few gray strands stuck to the side of her face.

"State your names," she said.

"I'm Tom McKinney," Tom said, "and this here is Eveline Deal."

The woman kept her eye on the rifle sight. "What business brings you here?"

It came to Eveline, then, that the braces the woman was wearing had once belonged to her father. She thought of the first time she'd seen him when he came back from Dark Bend, the time he surprised her in the woods, and he had a hank of rope to keep his trousers up because his braces were gone. Now, Eveline knew where.

"My father lived here at one time," Eveline said in a clear, strong voice. "I'd say you knew him."

The end of the long rifle drooped just a tad before the woman got it back to level. "Your father?" she said.

"Those are his braces you're wearing."

"You don't mean . . ."

"Yes, I do mean," Eveline said. "My father was Moses Deal."

"Don't say that name." The woman advanced on them, her rifle still at the ready. "Not if you want to get out of here alive. There are folks here who'd kill you if they heard you were his daughter."

Eveline wanted to ask why that might be, but the woman was nudging her with the rifle, herding her and Tom off the trail onto a deer path.

"Where are we going?" Tom said. "I've got my horse and wagon back there."

"Somewhere we can talk," the woman said. "You can forget that horse and wagon, Mister. I wouldn't be surprised if someone's already made off with them. Now get to hiking, and don't even think of trying to use that revolver on me. I'll shoot you dead."

As they walked along, Eveline in front now and Tom behind her, she thought, *so this is the woman my father left us for.* She was, it came as no surprise to Eveline, a woman who was used to getting what she wanted. She'd had her father for a time, and then something had happened to send him back home, and, if what the woman said was a fair indication, it seemed he'd left a good bit of ill will behind him.

A gunshot sounded somewhere north of where they'd left the trail, and Eveline stopped and turned around, only to find the barrel of the woman's rifle lying over Tom's shoulder and touching the tip of her nose.

"Keep walking, missy," the woman said.

"But that shot . . ."

"Happens all the time up here. That's one thing your daddy knew for sure."

Eveline wanted to ask what she meant, but there was that rifle barrel pressing against her nose now, telling her to keep quiet, to turn back around, to keep walking.

"Your daddy couldn't keep himself straight," the woman said. "He got himself on the wrong side, and the only way he could get himself free from it was to run."

"I didn't know there were sides," Eveline said.

"Honey, there are always sides."

Eveline saw a shack ahead with an open fire out front, where a man squatted on his haunches, three dead rabbits at his feet.

He looked up as they approached, but he didn't stand. Just sat there, frozen, like he was one of the dead rabbits, waiting to be skinned and gutted.

"Looks like someone had some luck," the woman said.

The man nodded in a sly way, a quick pulse of his head that Eveline thought must be the custom of people with things to hide.

"You seen a hog come through here?" the woman asked.

The man lifted his arm and pointed a finger on down the trail.

Now it was the woman's turn to nod. "Obliged," she said, and the three of them went on.

Eveline could see the river now to her right, a clotted mess of tree stumps and sandbars. Then she smelled meat cooking somewhere ahead of her, where the shacks were closer together and the wood fires of a greater number. Wet clothes hung from branches to dry. A group of men played cards atop a tree stump. Another man played a mouth organ and shuffled his feet, dancing in the dirt in front of a canvas tent.

Just then, the hog came running out from behind a shack, a man chasing after it, his knife raised.

The woman fired her rifle before Eveline knew what was happening. She smelled the powder on the air and heard the whizz of the lead ball as it flew past her left ear. The man stopped, his knife still raised, and Eveline saw that it was Mr. Shank, whose appearance at Ethan Delz's Dry Goods Store had made her know that there was nowhere else Heinz Ernst might be but here. The men who were playing cards lifted their heads to see what the fuss was all about. Then they went back to their game, unimpressed.

"Otis," the woman said, "you know that hog belongs to me."

"Aw, Lucy." Mr. Shank laughed and lowered his arm. He took the slouch hat off his head and examined it for a bullet hole. Finding none, he settled it back on his head. "Jesus, Lucy," he said with another laugh, joyful with the knowledge that she had aimed high. "You hadn't ought to do me that way."

"And you hadn't ought to go after my hog."

Mr. Shank took a few steps toward them. "Who you got there?"

"It's me, Mr. Shank," Eveline said.

"Oh, Lordy," said Mr. Shank. "Girl, I didn't think you'd come."

In short order they were all inside Mr. Shank's shack, sitting on empty whiskey casks around a trestle table made from leaf-stripped branches bound together with rawhide, and it was there, as the sun moved overhead and spread dappled light over the table, that Lucy and Mr. Shank told Eveline and Tom the story of why it was a danger for them to be in Dark Bend.

It started back in the spring, when Moses Deal made a bargain with Lucy's brother, George Adair. Moses agreed to throw in with him on a moneymaking proposition. Moses would buy up livestock, a perfectly legitimate business if only the silver dollars that changed hands hadn't been counterfeit.

"That's where George came in," Lucy said. "He had the dies and the press."

"He was an artist at it, too," said Mr. Shank. "Sometimes even he couldn't tell the difference."

So Moses bought the stock with homespun money, and then sold the cattle and horses and hogs for the genuine article.

"A hundred percent profit," Tom said.

"A right smart business enterprise," said Lucy. "All those fake coins just went whirling by and no one was the wiser. People planked down their dollars, and George and Moses raked them in." She looked down at her hands, which were red and chapped. The flintlock rifle lay on the floor at her feet. "I really thought we were on our way," she said in a faraway voice. "I thought we were finally going to see the elephant."

The trouble started when Moses decided to cheat George on the return. Moses kept selling the stock, but he only turned over a portion of the cash he received. He skimmed off a little something for himself, and he felt justified, Lucy said, on account of he was doing all the legwork. To his way of thinking, it was only fair that he got a bigger share of the take.

"You mean you knew all along?" Eveline said.

Lucy chewed on her bottom lip, trying to decide, Eveline could tell, whether to say exactly what was on her mind. Finally, she lifted her chin and drew back her shoulders, and she said, "Well, mercy, girl. Why wouldn't I know? He was my man."

Eveline thought of her mother, waiting for her at home, unable to understand why it was so important that she go to Dark Bend. *Goodness' sake, Eveline. You're not the law. Let John Wynn do his job.*

But John Wynn hadn't been able to deliver Heinz Ernst.

"George was your brother," Tom said, "and you just let him get cheated?"

"People up here are out for themselves," Lucy said. "Families get made in funny ways when everyone's crooked or desperate or lonely or all three wrapped up together. Things would have been fine if Moses hadn't got greedy. Girl, your father was a stubborn man. He'd got the urge for California by that time, and he was bankrolling money for the trip. It wasn't just George he was stealing from. It was other folks, too." Lucy's eyes were wet. "Him and me." She shook her head, overcome, Eveline guessed, with the thought of all she'd imagined for the two of them. "Him and me," she said again.

Moses started taking whatever he could get his hands on and turning it into cash. He didn't care what it was, just as long as he could sell it for profit: a woman's gold ring, a silver tray, a spinning wheel, a butter churn. He sneaked into people's shacks and huts and made off with what he wanted.

"I'm sorry you have to hear this," Mr. Shank said to Eveline.

"He wasn't always like that," she said—a weak defense, she knew. "And he wasn't like that at the end. He died because he spoke up for me."

At this point, Lucy reached across the table and took Eveline's hand. "He wasn't a bad man, your father. He just had the fever."

And like a sickness, greed consumed him. He grew bolder, and finally he was caught.

"They beat him plenty good," said Mr. Shank. "That's when he got spooked and he lit out. Guess he went back to you and your ma."

"I'm looking for Heinz Ernst," Eveline said.

Lucy and Mr. Shank exchanged a glance. Eveline saw him give her an almost imperceptible nod.

"We can take you to him, if you're sure that's what you want," Lucy said.

"It's why we've come." Eveline stood up. "He killed my father." She placed her hands on the table and leaned toward Lucy. "I don't know how you can stand to look at him."

Lucy picked up her rifle and got to her feet. "You think you know how a body makes a life, but you're just a girl. You'll find out. You'll see how many lives one woman can have, if you're lucky to get to be my age. You'll see what it takes to go on once you've lost enough."

"I lost my father."

"Girl," Lucy said, "I lost him before you."

Now there were loud voices outside the shack, the shouts of men who were riled and about to be at one another's throats. One of the men, Eveline could tell, was Heinz Ernst.

"You stay here with Otis," Lucy said, already headed to the door with her rifle in hand. "Let me see what this is all about."

But Eveline could no more stay in that shack than she could ascend to Heaven, not when she knew the man who killed her father was just outside the door.

And in quite a state, too, if what she heard was any indication.

"Get him, get him. Gott damn. I'll put a bullet in his head."

It was the hog. Eveline could hear it squealing.

Then Lucy said, "Do it, Heinz Ernst, and I'll put a bullet in you."

Inside the shack, Mr. Shank tried to dismiss the disturbance. "Nothing to pay any mind to. Someone's always ready to fix someone else's flint up here." Mr. Shank made a show of yawing and stretching his arms over his head. "Gets a little teejus. Ho-hum."

But Eveline was already at the door, and Tom was close behind, his revolver in hand.

Outside, the men who'd been playing cards had tossed some apples to the hog, making a trail that led to a sty. With the hog finally confined, the discussion of his possession could continue in earnest.

"You're trying to steal that hog from me," Lucy was saying.

"I don't steal," Heinz Ernst said. "Dat man of yours. He vas the thief, and look vat happened to him."

It was the first time since the night her father died that Eveline had seen Heinz Ernst. She'd thought she'd know exactly what to do with him, but now here he was, and she had no idea. His face was the same as it'd been the night he killed her father, distorted with rage, swollen and red, his eyes mere pinpricks of light.

"You killed him," Eveline said. "That's what happened to him."

She felt Mr. Shank's hand squeeze her elbow, warning her to take care, but the men suddenly took note of her. "Who's this?" a tall man wearing a stovepipe hat asked.

A man with no teeth said, "I can't say, but I'd like to get to know her."

He took a few steps toward Eveline, but stopped when Tom leveled his Colt in his direction.

"Hold it right there," Tom said.

The man scowled at him. "Looks like her friend is a mite tetchy, boys."

Heinz Ernst stepped forward. He pointed his finger at Eveline. "I know you," he said. "You're Moses Deal's daughter. Vy are you here?"

"Moses Deal?" the man with no teeth said. "That bastard stole from me and nearly everyone hereabout. I don't suppose you've come to pay what he owes us, have you?"

"Leave her be," said Lucy. "She's not your concern."

"We've come for you," Eveline said to Heinz Ernst. The memory of her father's death had sent a rage to boil within her, and she couldn't help but speak.

Heinz Ernst sniggered. "And vat do you tink you'll do vith me?"

"We'll turn you over to John Wynn."

Now he was laughing. "Dat's a good story, dat one."

Eveline pressed on. "I know what I know. Ethan Delz hired you to kill Mr. Reed, isn't that the way it was?"

"You tink I killed Leonard Reed?"

"I think there are facts yet to come out," Eveline said.

Heinz Ernst looked around at the other men. The hog was long forgotten. "Vat do you tink, boys? Should I let this girlie take me in?"

That set the men to laughing. They bent at their waists and slapped their knees. One man actually fell to the ground and rolled around in the dirt, cackling.

Eveline felt her cheeks burning with humiliation. She looked to Tom, begging him with her glare to do something.

Then Heinz Ernst said, "No, I don't tink so. Not today."

He turned and started walking away. Tom took aim at him with his Colt. *Shoot*, Eveline wanted to tell him, but she knew that if he did—if he killed Heinz Ernst—everything would be lost for Miss Betsey.

She saw that he meant to do it. Tom. He was about to squeeze the trigger.

"No, Tom, don't," she said.

She grabbed his arm, and the gun went off. The bullet whistled through the tree branches overhead. The man with no teeth flinched at the sound of gunfire. He crouched, his arms crossed over his head. The man with the stovepipe hat drew a long knife. Other men hurried away to retrieve weapons of their own.

Heinz Ernst chose that instant to run, and Eveline feared everything would be lost.

The man with the long knife lunged toward Tom, and Tom pulled Eveline out of the way. Lucy shouted at them to follow her and Mr. Shank.

"You got to get clear of here," she said. "You can't start shooting at folks up here and expect to get out alive."

They set off, hurrying behind Mr. Shank and Lucy down a trail through the woods. Sapling branches whipped Eveline's arms. The soft earth of dead leaves and rot gave way to the sandstone of the river bluff and they broke out into the clear. Overhead, three buzzards flew lazy circles. The stink of something dead nearby filled Eveline's nostrils, and she put her hand over her nose and mouth. For an instant, she feared she might be sick, but there was no time. They were going down the path from the bluff to the river below them. She could hear the current running fast from the spring snow melt.

Mr. Shank had a raft made from logs. They'd soon be on it. Mr. Shank would be poling the river, using the current to take Eveline and Tom safely from Dark Bend.

"Don't come back," Lucy said to them at the river's edge. "Let us be. For God's sake, don't ever come back to this place."

⬿⬷

How would she tell all this to her mother, or would she even try? That's what Eveline was thinking about as she and Tom, back on dry land, made the long walk to Heathsville.

It would soon be dark. A sliver of moon hung overhead, and Eveline felt the chill creep into her. Somewhere in a distant pasture, a cowbell gave out its heavy, leaden ring as its wearer plodded along. Eveline thought it a somber sound, one to match her mood.

"Maybe we should think about leaving this place," she said to Tom, recalling the Mister's yearning for the West. "Maybe California or Oregon. Somewhere no one knows us."

Night was closing in. She could smell the wild onion in the pastures. A whippoorwill was calling. Spring peepers were trilling. It came to her so quickly, she had to stop walking and take a deep breath—the thought that this was home, the only one she'd ever known. These fields, these woods, these pastures, these log homes with the scent of cookfires rising from their chimneys. Eveline didn't want to lose any of it, but already she feared her mother was slipping away. She sat in her rocker most of the day, a blank stare on her face. Rarely did she speak. Once, she said, "Your father wasn't a bad man. He just got on a bad path for a while, but he always loved us. I have to believe that much is true."

"Eveline, are you all right?" Tom put his arms around her and drew her to him. "You said *we*. You said maybe *we* should leave this place. Does that mean you might consider marrying me?"

She let him hold her. She clung to his warmth, and she didn't say a word.

"Eveline?" he said after a while. "You know we can't go anywhere. You know you'll have to testify at Betsey Reed's trial."

Yes, she knew it, but she didn't want to think about it just now. She nodded her head to let Tom know that she understood. She couldn't bear to hear the sound of her own voice, so she nodded again, and then after a time, they started on up the road, getting close now to home.

Let the Jury Come

ON THE DAY THE JURY was elected, the Reverend Seed sat with Betsey in her cell and recorded her last will and testament:

2 bedsteads
2 frying pans
1 tea kettle
1 bureau-toilet
1 feather bed
1 falling leaf table
4 bed quilts
cupboard ware
some clothing

All this, she bequeathed to Eveline Deal. She also left her the *Godey's Lady's Books* and the Bible the Reverend Seed had given her, the one she read from every day.

"I hope you don't mind," she said to him. "Perhaps it will help her regain her faith."

"Betsey," the Reverend Seed said, "you mustn't give up hope."

"What comes will come," she said.

She was now a believer. She'd turned herself over to Reverend Seed and to God. Funny, she thought, how she'd considered Eveline's faith in the hereafter silly. Now, facing the possibility of the gallows, she took comfort from the words of Jesus in Mark 6:36—*Be not afraid, only believe*. As she listened to the gallows being built, and as the jury selection continued above her in the courthouse, she prepared herself for the afterlife, which Reverend Seed assured her would be glorious. She understood why Eveline had been so filled with joy in what now seemed a long-ago age, the summer just before Leonard had taken ill.

All that was left was for Betsey to be baptized, immersed in water so she could wash away all her sins and rise to a new life, made pure by redemption—that is, if that's what she wanted. She assured Reverend Seed that it was. But she would need special permission to leave the jail, and as of yet, that permission hadn't come.

The Reverend Seed had encouraged her not to give up hope. "And I don't just mean the baptism," he said. "The trial, too. The innocent don't go to the gallows."

"Oh, Reverend," she said with a sigh, "if only that might be true."

"Faith," he said.

She went on with the will. All of Leonard's belongings from the glasshouse should go to the Bakewell, Page, and Bakewell glasshouse in Pittsburgh, the place where he'd first started to learn his craft. She didn't know that everything from the glasshouse was already gone.

Her voice broke. She remembered Leonard on the last morning of his life. He told her he meant to finish the candlestick holders for her and then he went to the glasshouse only to return shortly thereafter, a horrible pain in his stomach. She tried to get him to drink some sassafras tea, but he wasn't able. "Betsey, I don't want to die," he said to her, and she told him he wouldn't. She said she'd stay right there with him until James Logan came with his apothecary bag. She sent the girl, Eveline, running to the village. It wouldn't be long, she told Leonard. Not so long, and Mr. Logan would give him something for the pain.

The Reverend Seed had stopped writing. Footsteps were sounding on the stairs. Soon Augustus French was standing outside the cell with Mr. Fyffe, who was about to turn the lock.

"I'm afraid I have some bad news," Mr. French said.

Betsey braced herself.

"Heinz Ernst is nowhere to be found." Mr. French drew his shoulders back. "The jury has been seated. The trial will begin tomorrow."

Then, a Surprise

AND NOW AT THIS DAY, April twenty-first, came Aaron Shaw, States Attorney for the 4th Judicial Court, to tell the judge, the Honorable William Wilson, that he could not enter upon the trial without the presence of a key witness, the very witness, in fact, who would prove, without doubt, that the defendant, Elizabeth Reed, did feloniously willfully, and with malice aforethought, murder her husband, Leonard, with a large quantity (to wit two drachms) of white arsenic, put, mixed, and mingled into and with a certain quantity of cofee, which the said Leonard Reed did drink, and then and there became sick and greatly distempered in his body.

"And who might this witness be?" Judge Wilson wanted to know.

He was fair of skin and hair, soft-spoken and genteel, a native of Virginia. He sat at his bench, drumming his fingers on the wooden handle of his gavel.

Augustus French and Usher Linder were waiting, too. Betsey sat between them at the counsel table. Mr. French had brought her a new dress to wear—a dress of purple, very much like the one she'd made for herself to attract the attention of Ethan Delz.

Betsey turned in her chair, scanning the gallery, wondering if she might see him. No one knew where he was. His store was locked tight, but he was nowhere to be found. Behind her, to her left, sat Eveline Deal. The girl had her head bowed and wouldn't look up, not even when Tom McKinney, sitting next to her, whispered something in her ear. And the schoolmaster Lemuel Brookhart was there, as was John Wynn, and Mr. Logan the apothecary. The Reverend Seed sat just behind Betsey. Twelve men occupied the jury box. Everyone was gathered to try the case, but now Aaron Shaw was saying that wasn't possible without the presence of a certain witness whom he could produce in the space of forty-eight hours.

Betsey had no thought of who this witness might be.

Aaron Shaw was an angular man with a long point of a nose. His collar turned up from above his cravat. He hooked his thumbs into the pockets of his waistcoat and he rocked back on his heels. Then he gave the name of the witness.

"Mr. Heinz Ernst," he said.

What Can It Mean?

EVELINE, UPON HEARING THE NAME of Heinz Ernst, immediately fell into a faint, so that Tom had to catch her lest she fall to the floor of the courtroom. In the commotion that followed, Usher Linder said to Augustus French, "Most curious."

Mr. French was likewise mystified. Why would Aaron Shaw desire the testimony of Heinz Ernst, the very man Linder and French had been trying to find because they, like Eveline, suspected he was the murderer of Leonard Reed?

Augustus French was eager to get this Heinz Ernst on the stand for a cross-examination. He'd work the old hocus-pocus. Just see if he wouldn't, he told Linder once Judge Wilson had adjourned court for the day.

"By the time we resume two days hence," French said, "I'll be ready."

Later, after Judge Wilson had adjourned court for the day, Linder and French sat in Linder's room at the hotel. "What do you make of the girl?" he asked French. "The Deal girl. She was quite distraught at the mention of Heinz Ernst."

The two men sat in rocking chairs by the window, a small round table between them. They looked down on the courthouse square. More people were out and about than would have been common for a Thursday: men who had left their farms even though it was the time of spring planting, women who had their children in tow, rowdy young men with a day off from work at the tannery or the livery or the mill with a bottle to pass among them. A whole boodle of folks milling about now on this pleasant sunny day. Banjo music was playing somewhere, and on occasion the sound of a woman's bright laughter came through the window with the breeze.

French had slipped out of his coat and was enjoying the breeze in his waistcoat and shirt sleeves. "What do you make of it?"

"I'm not sure," said Linder, "but I'm about to find out. Makes me wonder if she knows something we don't." He'd uncorked a bottle of bourbon even though the hour wasn't nearly midday, but still a celebratory drink was surely in order, because the appearance of Heinz Ernst would mean the chance for cross-examination. French would work the hocus-pocus. Linder drank down the rest of his bourbon and rapped the empty shot glass onto the table with vigor. "It shouldn't be too hard to find her. What say we go snoop around a little?"

"You do that if you want." French stood and slipped his arms into his coat. "I'm going to have another talk with our client."

⌁

Betsey paced the length of her cell. She dragged her stool to the window so she could look out. She heard people talking outside.

"They say Betsey witched Heinz Ernst once," a man said.

Oh, that talk. She couldn't stand it. She'd had nothing to do with that milk cow going dry. Nothing at all.

She heard footsteps coming down the stairs to her cell, and she assumed it would be Mr. Fyffe bringing her noon dinner. Not that she thought she could eat a speck. Her stomach was all in knots since hearing Heinz Ernst intended to testify against her. Crazy German. What would he say?

It was Mr. Fyffe all right, and with him, Mr. French. Mr. Fyffe carried her tray. Mr. French had removed his beaver hat and was holding it before him by the brim.

"Mr. French to see you," Mr. Fyffe said. He balanced the tray on one hand while he used his other to work the key into the lock. "What do you make of what Mr. Shaw came up with today, Mr. French?"

"That's what I'm here to talk to Mrs. Reed about," Mr. French said, and then he waited patiently for Mr. Fyffe to place the tray on the table inside Betsey's cell and then to lock the cell again and to make his way back up the stairs, casting glances behind him, pausing a while to see if there might be anything to hear.

Finally, when he was gone, Mr. French started in. "It's curious, most curious, that Mr. Shaw insists that Heinz Ernst will be his key witness."

Betsey couldn't sit down. "You said he'd be the one to prove I didn't do it."

"That's exactly what I intend," Mr. French said. "I'll have him cornered when it comes to cross examination, and I'll turn his story inside out." Here Mr. French paused and tried to get Betsey to meet his eye. But she was pacing again, and she kept her eyes cast to the floor. "That is," said Mr. French, "unless there's something else you think you should tell me."

Betsey stopped her pacing. She was at the end of the cell, her back to Mr. French, and she placed her hands on the brick wall.

"I'm afraid of what he might say," she said without turning around. "Heinz Ernst. He scares me."

"Let him talk." Mr. French laughed. "I'll have him right where I want him."

"No, you don't understand." Betsey turned to face Mr. French. "There's something you have to know."

It happened, she said, in the summer when Leonard was gone on his trip to St. Louis. "He had earth hunger," she said. "He wanted to sell our place and go west."

One day, she came back from a shopping trip in the village and found the scrap of paper weighted down on the table with a crock. Written on the paper, scrawled in an ugly hand, were the words *Everytink you have I can take.* It was the note that Eveline had seen.

"I knew who'd written it," she said to Mr. French. "I knew he'd been in my house, and I was scared to death."

"He threatened you because he blamed you for his son's death." Mr. French set his beaver hat upside down on the table beside Betsey's untouched tray. "I can't believe Shaw aims to put him on the stand. What could he have to say that would be credible? Not to mention the fact that everyone knows he killed Moses Deal." Mr. French snapped his fingers. "I'll wager he's worked out some sort of bargain to save him from hanging. His testimony in exchange for his life."

"It wasn't the note that scared me." Betsey's voice was barely a whisper, and Mr. French had to ask her to repeat herself. "Nor the fact that he'd been there in the house. It was the parcel that came later. A paper the weight of a book leaf, tied up with string. On the paper he'd written, *Tink and do.* It was what was inside that paper."

With that, she sat down on the edge of her bed so that her knees were nearly touching those of Mr. French.

"Mrs. Reed," he said after a time, "what have you been keeping from me?"

She couldn't bring herself to say it, but she knew she must. "It was white arsenic in that paper. At first, I hoped it was flour or maybe salt, but, no, it was arsenic. I finally had to face that fact."

"How did you know it was arsenic?"

"I showed it to Ethan," Betsey said. "Mr. Delz. I showed it to him, and he told me that's what it was. He said I should put some in Mr. Reed's coffee. 'I can't do it,' I told him. 'I just can't.'"

"Mrs. Reed, what did you do with that paper of arsenic?"

"I didn't know what to do with it. I thought of tossing it out, but every time I came up with a plan, I couldn't bear to think of it out there for some child or animal to find. I couldn't have lived had any harm come." Here, her voice shrank a little more. "So, finally I decided to hide it."

"Hide it, Mrs. Reed? Where?"

"In the step-back cupboard," she said. "Back behind the tea plates."

Mr. French leaned forward. Betsey couldn't bring herself to look at him. She looked at her hands instead, the right gripping the left as they lay in her lap. "Are you telling me that you knowingly kept arsenic in your house, hidden in the very spot where Eveline Deal says she saw you put a pinch of something in Mr. Reed's coffee? This is what you're afraid Heinz Ernst will say?"

Betsey nodded. Betsey nodded. "And the rest of it. He'll say the rest of it."

"Good God. There's more?"

She told him how from time to time that summer, she'd peek behind the tea plates and find other notes.

"Where are those notes now?"

"Where Eveline found the first one. I hid them all in a *Godey's Lady's Book* in my trunk at the foot of the bed."

Mr. French was calling for Mr. Fyffe. "Fyffe, Fyffe." Betsey had never heard him shout so, had never seen him in such a state. "I must find Linder," he said. "If only you'd told us this from the beginning."

❧

Linder, at that moment, was approaching Eveline and Tom, having spotted them on the courthouse lawn engaged in conversation.

"Inside the glasshouse?" Tom was saying as Linder approached them. "How many times?"

"Too many to count," Eveline said.

She spotted Linder approaching, and she and Tom both went quiet.

"It seems that I've arrived in the middle of something," Linder said, but neither Eveline nor Tom made a response. "I guess you're all right now, Miss Deal? I noticed that you looked a bit peaked just now in the courtroom."

"It was hot in there," she said. "I needed some air."

"Yes, quite," said Linder. "So warm for this time of year."

It was indeed warm for a late April day. A bright sun beat down. Crows called overhead and swooped down to roost in the tall oaks. The storekeepers around the square had their front doors open, and Linder could hear the currents of conversations swirling inside, everyone wanting to speculate on what Heinz Ernst's appearance might mean.

"Miss Deal," he said, "have you told us everything there is to tell about Heinz Ernst?"

She looked at him for a good while, her eyes gradually narrowing until they were slits. Then she said, "Yes. Yes, I have."

She took Tom's arm, and Linder noticed how he covered her hand with his, there at the crook of his elbow, as if to say, *All right, all right, there, there, it's all right.* Linder imagined some secret that they were swearing to protect, but he couldn't for the life of him figure out what it might be.

"We were just going," Eveline said.

But before she and Tom could make their escape, French was there. He was out of breath from hurrying across the courthouse lawn.

"God's sake," said Linder. "What is it?"

French told him about the notes that Betsey claimed Heinz Ernst had left for her. "She says she left them in a trunk in her bedroom. We have to send someone to retrieve them. We have to prove that Ernst was threatening her."

This time when Eveline spoke, she did so with a flat voice, as if she'd been expecting this moment would come and she was glad now to follow her script.

"You don't have to send anyone." She loosened the drawstring of her reticule and reached inside. "I have what you need." She pulled out a few scraps of paper and handed them to Mr. French. She'd gone back to the Reeds' and gathered them after the Great Disappointment. She knew they were the first step toward a story she didn't want to tell, so she'd merely held them and waited until she knew she could wait no longer.

"Why didn't you tell me about these before?" Mr. French asked Eveline.

She didn't answer the question. She tugged on Tom's arm, and the two of them made their way across the courthouse lawn.

"There's something that girl's not saying," Linder said.

"I expect you're right," said Mr. French. "But what?"

The Trial: Day One

Two days later, on April twenty-third, the trial began, this time in earnest. The intent, Aaron Shaw said in his opening remarks, was to prove that Elizabeth Reed, not having the fear of God before her eyes but being moved and seduced by the instigation of the Devil, wickedly poisoned Leonard Reed to murder him on the fifteenth day of August in the year of our Lord one thousand eight hundred and forty-four. To be more precise, Mr. Shaw said, the State of Illinois would prove that Elizabeth Reed feloniously, willfully, and with malice aforethought did mix a large quantity of white arsenic, to wit the quantity of two drachmas, into a certain quantity of coffee which Leonard Reed did drink, not knowing he was consuming any white arsenic or any other poisonous or hurtful ingredients, and that, furthermore, once he drank the coffee he became sick and greatly distempered in his body and languished until the nineteenth day of August, at which time he slipped away from the living, his life taken by the hand of the one he most loved and trusted.

"Elizabeth Reed murdered her husband," Mr. Shaw said. "This the State will prove without a doubt."

The benches in the courtroom were full of people, even more so than when the Court had gathered two days prior, for now the word had spread that Heinz Ernst had been found and his testimony would be the very thing the State needed to make its case.

He was, though, Betsey noticed, nowhere to be seen. She sat at the table with Misters Linder and French, glad for the sunshine that fell across her face—so warm it seemed after so much time spent in her basement cell—and had she not been on trial for her life, she might have said she was almost happy.

The jurymen were solemn-faced in their chairs to her right, but even their dour expressions couldn't damper what had become a growing coal of optimism, a fierce belief she had somehow stoked during the night that told her all would be well.

"How does the defendant plead?" the Honorable William Wilson asked from his judge's bench.

Mr. French stood and said, "Not guilty, Your Honor."

"Call your first witness, Mr. Shaw," said Judge Wilson.

Mr. Shaw spoke in a clear, loud voice that was deep and calm. "The State calls Dr. Harrison Kirkwood."

Betsey's heart nearly broke when she imagined what was soon to come—Dr. Kirkwood's testimony regarding Leonard's autopsy. She couldn't bear to think of Leonard's body raised from the grave and intruded upon with Dr. Kirkwood's instruments. Her poor Leonard, a man who deserved a better end than the one he came to. Oh, how he'd suffered those days before his death. *Betsey, I don't think I'm going to live to see another day,* he'd told her that last day, and she'd said, *My darling, I'm right here, and I'm not going to let you go.* All of the hurt between them had been nothing compared to the thought of his dying. Thinking of it now, thinking of how he'd finally let go and left her to mourn his passing, she felt an ache in her throat and she tried to swallow it down, determined that she wouldn't cry, not here in this courtroom where everyone could see her.

Dr. Kirkwood placed his right hand on the Bible that Mr. Fyffe held and swore that he would tell the truth. He was a tall man who stood very straight with his shoulders back. His hair was white and so thin it barely seemed to be atop his head at all. A pair of small, round spectacles rested just above his nostrils so he could look over them at ease, as he did when he scanned the courtroom, or through them by tipping back his head, which he did when Mr. Shaw presented him with a sheaf of papers.

"Dr. Kirkwood, could you please tell us what you're holding now in your hands?" Mr. Shaw stood before the witness stand, his thumbs hooked into the pockets of his waistcoat. Betsey thought he looked very sure of himself. "Take your time," he said to Dr. Kirkwood, even though it was fairly obvious that the good doctor knew right away what Mr. Shaw had handed him.

"This is the autopsy report," he said. "The report I did concerning the death of Leonard Reed."

Betsey remembered that day and how she watched them carry Leonard's coffin into James Logan's apothecary shop. She could still hear the groan and creak of the nails being prized from the lid and the delicate chime of the surgical instruments against the rim of a glass bowl. She shut her eyes now and gave her head a quick shake to clear that memory away.

"Could you please explain your method during this autopsy?" Mr. Shaw said.

Dr. Kirkwood explained the Marsh test that he'd performed on bits of tissue from Leonard's stomach and intestines. He'd put the tissue into a glass bowl containing sulfuric acid and then had heated the bowl over a flame.

"Is this the bowl?" Mr. Shaw retrieved a glass bowl that had been covered with cloth on the prosecutor's table. He showed it to Dr. Kirkwood. Betsey could see that the bowl was coated with something. "Is this the bowl that you used for the test on Leonard Reed?"

"It is. You can see the residue left on the glass was silvery-black."

"Indicating what?"

"The presence of arsenic."

Here, the court erupted in a clamor of voices, and Judge Wilson had to use his gavel to call it back to order.

"Proceed, Mr. Shaw," he said, and Mr. Shaw went on to ask Dr. Kirkwood about the Marsh test and why it had been necessary to develop it.

"Before the Marsh test, the evidence of arsenic didn't preserve well." Dr. Kirkwood took a long breath and let it out. "A man in England was acquitted of murder because the yellow precipitate that the test produced had deteriorated by the time it was presented to the jury."

"And now?"

"Now the stain lasts. There can be no doubt."

Mr. Shaw turned to the jury, letting his gaze linger, making sure each one of them was giving his attention. He went down the length of them, letting each man take a good look at the glass bowl. Then he said to Dr. Kirkwood, "In your opinion, sir, how did Leonard Reed die?"

"Death came as the result of Mr. Reed ingesting arsenic," Dr. Kirkwood said. "About two drachmas, I'd say. Definitely enough to kill him."

Mr. Shaw walked across the courtroom, letting the silence linger as he returned the bowl to his table. Then, in a very quiet voice, he said, "Thank you, Doctor. I have no further questions."

Judge Wilson said to Mr. French, "Counselor?"

"I have no questions," said Mr. French. "At least, not at this time."

"Very good," said Judge Wilson. "Mr. Shaw, call your next witness."

It seemed to Betsey that Mr. Shaw was a bit flustered, expecting, as he must have been, that Mr. French would cross-examine the doctor about the Marsh test and what he believed it proved. But Mr. French sat quietly, staring straight ahead. Mr. Linder was whistling softly under his breath so that a barely imperceptible sound could be heard in the courtroom—"Barbara Allen," if Betsey was any judge. A number of people strained their necks and looked around, trying to figure out who or what was making that noise.

"Mr. Linder?" said Judge Wilson.

"Yes, Your Honor."

"Enough."

❧

The second witness for the prosecution was James Logan. He told the story again of the morning—yes, it was the fifteenth day of August—when the Reeds' hired girl, Eveline Deal, came running into his apothecary shop to say that Mr. Reed was grievously sick.

"And what did you do?" asked Mr. Shaw.

"I gathered up my bag and went straightaway to the Reeds' place."

"And the girl?"

"She came with me in my buggy."

Mr. Shaw took two steps toward the side of the courtroom where Eveline was sitting, and it seemed to Betsey that he looked straight at Eveline when he asked Mr. Logan the next question. "Can you please tell us what you found when you arrived?"

"Mr. Reed's stomach was inflamed. It was in a state of incipient mortification."

"Meaning?" Here Mr. Shaw turned back to the witness. "Please forgive me, Mr. Logan, but for those of us unschooled in the medical arts."

"Meaning someone had poisoned him."

At this point, Mr. Shaw entered into the court record his second piece of evidence, the scorched paper Eveline had found in the dooryard that morning.

"Do you know what this is, Mr. Logan?"

Mr. Logan pursed his lips, and his hollow cheeks sank in even more deeply. "Yes, I most certainly do," he said. "I use a paper like this to wrap herbs and medicines for people when they purchase them."

"Is this the sort of paper that you'd use to wrap arsenic in?"

"It is."

"Do you generally have call to scorch the paper as this one has been?"

"Scorch? No."

"Do you know how this one came to be scorched?" Mr. Shaw held the paper aloft, turning it from front to back so everyone in the courtroom, particularly the jury, could clearly see it. "It appears it got too close to flame, wouldn't you say?"

"Yes, I would," said Mr. Logan, "but I'm afraid I don't know how that came to be."

"Do you know where the paper came from?"

"From what I understand, it came from Elizabeth Reed's dooryard."

"Is it safe to assume, then . . . that is, in your opinion of course, as a man schooled in scientific observation . . . that Mrs. Reed may have tried to burn the paper, and failing at that, tossed it out into the dooryard?"

"I'd say that would be very reasonable. Yes, indeed."

At this point, Mr. French could no longer restrain himself. He jumped to his feet and said, "Your Honor, I must object to this line of questioning. Counsel is clearly leading the witness toward assumptions no one can safely make."

Judge Wilson squinted at Mr. French, appearing to give the matter some measure of study. Then he said, "I'll permit it, curious as I am myself. Continue, Mr. Shaw."

Mr. French sank back down in his chair and gave Betsey an apologetic look.

Mr. Shaw was now at the question Mr. French had tried his best to prevent. "Mr. Logan, is it your opinion that Leonard Reed died of poisoning by arsenic that Elizabeth Reed purchased from your shop?"

The courtroom was silent as James Logan prepared his answer. A chair creaked once, as someone leaned forward. Outside, the crows were calling from the tall oaks. Then a sash weight on one of the open windows failed, and the window came down with a loud noise that startled one woman into saying in a very loud voice, "Oh, mercy mother of God."

That caused folks to break out laughing, and again Judge Wilson had to bang his gavel to bring things back to order.

"Answer the question, Mr. Logan," he said.

"Yes," said Mr. Logan. "That is precisely my opinion."

∽❧∾

This time, Mr. French accepted his opportunity for cross-examination. He sat with one leg folded over the other and questioned Mr. Logan from his chair beside Betsey. "Mr. Logan, you say that it's your opinion that Mrs. Reed purchased arsenic from you and that you wrapped it in this paper. But with the same breath, you say you have no memory of selling the arsenic to her." Mr. French picked up a paper and studied it. "Reading now from the record of your testimony to the coroner's jury on August twentieth of last year: 'He has no personal knowledge of Elizabeth Reed getting said poison at his shop, but has good reason to believe she did get it there, and further this deponent saith not.'"

Mr. French let the paper fall back onto the table. Then he stood, taking a long time before he began to walk. He walked to the witness stand, and he said, "Mr. Logan, it appears that you didn't feel like elaborating before the coroner's jury. Perhaps you'd be more inclined to do so now. Could you please tell us what gives you such confidence that Elizabeth Reed came into your shop for the purpose of buying arsenic?"

Mr. Logan slowly drew back his head until his pointed chin seemed to be aimed at Betsey. "Everyone knows she's an odd bird. Ask Heinz Ernst about the cow she made go dry, or John Wynn about how she managed to set a fire in her cell with no matches or any other means at her disposal."

"In due time," said Mr. French. "Right now, you're the one answering the questions. So I say again, how can you be sure that Elizabeth Reed came into your shop for the purpose of buying arsenic?"

Mr. Logan placed his hand over his heart. "I know it. I know it in here. Like I said, she's an odd bird. Everyone knows she was angry with Leonard for selling part of their land to Tom McKinney. I wouldn't put anything past her."

"I'm afraid that's not a very convincing argument, Mr. Logan. Frankly, I'm surprised it held any weight with the coroner's jury, but, alas, here we are, deliberating the fate of Mrs. Reed." Mr. French took in a long breath and let it out. He scratched his head. "But let's say I'm willing to indulge you, Mr. Logan. Let's say that indeed my client purchased a quantity of arsenic from you and you wrapped it in this paper. Aren't there other reasons, sir, that someone might have purchased that arsenic other than for murdering her husband?"

"I suppose so, yes."

"Rats, for instance. Don't you sell arsenic to folks who want to rid themselves of rats?"

"Yes."

"And wouldn't you think that someone who lived on a farm the way the Reeds did might have rats they wanted to get rid of?"

"She's a mean-spirited woman," Mr. Logan said.

"Your own opinion aside for the time, isn't it true that you yourself include arsenic in medicines that you sell to the public? Medicines for breathing difficulties, or cancers, or eruptions of the skin?"

Mr. Logan hesitated. "Yes, sir," he finally said. "It is."

"So," said Mr. French, "it's possible that even if Elizabeth Reed did purchase arsenic from you, she did so for a purpose other than murder. Please answer this question, Mr. Logan, and then I'll be done with you. Would you agree that first you can't say with any certainty that Mrs. Reed made such a purchase, and if she did, you can't say for sure that she did so with the intention of poisoning her husband?"

"I suppose that's right."

Mr. French turned to Judge Wilson. "That's all I have, Your Honor."

With that Judge Wilson dismissed James Logan from the witness stand.

◦◦◦

Mr. Shaw next called Eveline Deal to the stand. Betsey's heart went out to her. In spite of all the times the girl had irritated her, and in spite of how Betsey had once jeered at her belief in the Ascension, she couldn't forget the afternoons they'd spent reading the letters from the lovelorn in *Godey's Ladies Book*. Eveline's true heart showed through then, the heart of a young girl yearning for love, not so different from Betsey herself; no, not so different at all. Those days by the fire, when Eveline read in a breathless voice, Betsey could almost think of her as a friend, a daughter even, a soul as lost as she was.

Seeing her now in her drab calico dress, a homespun shawl over her shoulders, made Betsey regret that she'd called her an ugly girl the morning of Leonard's illness. She'd been so frantic for Eveline to fetch help, and the girl had seemed frozen in some sort of paralysis. Surely anyone would understand why Betsey had to speak sharply to her. Betsey went through all the possible things Eveline might say about her. She'd treated her poorly, spoken to her with venom, derided her for being a Millerite, tried to hide Ethan Delz from her. Forgive me, God, of all my sins, Betsey mumbled. Amen.

She'd already forgiven Eveline for her testimony to the coroner's jury. The girl had merely said what she'd seen—Betsey reaching behind the tea plates and putting a pinch of something in Leonard's coffee. She'd also forgiven Eveline her closeness to Leonard. Eating glass. Mercy. What a thing to do.

A home-stitched reticule dangled from Eveline's wrist, and it was that above all else that nearly broke Betsey's heart, so eager the girl was to make a fine impression.

Mr. Shaw got right to the point. "Tell me, Miss Deal, exactly what you saw on the morning of August fifteenth inside the Reed home."

Eveline took her time. She looked all about the courtroom as if she wasn't afraid at all. Then she said, "I saw Miss Betsey reach back behind the tea plates in the step-back cupboard and take a pinch of something white from a paper and put it into the Mister's coffee." She stopped and looked at Judge Wilson. "I said all this before, back in August."

"If you'll kindly just answer Mr. Shaw's questions," said Judge Wilson.

Mr. Shaw said, "And what happened then?"

"The Mister took sick, grievous sick in his stomach. Miss Betsey told me to run quick for Mr. Logan, and that's what I did."

Betsey's heart gladdened at the fact that Eveline had left out the part about her calling her an ugly girl.

Then Mr. Shaw picked up the paper, the one that Mr. Logan had identified as one that he would use to wrap arsenic for a customer in his shop. "Have you seen this paper before, Miss Deal?"

"I found it in the courtyard that morning after I got back with Mr. Logan."

"Did it look familiar to you?"

Eveline nodded. "It looked like the paper in the step-back cupboard."

"The one you said you saw Mrs. Reed take a pinch of white powder from."

For the first time since taking the stand, Eveline looked at Betsey, and Betsey saw the fear in the girl's eyes. Go on, she wanted to tell Eveline. It's all right. Say what you have to say. She gave the girl what she hoped was an understanding look.

Only then, did Eveline answer the question. "Yes," she said. "Yes, it was that paper."

"Now, Eveline," Mr. Shaw said. "Perhaps you remember the evening of July eighth."

"That depends on what you want to know," Eveline said.

That brought chuckles from a few folks. Imagine the nerve of that girl. Even Mr. Shaw allowed himself a smile.

"Very good, Miss Deal," he said. "Wasn't there a time back in July when Mr. Reed went on a trip to St. Louis?"

"It was sometime back in the summer."

"Just after the Fourth, wasn't it?"

"Might have been. I'm really not sure."

Mr. Shaw ignored her indecision. "He told you to milk the cows while he was gone, didn't he? Do you at least remember that much, Miss Deal?"

Betsey felt sorry for her. She'd twisted the drawstrings of her reticule around her wrist. "Yes, he asked me would I please do the milking."

"But what did Mrs. Reed tell you?"

"She said I wasn't to bother. She'd do it."

Mr. Shaw leaned on the rail in front of the jury members. "So Mrs. Reed told you to stay away, to give her, as it were, the whole place to herself."

"All I know is she told me she'd do the milking."

"Then why did you end up coming to the Reeds on the evening of July eighth?"

"I wasn't sure I could trust her to do it. Sometimes she got her mind on other things. I didn't want to disappoint the Mister."

"So you thought Mrs. Reed was somewhat . . . shall, we say . . . distracted? What would make you think that?"

Eveline paused a good while, trying to untangle the reticule's drawstring from around her wrist. "The Mister was talking about picking up and going west," she finally said.

"And Mrs. Reed didn't like that, did she?"

Eveline bit her lip and looked away toward the window, wishing,

Betsey felt sure, that she was outside the courtroom.

But Mr. Shaw wouldn't let up. "Nor did she like the fact that Mr. Reed sold twenty acres of their land to Tom McKinney, did she?"

"How am I to know that?" Eveline said.

"You were Mrs. Reed's hired girl, weren't you? You were in her home. Surely there were times when you heard things between Mr. and Mrs. Reed, the sorts of things husbands and wives usually prefer to keep to themselves."

"I never eavesdropped."

"I'm sure you didn't," Mr. Shaw said, "but weren't there times when you didn't have to eavesdrop, times when Mr. and Mrs. Reed expressed their dissatisfaction with one another openly for you to hear? I'm thinking of one time in particular. Mr. Reed was letting snow melt from his boots onto the floor, and Mrs. Reed took issue with that. Do you remember?"

Eveline said, "Miss Betsey was sewing a dress. A purple wool dress."

How in the world, Betsey wondered, did Mr. Shaw know everything he seemed to know? From the reluctance that Eveline showed to speak of it now, Betsey felt sure she hadn't been the one to divulge it. That left only her and Leonard, and of course . . . of course, oh my word that must be it. Someone peeking in from the outside. Someone listening to their conversation. Someone who now was willing to talk. Surely, Betsey decided, it must have been Heinz Ernst.

"Yes, purple wool," said Mr. Shaw. "We'll get to that in time. But back to that day when Mrs. Reed was angry with Mr. Reed. Could you tell what she was really angry about?"

"It was the fact that he'd sold Tom those twenty acres without talking to her about it first."

"Would you say she was enraged?"

"She was pretty mad."

"Did she often get mad at Mr. Reed?"

Mr. French raised his voice. "I must object, Your Honor. All married couples have their squabbles. What makes this girl an expert on gauging the level of the anger?"

Betsey saw Eveline's head jerk toward Mr. French. She saw the heat in her eyes.

"I'll allow the witness to answer," said Judge Wilson.

"Miss Deal?" said Mr. Shaw.

"She was angry a lot of the time. Yes."

Betsey regretted now all the times she'd spoken sharply to Eveline and all the times she'd let her temper get the better of her with Leonard. She feared where Mr. Shaw's questions would next point.

"Now about this purple dress," he said.

"Mr. Shaw," said Judge Wilson, "you seem far afield from your original line of questioning concerning July eighth. Will you please quickly come back to it?"

"I intend to, Your Honor, as I believe you'll see. It's this purple dress that connects everything."

The purple dress, he said, was sewn from cloth purchased from the dry goods store of Ethan Delz.

Betsey stared straight ahead of her, sitting upright. Later, people would say she seemed haughty, like she had no feeling for anyone but herself. She'd tell them if she could. She'd say the truth. Love finds you, and when it does, watch out; you're no one you know. You've left the person you were behind you. You may be better, or you may be worse, but one thing's certain: you're changed in an instant, changed forever.

"Did you ever know Mrs. Reed to speak of Mr. Delz?" Mr. Shaw asked Eveline.

"Maybe," she said. "I don't know."

"You don't know?"

"I don't remember."

"But you remember coming to the Reeds' on the evening of July eighth, don't you, Miss Deal?"

"I came to do the milking that night," Eveline said.

"And what happened while you were doing the milking?"

"Sir?" Eveline said, as if she didn't understand the question.

"Wasn't it on that night that you saw Ethan Delz and Elizabeth Reed step from her house?"

She sat up straight now. She drew her shoulders back. Betsey knew she was accepting the fact that she'd have to go head-on into this tangled territory.

"He brought her a parcel of salt that he'd forgotten to put in her basket earlier that day at his store."

Mr. Shaw quickly went on as if she hadn't said a thing about that parcel of salt.

"Didn't you and Mrs. Reed used to look at the letters from the lovelorn in *Godey's Lady's Book*?"

"She liked for me to read them to her. Yes."

"A woman reading love letters. A woman pining. A visit from a gentleman on a night when her husband was away. A dress sewn from cloth that this same gentleman sold her. A purple dress. Such a bold color, wouldn't you say, Miss Deal?"

"I don't really know."

"But you know that Mrs. Reed and Mr. Delz were more than friends, don't you?"

Eveline's lips were trembling. Her mouth was open but she'd yet to find the courage to say the words. Betsey waited for them, her heart pounding in her chest.

After a good while, Mr. Shaw said, "You really don't have to answer, Miss Deal. Your silence is answer enough. Your Honor, I have no further questions for this witness."

❧

Mr. French went right at the issue of Betsey and Ethan in his cross-examination.

"Did you see anything inappropriate between Mr. Delz and Mrs. Reed?"

"No."

"Did you see Mrs. Reed touch him in any way?"

"No."

"Did you see him touch her?"

"No."

"And what exactly did you hear them say to each other?"

"They talked about sin. Miss Betsey said something was a horrendous sin."

"And what did Mr. Delz say?"

"He said it was no one's fault."

"Miss Deal, did Mrs. Reed ever know that you were eavesdropping."

"I wasn't eavesdropping. It wasn't my fault that I was within hearing range."

That sent a gentle laughter rippling through the courtroom, but it died out quickly, and though Judge Wilson raised his gavel, he had no need to bang it against the block.

Mr. French continued. "Call it what you will. Did you and Mrs. Reed ever discuss the events of that evening?"

"I told her." Eveline mumbled the words, and Mr. French had to ask her to repeat them. She snapped up her head and said in a loud, clear voice, "I told her that night what I'd heard."

"Yes, and what did Mrs. Reed say when you told her that?"

"She said I was being silly. She said Mr. Delz had brought her a parcel of salt that he forgot to put in her basket when she was shopping earlier in the day. She said I'd heard them talking about salt."

"As in, it was a sin to forget the salt?" Mr. French was leaning in close to Eveline now. "As in, it was no one's fault?"

"Yes."

Betsey wished Mr. French might cease for she knew that what he was leading the jury to believe was a lie. She had indeed kissed Ethan that night when she didn't know Eveline was there. She'd kissed him first, and then he'd kissed her back. That had been the start of them, the start of what she dreamed would be a new life, one free from Leonard who granted her no respect, no rights. A glorious life as the wife of a merchant, a handsome man with the loveliest hands. No more sharp smells of the chemicals of the glasshouse, no more burns on the skin, as Leonard always had on his own hands. A gentler life.

It was true; she'd convinced herself of all of this without really stopping to imagine all that it would take to deliver her to it.

Just when it looked as if Eveline would be allowed to step down, Mr. French had one question more. "Miss Deal, can you say for certain that Mrs. Reed murdered her husband by putting white arsenic in his coffee?"

She'd made this clear to the coroner's jury. She'd told the truth. "I already said this. I saw her take a pinch from the paper in the step-back cupboard."

"A pinch that could have been salt, couldn't it, Miss Deal?" A murmur rose up in the courtroom. Eveline bit her bottom lip and looked down at her hands. "Miss Deal?"

She knew she should agree, but still she hesitated. Mr. French lowered his head. He spoke to her with a soft voice.

"Isn't it true that you never much liked Mrs. Reed? You didn't like her because she scoffed at your religious beliefs—you're a Millerite, aren't you? And you didn't like her because she sometimes spoke sharply to you about the performance of your duties. On the morning of Mr. Reed's illness, she called you an ugly girl, isn't that right?" Mr. French didn't wait for Eveline to answer. His voice grew softer and softer, until people were leaning forward to hear it. "You had every reason to lie about what you thought you saw the morning of Mr. Reed's death."

Eveline finally lifted her head, and her cheeks were shiny with tears. "Yes," she said, "it could have been salt."

An Uneasy Repast

EVELINE WAS SO SHAKEN SHE couldn't bring herself to eat no matter how sweetly Tom tried to coax her to take just a few bites of the dinner he'd carried to her room on a tray.

"I can't," she said. "I just can't. Oh, Tom."

She began to cry, and Tom patted her hand and said, "Shh, there, there. Calm yourself. You wouldn't want the lady of the house to hear. Or worse, Mr. Brookhart."

The lady of the house was Constance Musgrove, the wife of Mr. Ridgley Musgrove, who owned the local livery, and the sister of the schoolmaster, Lemuel Brookhart. Mr. Brookhart had arranged a room for Eveline at his sister's home. He and Tom were sleeping on pallets in the stables.

"Mr. Brookhart was there in the courtroom," Eveline said. "He's already heard it all. Mr. French made me out to be a liar, and that's what Mr. Brookhart has thought of me all along."

"That's not true, Eveline. No one thinks you're a liar."

"How can you say that, Tom? Really, how can you? Everyone thinks I'm an evil gossip, an ugly girl who's telling lies to get revenge."

Mr. Brookhart was downstairs eating with his sister. Constance Musgrove was a tall, slender woman with a pinched face who wore a cameo brooch pinned at the throat of her dress. The brooch was a carving of a lady's profile, and to Eveline it gave Mrs. Musgrove an air of propriety—her upright carriage, the lift of her chin that pointed the tip of her nose upward—as if the woman in the brooch was pressing into her throat, reminding her to be on her guard, to be ever forthright. Eveline despised the way she called her "dearie." *Dearie*, she'd said that morning, *don't slurp your tea like that. Honestly.* Eveline could hear her downstairs now, talking in her high-pitched voice, chirping like a cardinal—*birdie, birdie, birdie.*

"Such a strange girl, Lemuel," she said. "Such a strange, strange girl."

"You see?" Eveline said to Tom. "Mr. French has succeeded in changing everyone's mind about me, and after all I tried to do to help him."

⁊⧢⳩

In the basement of the courthouse, Mr. French forsook his own dinner and sat with Betsey in her cell while she had hers.

"Did you have to do that to poor Eveline?" she asked.

Mr. French looked aggrieved. His lips were set tight together in a frown, and the worry line just above his brow was deeply creased. He sat on the edge of Betsey's bed, his hands clasped in his lap as if he were a boy waiting for his punishment.

"I always hate it," he said, "but I had to discredit her story of what she saw the morning your husband fell ill. I had to show that she might have a motive for lying."

"But she's not lying." Betsey stopped with her fork lifted in midair above her plate. "It's true that Ethan and I had a dalliance."

"Mrs. Reed, I have to make the jury believe that you didn't."

"Your job might get a bit harder this afternoon, Mr. French, once Heinz Ernst testifies."

"I'll admit he worries me. He's the wild card neither I nor Mr. Linder could predict." Mr. French pressed his palms together and brought his fingertips to his lips as if in prayer. Then he said, "I'll do what I did with Eveline. I'll think fast and figure out how to spin his story, whatever it might be, a different way."

"But what if what he says is the truth?"

"Mrs. Reed, I'm trying to save your life."

Upstairs, in his office, Mr. Shaw paced back and forth before Heinz Ernst, making sure his witness was ready. He'd made certain the man was freshly shaved and dressed in the black suit of clothes he'd provided him so he'd look as sober as . . . well, as sober as a judge. One of Mr. Shaw's law clerks, a beefy lad named McDonald who brooked no guff, had been put in charge of Mr. Ernst overnight to make certain he didn't find his way to a jug. It wouldn't do to have him appear in court corned. He had enough of a devilish past to overcome as it was. Mr. Shaw needed him to be above board, perhaps even sympathetic—a man who lost his beloved son and made a few mistakes as he tried to recover from his grief.

"Just tell the story the way you told it to me," Mr. Shaw said. "I'll ask questions to help you, the questions we've already gone over, yes?"

"Ja, ja, the story," said Heinz Ernst in a guttural snarl.

Mr. Shaw stopped his pacing to take a good look at the man, to try to take his measure. There was something rodent-like about him: that narrow face, those deep-set eyes, the way he kept casting them about the room as if he wasn't sure whom to trust. Mr. Shaw took note of a few flecks of dried blood on Mr. Ernst's throat where the barber's straight razor had nicked the skin. Mr. Shaw knew he'd have to get McDonald to clean that up. Oh, it was going to be a hard sell. Mr. Shaw knew that as sure as he knew anything, but if he could pull it off, there'd be nothing French and Linder could manage that would swing the jury in their favor.

"Listen to me, Ernst." At the sharp tone, Heinz Ernst snapped his head toward Mr. Shaw and waited. "You know our deal." Mr. Shaw, no matter how much he'd managed to persuade himself that Ernst's story was true, still felt a sliver of doubt worry itself up inside him each time he thought of the way Ernst had come up from Dark Bend to tell it to him. *I've got something you should hear, ja?* he'd said, and Mr. Shaw had agreed to listen. "If you get caught in a lie," he said to Ernst now, "our bargain is off, and I'll prosecute you to the full extent of the law."

The agreement was one that would keep Heinz Ernst from the gallows, and only sent to the penitentiary for the killing of Moses Deal, in exchange for his story of what went on at the Reeds' farm that summer.

"Sure, sure," said Heinz Ernst. "Don't you fret. I tell the story. I tell it just the way it happen. I tell it true."

When the Ear Heard Me

IT WAS LIKE THIS, HE said that afternoon from the witness chair. He sat very straight, his shoulders pressed back, his hands flat on the tops of his legs while Mr. Shaw leaned toward him.

"I used to go out dat vay," Heinz Ernst said. "I made a friend of Mr. Reed."

"You had a son, didn't you?" Mr. Shaw was speaking in a very soft tone. His voice was that of a kindly parent, and Eveline could tell by the way the faces of the men on the jury softened that they felt it, too, that soothing. "A little boy," Mr. Shaw said, pausing a moment for effect. "A fine little boy named Jacob."

Heinz Ernst bit his lip and tilted his head to the side. There was such pain in the way he held himself. Finally, he managed a nod. "My son, ja," he said. "My son, Jacob."

"Did Jacob go with you when you visited Mr. Reed?"

"I went to talk farming with Mr. Reed. I'd take a look at his stock. The Missus always had sometink for Jacob."

"By the Missus, you mean . . ."

"Betsey Reed."

Mr. Shaw walked over to the window and paused a moment, looking out into the bright sunshine still spreading across the courthouse lawn.

"So you were friends with the Reeds. Neighbors. You trusted them."

"Ja. But den there was dat business vit da cow."

"What business was that, Mr. Ernst?"

So Heinz Ernst told the story of buying the cow from Leonard Reed, a milk cow that never gave milk because Betsey Reed put a spell on it, a red roan Shorthorn that dried up the instant Betsey came out into the dooryard to shake something from an apron.

"I vas leading the cow past da house," Heinz Ernst said, "and Betsey came out." He raised his arms above his head. "She had an apron and she lifted it up and brought it straight down." He brought his arms down and his palms slapped the wood rail in front of him with a slap. "Just like dat, the milk started leaking from dat roan cow's teats, and it never gave milk again."

Once Heinz Ernst started, he couldn't stop. His story came out in a rush and kept going, from the spell he claimed Betsey put on that roan cow to the way she used to hypnotize chickens, and why was it she wore veils on her bonnets to hide her face whenever she went out if not because she was some sort of witch who couldn't look directly at the sun, and, of course, it stood to reason that she changed her appearance through some sort of hocus-pocus so she could buy that arsenic from James Logan and not be recognized.

"Your Honor, please," Augustus French finally said in objection. "This is all mere hearsay and speculation. Surely, you won't allow it."

"Bring your witness to the point, Mr. Shaw," Judge Wilson said.

Mr. Shaw nodded. "Mr. Ernst, I hesitate to put you through this, but could you please tell us the story of what happened to your son?"

It took Heinz Ernst a good while before he could begin to speak. He bowed his head and brought his hands together and shook them as if he held something alive and pulsing between his palms. The motion mesmerized Eveline. She half expected to see him unclasp his hands and a small songbird come winging out.

"Mr. Reed, he vouldn't make it right about dat milk cow. I told Jacob not to go over dere anymore, but he did. I couldn't keep track of him every minute, and he'd sneak across the fields to see Betsey. He vasn't a bad boy. It was like he couldn't go vitout seeing her, like she had a spell on him with all the tricks she showed him. I even spanked him—I'm ashamed to say it—but it didn't do any good. He kept going."

"What sorts of tricks, Mr. Ernst?"

"How to dowse for water. How to catch a bird vit salt. Tinks like that. Tinks a boy vould like to know."

"So he kept going back."

"Ja. One day, I caught him over dere. He was drinking milk she'd given him, milk she'd gotten from her own cows, mind you, ven she'd taken it all from the one Mr. Reed sold me. 'Vat's this?' I asked her, and she told me Jacob had sometink vrong vit his stomach."

"Mr. Ernst," said Mr. Shaw, "was your son sick in any way that day?"

Heinz Ernst shook his head with vigor. Eveline could see his anger building the way it had the night he'd killed her father. "Nein, nein, nein. My Jacob vas just fine." Heinz Ernst pointed at Betsey. "Until she got hold of him. I said, 'Vat's in dat milk?' And she told me just a little bloodroot. 'Vat call do you have to give him dat?' I asked her, and she said she just vanted him to feel better."

"And did he?"

"I took him home." Heinz Ernst was staring directly at Betsey now, his eyes narrowed. "By nightfall, he vas on fire vit the fever, and his arms and legs vas jerking like someone vas pulling on dem vit ropes. Den the sickness on his stomach set in. He couldn't keep anytink down. By da time it vas mornink, he vas dead. All because of her."

Augustus French slammed his hand down on the table. "Your Honor, since when does superstition count for testimony?"

Judge Wilson thought for a moment and then said, "I'll entertain this. I want to see where it might be going."

Eveline knew where it was going. She knew because she'd been there at the Reeds' the first time Heinz Ernst came.

He came one morning when she was gathering eggs in the henhouse. She stepped outside, her wicker basket full of eggs, and saw him walk into the Reeds' house just as big as day.

The Mister and Miss Betsey had gone into the village on some matter of business that Eveline didn't know. She only knew they'd been squabbling when they left, the Mister saying, yes, by God, she'd do exactly what he said, and Miss Betsey insisting that hell would freeze over first.

Eveline wasn't sure what she was to do. Should she march into the house and ask Heinz Ernst exactly what he thought he was doing? Or should she go back into the henhouse and wait until he was gone? Before she could decide, he came out of the house and saw her staring at him. He lifted his arm and pointed a finger at her.

"I've got my eye on you, too," he said, his voice low with menace. "Don't tink I don't, Missy."

Then he set off across the fields toward his farm.

Eveline stayed where she was until she could no longer see him, but still, when she finally started to the house, she had a shaky feeling in her legs for fear that he'd come back.

The house was as she'd left it. The breakfast dishes washed and dried and put away in the cupboard. The bed made. The floor swept. A bouquet of spring daffodils in a crock of water on the table. No sign at all that Heinz Ernst had been there, but Eveline could smell the odors he'd left behind—the smells of sweat and tallow and corn whiskey. She looked around the cabin but could see nothing that he'd disturbed. She couldn't figure out for the life of her why he'd come. Had he only been looking for the Mister, and finding the house empty, quickly left it? Or had he been looking for Miss Betsy, the woman he claimed put a spell on his son and killed him? Had he come for his revenge?

Eveline spun around, looking first in this direction and then in another, thinking she'd finally see something that would explain Heinz Ernst's intentions, but there was nothing.

Then the Mister and Miss Betsey were back, and they were still in the middle of some soreness.

"He expects me to pack off to Oregon," Miss Betsey said to her. "Can you picture that?"

"Just you hush, Mrs. Reed," Leonard said. "What's between us is between us."

Now, in the courtroom, nothing was private.

Heinz Ernst said, "So I brought it to her. The arsenic."

"Where did you get the arsenic, Mr. Ernst?" Mr. Shaw asked.

"I bought it from James Logan."

"For what purpose?"

"On account of vat he told me."

"Mr. Logan?"

"Nein. Ethan Delz." A murmur was already starting to rise in the courtroom, and Heinz Ernst had to raise his voice to be heard. "He vas da one vat gave me da money to buy it."

Eveline felt as if she might faint.

Mr. Shaw said, "Did Mrs. Reed have a rat problem?"

Several in the courtroom laughed.

"I can't say," said Heinz Ernst. "I only know I vas to deliver da arsenic. I vas to put a message on da paper it vas in."

"And did you? Write a message on the paper, I mean."

"Ja. It said, 'Tink and do.' Dat's vat Delz told me to say, and dat's vat I did."

"Mr. Ernst, let me make sure I understand you," Mr. Shaw said. "Mr. Delz told you to take a parcel of arsenic to Mrs. Reed?"

"Ja, he gave me money to buy da arsenic, and he paid me to keep bringing da notes."

"What sorts of notes?"

"Notes dat made it plain she vas to use dat arsenic."

Mr. Shaw turned from the witness stand and made a slow walk to the window. He looked out for a moment. Then he turned around and made another slow walk back to where the jurors were sitting.

"Mr. Ernst, are you saying that Ethan Delz wanted Mrs. Reed to poison Mr. Reed?"

"Ja, dat's vat I'm saying. He vanted Leonard Reed dead, and he meant for her to do the job."

The courtroom erupted. Judge Wilson banged his gavel.

Eveline couldn't stand it anymore. She got to her feet. She was thinking of the scripture from the Book of Job: *When the ear heard me, then it blessed me; and when the eye saw me, it gave witness to me.* She knew what she had to do. In her loudest voice, she said, "You have to listen to me. You have to let me tell you what I know."

But it was no good. No one could hear her.

A Secret Made Known

FINALLY, JUDGE WILSON TOOK CONTROL of the courtroom, and when it was quiet, he ordered a recess. Court would readjourn in one hour.

"And if you can't control yourself," he said, looking out over the spectators, "then go home. Don't come back. If this behavior repeats itself, I'll have Sheriff Fyffe throw you all in jail."

Heinz Ernst still sat in the witness chair, a smirk on his face, lording over all that he'd wrought.

Mr. Linder must have taken note of him, too. Eveline saw him lean toward Mr. French. She heard him say, "I'll take the cross-examination. I'll fix that bastard's flint."

During the recess, Eveline lingered in the hallway outside the courtroom, hoping to have a word with Mr. French. He stayed inside a long time, speaking, so she assumed, with Mr. Linder and Miss Betsey. Most of the other spectators had gone out to the courthouse lawn to enjoy the sunshine. Eveline could hear their voices through the open door. She could see men standing in small circles, talking and smoking. Some of the ladies sat on the grass, their legs folded to the side and covered with their long skirts. Everyone was animated. The men waved their arms about; the ladies nodded their heads with vigor. From time to time, Eveline heard a few words. She heard "Ethan Delz." She heard "love affair." She heard "murder."

Eveline sat on a bench while Tom paced about in front of her. He had a slouch hat rolled up in his hands as if he was wringing water from it, and that's what he kept his eyes on. She knew what she had to do. She'd have to say the things she'd tried so hard not to say, the ones that were so private she wanted them only to be in her heart.

She thought of her mother, who waited for her at home, and how she would feel when finally the news came to her, and Tom, poor Tom—already, she feared he might slip away from her before she could admit how much she'd come to rely on him, how much she loved him. But it couldn't be helped. A time came—she was learning this now—when she had to pay for her life. Her father must have known it to be true. He'd made the choices he'd made, and they'd brought him to that hill in October when Heinz Ernst came out of the fog. She'd made her choices, too, and she knew as well as she knew her own name that everyone's lives were connected. The Mister had shown her how to blow glass, how the slightest breath could change forever the shape or texture. It was the same way with their living. She was sure of that now. Everything she did or didn't do, everything she allowed—it all touched the lives of those around her. Some she loved, and some she didn't. Some, like Heinz Ernst, she'd never given much thought at all. They were all brushing together now in ways she never could have imagined when she went to work for the Reeds. She was just a girl. It was winter. The furnace in the glasshouse was warm. The Mister showed her how to eat the glass. He painted her eyes. That's where she'd begin to tell her story.

She waited until finally Tom lifted his head to look at her, and she held his gaze.

Then the door to the courtroom opened, and Mr. French stepped out into the hallway.

"Mr. French," Eveline said, "you must put me on the witness stand. You simply must."

"And why is that, Miss Deal?"

Even after the way he'd treated her during his cross-examination, Eveline could forgive him, all for the sake of Miss Betsey.

"I can save her," Eveline said. "Tom, will you please run to Mrs. Musgrove's and bring me my carpet bag?"

He nodded and said, "I can do that."

"Tom," Mr. French said, "when you get back with that bag, you bring it to that office there." He pointed to a door at the end of the hall. "We'll be there waiting. I'll fetch Linder, and when you get back, Eveline will tell us what she knows."

⌒⊘⌒

And so it was, when the court was back in session, that Usher Linder approached the stand, and said to Heinz Ernst, "Would you say that you're a man of temper?"

"Temper?" said Heinz Ernst.

"Get your back up, do you?" Mr. Linder's Kentucky twang was mesmerizing to Eveline. "Go off half-cocked? Chew nails and spit bullets?" Mr. Linder approached Heinz Ernst and stood as close as he could to him. "Do you get angry easily, Mr. Ernst. Are you a man of temper?"

"I don't let no man push me around." Heinz Ernst folded his arms across his chest. "I push back."

"Is that what you did the night of October twenty-second when you killed Moses Deal?"

Mr. Shaw voiced his objection. "Your Honor, the witness isn't on trial."

"Not yet," said Mr. Linder. "Maybe not ever. I assume that the State has made a bargain with Mr. Ernst."

"Gentlemen," said Judge Wilson. "Stay to the matter at hand. Don't force me to cite you for contempt of this court. Proceed, Mr. Linder."

Heinz Ernst didn't need Mr. Linder to coax an answer for him. He said, "Moses Deal started all dat business. He hit me first, and I hit him back."

Mr. Linder was quick to respond. "So you believe in an eye for an eye? You believe that what someone does to you should be returned."

Eveline could tell that Heinz Ernst was too dim to see where Mr. Linder was leading him. Heinz Ernst charged ahead.

"If anyone hurts me, I hurt dem back."

Mr. Linder was quick to attack now. "Like Mrs. Reed. She hurt you, or so you thought, by having some sort of witchy hand in your son's death. You wanted to hurt her back, didn't you, Mr. Ernst? You still want that."

Mr. Shaw tried to save Heinz Ernst. He said, "Your Honor, Mr. Linder is putting words in the witness's mouth."

But Judge Wilson wouldn't uphold the objection. "Answer the question, please, Mr. Ernst."

"She *is* some sort of vitch." Heinz Ernst was standing now. He was standing and pointing his finger at Miss Betsey. "She took my Jacob from me. Vat sort of father vould I be if I didn't vish her dead?"

"Wishing and doing are two different things, Mr. Ernst. You placed that parcel of arsenic in Mrs. Reed's cupboard and there it sat, and sat, and sat, gathering dust along with the threatening notes that you left. Ethan Delz may have wanted Leonard Reed dead, but your grievance was with his wife. That's why you made it appear that she was the one to poison him, when all along you had no way of knowing that couldn't possibly be true."

Eveline had known that this moment would eventually arrive, and she found herself longing for some dark place where she could shut her eyes and close out the world and everyone in it. She dreaded what Mr. Linder was about to make known.

"It couldn't be true," Mr. Linder said, "because that paper didn't contain arsenic at all, at least not for some time before Leonard Reed's death."

Mr. Linder turned and made the short walk to the table where Miss Betsey and Mr. French were sitting. Mr. Linder held out his hand, and Mr. French handed over the paper parcel that Eveline had taken from her carpet bag, handing it to him in the office outside the courtroom only moments before. It was this parcel that her father had seen her unearth behind the Reeds' granary, not the one containing the pieces of Miss Betsey's hand mirror as she'd claimed.

Mr. Linder returned to the witness stand and showed the parcel to Heinz Ernst. "Mr. Ernst, is this the parcel of arsenic that you left for Mrs. Reed to find?"

"It could be. I don't know." Heinz Ernst stammered about. "It might."

Mr. Linder had been holding the parcel so Heinz Ernst could only see one side of it. Now he turned it, and said, "Mr. Ernst, will you read what's written on this paper?"

Heinz Ernst leaned forward and squinted. "My eyes," he said. "They're not so good."

"Do you have spectacles?"

"Nein."

"Very well," said Mr. Linder. "I'll read the writing for you. It says, 'Tink and do.' A simple message meant to prompt Mrs. Reed to act, to use this arsenic to murder her husband. Three words, the first misspelled, spelled the way a German would say it. I know you remember writing this, Mr. Ernst. You've already said as much under oath."

Heinz Ernst said, "Yes, I said dat tink."

Mr. Linder showed the parcel to Judge Wilson so he could see that what Mr. Linder had read was indeed what was written on the paper.

Then Mr. Linder set the parcel on Judge Wilson's bench and prepared to untie the string that held it closed. "With your permission, Your Honor?"

Judge Wilson nodded, and Mr. Linder undid the string. The paper loosened, and soon everyone could see the mound of white substance that it contained.

Mr. Linder took some in his hand, held it aloft, and then let it drizzle back down onto the paper. He wet his finger with his tongue, and pressed it into the white substance. He put some into his mouth.

"Care for a taste, Mr. Ernst?"

Heinz Ernst pressed his palms into the air between him and Mr. Linder. "Nein. I'm not a stupid man."

"It's salt, Mr. Ernst. Plain salt. That's all." Mr. Linder nudged the paper toward Judge Wilson. "Your Honor?"

Judge Wilson took a taste. "Salt," he said.

"Mr. Ernst," said Mr. Linder, "you had no way of knowing that Eveline Deal finally found this parcel, which once contained arsenic, and she recognized it for what it was, and she worried over what it could mean, so she emptied the contents into a crock and took it away to bury, and she replaced the arsenic with salt and put it back where she'd found it."

"What a preposterous claim," Mr. Shaw said. "Where is the proof? Where is the proof?"

That was the secret Eveline had carried. She'd done exactly what he said she'd done, because she'd known all along there was a danger lurking. She knew that Miss Betsey loved Ethan Delz as surely as she knew that there was trouble between her and the Mister. She would have known it on her own, but one day in the glasshouse the Mister made it plain.

He was painting her eyes with the stibnite. He said, "Don't let Mrs. Reed see you like this, you understand?"

Eveline knew she couldn't nod her head without disturbing the Mister's hand that was so gentle as he traced her eyelids. His other hand held her jaw, not with force, but with just the slightest pressure that told her she was to hold still. He smelled of the lime and the sand that he used to make the glass. He smelled of that and the stibnite, but she didn't mind.

She found her voice. "Yes," she said in a whisper. "Yes, I understand."

"That woman," said the Mister. For a good while, he didn't say another word. Eveline felt his fingers tremble ever so lightly, and she held her breath, sensing the pain—now she wondered if it was also fear—rising in him. "You never know about her," he said. "Be careful, Eveline. You never know what she might do."

Then he was finished with the stibnite. "Open your eyes, Eveline." He was gazing on her with such a look of rapture. "Beautiful," he said, as if the word was dangerous in his mouth and he had to say it carefully. "Simply beautiful."

The warmth from the glass furnace was on her face. Outside, sleet was falling. She could hear it striking the tin roof of the glasshouse. But inside, it was dry and warm, and here was this man, the Mister, who had taken her hands in his, who was looking at her the way he did the beautiful glass he made, and she couldn't help herself. She laid her head on his chest, just gave herself over to him that way, and in time, he put his arms around her, gathered her in, and held her.

They never spoke again of that moment. How long had it gone on before he gently nudged her away from him? She knew she should be ashamed. Anyone else would have thought that embrace a sin, but she couldn't agree. She knew nothing about love, but she knew that what she and the Mister had just done, holding on to each other in the warmth of the glasshouse, wasn't wrong. How could it be when it had brought her such comfort?

"She can get crazed," the Mister finally said. "I mean it, Eveline. Sometimes . . . well, I shudder to think."

A few days later, Eveline found the arsenic in the step-back cupboard. Arsenic behind the tea plates? A hotheaded woman in love with another man and angry with her husband? Lord have mercy. Eveline knew right away what she must do. She went to Ethan Delz's dry goods store and bought a parcel of salt. At the Reeds', she took the parcel of arsenic from the step-back cupboard. Then, so Miss Betsey wouldn't know she'd had her nose in business that didn't concern her, she copied Heinz Ernst's hand and wrote the words *Tink and do* on the new parcel of salt that she'd bought. She put that parcel behind the tea plates next to the one that Ethan Delz had brought Miss Betsey in July. Eveline placed the parcel of arsenic inside a crock, set the lid on it, and buried it behind the granary. So there were two parcels of salt behind the plates, and Eveline felt pleased that she'd done what she could to make certain no harm would come.

That should have been the end of things, but then the Mister took sick, and Miss Betsey called her an ugly girl, and the coroner's jury asked her what she'd seen, and she told them. She found herself, much to her surprise and disgust, sticking to the facts: Miss Betsey reaching behind those tea plates and putting a pinch of something in the Mister's coffee, the paper found later in the courtyard, the one James Logan said was the sort of paper he'd use to wrap arsenic. Eveline let the jury believe what she knew was impossible. Miss Betsey couldn't have poisoned the Mister because Eveline made sure that the only thing in those parcels behind the tea plates was salt. That was the one thing she didn't say in front of the coroner's jury. She kept that to herself because Miss Betsey had called her an ugly girl.

But now the secret was known.

Mr. Linder was finished with Heinz Ernst, and Eveline heard the name of the next witness being called—her schoolmaster, Lemuel Brookhart.

Mr. Brookhart took his time approaching the stand and settling into his chair. He folded one long leg over the other at the knee. The sleeves of his coat were too short. His knobby wrists showed beneath them, and his hands seemed so big as they rested on the arms of the chair. He sat stiffly in his chair, his chin slightly lifted, as Eveline had seen him do when he looked down upon his pupils from the front of the schoolhouse.

"Mr. Brookhart, you're the schoolmaster at Heathsville," Mr. Shaw said. "Is that correct?"

"Yes, sir." Mr. Brookhart's voice was louder than necessary for the small courtroom. "I am indeed the schoolmaster."

"And Eveline Deal is one of your pupils?"

"Eveline is a bright girl," Mr. Brookhart said, "but her head is too much in the clouds."

"Meaning?"

"She gets caught up in stories and dreams too much. The story of the Ascension, for example. Well, we all saw how that turned out."

Eveline thought how unfair it was to characterize her this way. Yes, it was true that she loved reading the books that Mr. Brookhart lent her, just as she loved the letters from the lovelorn in the *Godey's Lady's Books* that belonged to Miss Betsey. But that didn't mean she was a mooncalf. That didn't mean she didn't know what was what.

"Did Miss Deal come to see you shortly after Leonard Reed died?" Mr. Shaw was coming now to the point. "Did she tell you what she told the coroner's jury?"

"She did. I told her those were serious accusations. I told her she needed to be sure of what she said."

"And was she?"

"No, I judged from the way her voice shook that she wasn't sure at all. In fact, I'd say she seemed quite uncertain. I hesitate to say this since Eveline is one of my favorite students, but it seemed quite likely that she was lying."

"Very good, Mr. Brookhart," Mr. Shaw said. "I have no other questions."

When Mr. Linder conducted the cross-examination, he asked Mr. Brookhart if it was possible that Eveline was simply nervous, caught up as she was in something far beyond her years, this tale of adultery and murder.

"I'll admit that's possible," Mr. Brookhart said after some consideration, "but I can tell you this. She seemed haughty about it, like she was challenging me to call her a liar."

"I suppose that's one man's interpretation," Mr. Linder said, "but you must know, learned man that you are, an interpretation is just an interpretation and nothing more. It may be far away from the truth. Isn't that so, Mr. Brookhart?"

Mr. Brookhart opened his mouth to make his answer, but Mr. Linder wouldn't allow it. "That's all," he said. "I've nothing more."

Lemuel Brookhart was the last witness that Mr. Shaw called. The State, he told Judge Wilson, rested.

"Mr. French?" Judge Wilson said.

"Your Honor," said Mr. French, "the defense calls Eveline Deal to the stand."

Antimony

AT LAST, IT WAS SO simple for Eveline to tell the truth. She sat very still in her chair on the witness stand, and she answered Mr. French's questions in a calm voice. Yes, she'd found the arsenic. Yes, she'd known right away what it was because her mother often kept some on hand to put out for the rats. Yes, she'd put it inside a crock and buried it behind the glasshouse. Yes, she'd replaced it with another parcel of salt that she bought from Ethan Delz.

Why had she done that? Because she feared what Miss Betsey might do with it. She knew about her and Mr. Delz. She knew Miss Betsey and the Mister were often at odds. Why take the chance that she might one day reach for a pinch of salt to put in the Mister's coffee and find herself taking up the white arsenic instead?

"I was looking out for the Mister," Eveline said. "He was always good to me."

So good she'd felt herself draw close to him, the way a daughter would to a father, and yet with something else mixed in, something she didn't know how to name, something she only knew to keep quiet. She wouldn't tell the court that, but as she sat there answering Mr. French's questions, a part of her mind strayed and she wandered back to the girl she'd been, the one who'd spent so much time with the Mister in the glasshouse. The first time he showed her how to eat glass, her heart thrilled with the danger of it. Then he painted her eyes. He made her feel beautiful and loved. After that, she would have done anything he asked.

She told the court how he used the stibnite to make the paint. "Antimony," she said, and then she explained how it was found in nature as the mineral, stibnite. She knew she was showing off to spite Mr. Brookhart, who had cast her as a dreamer. It came all the way from China, she said. The Mister used it so there'd be no bubbles in the glass after he shaped it.

"And what else did he use it for?" Mr. French asked. He paced back and forth in front of the witness stand.

"He made a powder from it and mixed it with sulfur to settle his stomach, and sometimes . . ." Eveline paused and glanced away for just an instant. Then she looked straight ahead, and she said, "Sometimes, he painted my eyes."

"Painted your eyes," said Mr. French. "You mean the way some women do?"

Eveline nodded. "Egyptian women used to line their eyes with antimony. They called it kohl."

"How did Mr. Reed . . ." Here, Mr. French hesitated. He stopped pacing and considered his words. "How did he . . . apply . . . yes, apply . . . the paint?"

"With a horsehair brush. He licked the tip of it to get a finer point."

Mr. French made a slow walk to the jury box. He stood there, his thumbs hooked into the pockets of his waistcoat, his stare taking in all twelve men. He kept his back to Eveline. He held the gaze of each of the jurors, letting what Eveline had said sink in. Leonard Reed licked the point of the brush that he dipped again and again—who knew how many times—into the paste he made from stibnite. He took some of the powders from time to time to ease his stomach.

Finally, Mr. French turned back to face Eveline. He said in a very calm voice, "Wouldn't Mr. Reed know that antimony can be toxic?"

"I wouldn't know about that."

"I assume, then, that you also wouldn't know that the effects of antimony poisoning are similar to those of arsenic?"

"No," said Eveline. "How would I have known?"

"Of course. You aren't a doctor, are you? You're just a girl."

As much as it pained Eveline to say yes, she knew she had to for the sake of Miss Betsey, who was watching her now with a flat stare. "I just knew I liked the way I looked when he painted my eyes."

"And he did this many times?"

"Yes." Eveline bowed her head. "There were many times, so many times I wouldn't know how to . . ."

Mr. French interrupted her. "That's fine, Miss Deal," he said. "Your Honor, I have nothing more for this witness."

Mr. Shaw's cross-examination was brief.

"Miss Deal," he said, "have you ever been in love?"

Eveline looked out at Tom. He sat hunched over, with his elbows on his thighs and his slouch hat rolled up in his hands that dangled between his knees. He looked up at her with wide eyes, waiting, she knew, to see what she would say.

"I am," she said. "I'm in love with a man right now."

Tom bowed his head and looked at the floor an instant, embarrassed. Then he looked at her, a grin on his face.

"So you know what love can do to a person?"

"I do. It can be the most wonderful thing and also the most horrible thing."

"Makes you feel all at loose ends, wouldn't you say, Miss Deal?"

"I suppose," she said. "Like you're not quite sure who you are anymore."

"Exactly," Mr. Shaw said, "and when that's the case, what can you trust? What can you know for certain? Everything is suspect, isn't it?"

She didn't know what to say. She sat there with no tongue in her head at all. She was thinking about what Mr. French had said about antimony poisoning. Each time the Mister touched the bristles of that horsehair brush to his tongue, he took a bit of the stibnite—the antimony—into his body. All because she liked him to paint her eyes.

Finally, Mr. Shaw said, "That's all I have, Your Honor."

Then Judge Wilson adjourned the court for the day. But just then, Heinz Ernst leapt to his feet.

"I saw da two of dem," he said, his voice rising in the courtroom. "I saw Leonard Reed and the girl. Dey vere in the glasshouse. Dey had dere arms around each other. Like dey vere lovers."

Judge Wilson was banging his gavel. "Order! Order!" he said. "Mr. Ernst, I'll have you be quiet, or else I'll hold you in contempt." The Judge directed his last comment to the jurors. "You'll disregard what you just heard. It's to have no bearing on your deliberations. Do you understand?"

The foreman was a man named Emsley Wright, an elderly man of some dignity. He was an elder at the Christian Church. He was also a tall man, and it took him a few moments to unfold his lanky frame from the chair and to stand. "Yes, sir," he said, but Eveline could tell from the severe looks on the jurors' faces that it was too late. Once Heinz Ernst spoke, whatever she'd said, and whatever she might say, was suspect.

Dear Girl

EVELINE COULDN'T FALL ASLEEP THAT night, worried as she was over what had happened in the courtroom that day. She'd told the story of the Mister painting her eyes with stibnite. She'd said she'd had no idea that it was poisonous, but the truth was the Mister had told her that. He'd said in low doses it could be quite good for the stomach. He'd promised her he knew how much to take without doing himself harm, and she'd believed him.

She hoped Mr. French had adequately put a measure of doubt in the jurors' minds. If there was no arsenic behind the tea plates in Miss Betsey's cupboard, then how in the world could she have possibly poisoned the Mister? Wasn't it likely, then, that he'd died from overexposure to antimony, a hazard of his trade and his own miscalculations?

The thought threw Eveline into a fit of sobbing, grief-stricken with the knowledge that she'd been the reason he'd licked those brushes, adding just that much more stibnite to his system. She buried her face in her pillow in hopes that Mrs. Musgrove wouldn't hear her crying. She wondered what was happening between Tom and Mr. Brookhart in the stable. Was Tom calling him to task for casting suspicion on her, or had Tom given up on her? Had Heinz Ernst's words been enough to break what only moments before had seemed to her a dear moment she and Tom would cherish forever?

She'd said she was in love. He'd smiled at her. But then Heinz Ernst said what he did, and outside the courthouse she told Tom not to make a thing out of it, nothing at all.

"Is it true what Heinz Ernst said?" he'd wanted to know. "Were you sweet on Leonard Reed? Tell the truth, Eveline."

"No, it wasn't like that," she said. "It wasn't like that at all."

"How was it then?"

She had no way to explain what she'd felt for the Mister. She stood there trying to find something to say, something to make Tom understand. She tried to take his hand in hers, but he pulled away and started walking toward the Musgroves'. The only thing she could do was to follow.

Mr. Brookhart was in the house when they arrived. "Eveline," he said, but she wouldn't listen to him. She ran straightaway to her room and stayed there through supper, not wanting to face the company of anyone in that house.

Now, in her bed, she wondered how she'd ever be able to face Miss Betsey. Heinz Ernst had made her out to be some sort of strumpet intent on stealing the Mister. It wasn't true. No matter what Heinz Ernst saw—yes, she'd let the Mister hug her; yes, she'd held onto him— it wasn't like everyone would think. Mr. French was right; she was just a girl. A girl with no father, a girl who longed to feel pretty, a girl—yes, she had to admit it—who had always envied Miss Betsey. A girl who let the Mister paint her eyes and make her believe she was beautiful. A girl who loved Jesus. A girl who dreamed of beauty. A girl who longed to be swept up in drama. Well, she'd got what she wanted. More than enough to last her. Here she was in the midst of this tale of scandal and murder, her name forever linked with the death of Leonard Reed and whatever was going to happen to Miss Betsey because of it.

≈

In her cell in the basement of the courthouse, Betsey closed her eyes, but sleep refused to come. She couldn't forget what she'd felt for Eveline at the moment of Heinz Ernst's accusation. Such an understanding. If anyone knew what it was to be the subject of gossip, the object of people's fears and suspicions, she did.

If Leonard had painted the girl's eyes—even if he'd touched her the way Heinz Ernst claimed—surely it was out of loneliness, a loneliness that Betsey had contributed to, and surely God would forgive him that, as Betsey forgave Eveline.

"Dear girl," she whispered. Through the small window above her, she could see the night's first star, and she remembered what it had been to be Eveline's age, so uncertain of all that was to come, so eager for her real life to begin. Betsey knew she'd too easily forgotten all that when she dealt with Eveline. She was often too snappish, too haughty. If she'd only been kinder, maybe none of this would have happened. Maybe she would have been the one holding Eveline, rocking her gently in her arms, telling her *hush*, telling her *everything will be all right*. Betsey thought of how she used to look on the night's first star and make a wish.

And what would she wish now? Forgiveness for all her wrongs. A chance to walk in a new life. A life of goodness and love.

"I forgive you everything, dear Eveline," she said, "as I hope you'll be able to forgive me."

The Trial: Day Two

MR. FRENCH CALLED DR. HARRISON Kirkwood to the stand. Judge Wilson reminded the doctor that he was still under oath.

"Dr. Kirkwood," said Mr. French, "you say you performed the Marsh test on samples of tissue from Mr. Reed's intestines and stomach."

Betsey realized she'd scooted forward to the edge of her chair. Her elbows were on the table, and her hands were pressed together as if in prayer. She didn't know what Mr. French had in mind. She could only listen and hope he was intending to call into question Dr. Kirkwood's previous testimony. If she was praying, she was asking God to give Mr. French the knowledge and the cunning that he required.

"That's right," said Dr. Kirkwood. His jaw was set, his words deliberate and sharp. He didn't like having his expertise challenged. Betsey could tell that much. "The Marsh test is completely reliable when it comes to the detection of arsenic in the body."

Mr. French approached the bench and spoke in low tones. Betsey thought she heard the word "evidence" and the word "test," but she couldn't be sure. She leaned forward as much as she could, and she convinced herself that she heard Judge Wilson say, "most unusual." Then he summoned Mr. Shaw to the bench.

For a few moments, the three men seemed to be speaking at once, creating a low murmur. Betsey closed her eyes and listened to the hum of their voices. Then one voice broke clear. Mr. Shaw's: "I suppose you leave me no choice."

Judge Wilson said, "Mr. French, you may proceed."

"Dr. Kirkwood," said Mr. French, taking a few steps toward the witness stand, "you testified earlier regarding the bowl in which you performed this Marsh test on the tissue from Mr. Reed's body."

"Yes. The bowl, as you'll recall, Mr. French." Dr. Kirkwood paused just long enough to make it clear that he was chiding him. "The bowl was stained with a black residue. That was arsenic, Mr. French. Plain and simple."

Mr. French glanced over at the table where Betsey and Mr. Linder were sitting. She could see an amused look in his eyes, a slight twitch of his lips as if they wanted to stretch into a grin.

"Of course, Dr. Kirkwood. I do indeed recall that." Mr. French winked at Betsey. She was absolutely sure of it. Then he said, "I assume you know about sodium hypochlorite, don't you, Doctor?"

Dr. Kirkwood drew himself up even straighter in his chair. He tipped his head and glared at Mr. French over the top of his spectacles. "Chlorinated lime, commonly known as bleaching powder. Yes, Mr. French, I know about sodium hypochlorite."

"And you must know that the Marsh test isn't one hundred percent reliable."

"The test is very specific for arsenic," Dr. Kirkwood said. "I made that clear in my original testimony."

"That you did," said Mr. French, "but isn't it true that there's sometimes a false positive test?"

Betsey swore she saw Dr. Kirkwood grimace. He shifted his weight in his chair. "False positive?" he said. "Yes, I'm sure that's possible."

Mr. French swung around so he was facing the jurors. "So you agree that a false positive is possible. What, then, might be something other than arsenic that would leave the sort of black residue that you found in your bowl?"

Dr. Kirkwood unhooked his spectacles from around his ears and pinched the bridge of his nose as if he had a bad headache. He said something that Betsey couldn't make out.

"A bit louder, Dr. Kirkwood, if you please," said Mr. French.

"Antimony," Dr. Kirkwood said. He settled his spectacles back on his nose. "Antimony can sometimes leave a black deposit."

"Antimony," Mr. French said, still holding the jurors in his gaze.

"Yes."

"And just to be clear, antimony is found in stibnite. Is that correct?"

"It is."

"The stibnite Leonard Reed used in his glassmaking."

Dr. Kirkwood's voice shrank. "Yes."

"The stibnite he used to paint Miss Deal's eyes. The powder she said he took sometimes for his digestion."

"If that's what he did, then yes."

"Miss Deal testified under oath that Mr. Reed used a brush to line her eyes with stibnite, a brush he licked to give the bristles a fine point. Surely you remember that, Dr. Kirkwood."

At this point, Dr. Kirkwood gave in. "Yes, stibnite," he said. "That's where Mr. Reed would have gotten the antimony he needed for his glassmaking, and, yes, antimony can sometimes give a false positive in the Marsh test. Yes, Mr. French, you are correct."

"But this sodium hypochlorite." Mr. French turned from the jurors and was approaching Dr. Kirkwood. "You know why I asked about that, don't you?"

Betsey could tell that Dr. Kirkwood was now resigned. He slumped in his chair. He said, "Sodium hypochlorite, when applied to the residue, will not dissolve it."

"And when applied to the black stain of arsenic?"

"The stain will disappear."

Mr. French paused to let that piece of information have some space around it, and Betsey could hear the jurors' chairs creaking as they reacted to the shifts in weights of twelve men, now disturbed.

Then Mr. French said, "Did you use sodium hypochlorite to test the black residue left in your bowl from the Marsh test that you performed on the tissue samples from Mr. Reed's intestines and stomach?"

"No, sir. I did not."

"But, Dr. Kirkwood, you're a physician. A man of medicine and science. A man well-respected for his learning and his expertise. Why wouldn't you check your hypothesis? Why wouldn't you make certain that there was arsenic in Mr. Reed's system at the time of his death?"

"I don't know," Dr. Kirkwood said in a whisper, and Betsey could tell he was ashamed. "I'm not sure," he said.

"You don't know?" Mr. French spread his arms out as if pleading for a rational answer. "I find that hard to believe, Dr. Kirkwood. Very hard to believe."

"I made a mistake," Dr. Kirkwood said. "I erred."

Mr. French walked back to the table where Betsey and Mr. Linder were sitting. "Well then, let's correct that error, shall we?" He reached out his hand to Mr. Linder, who took a small, corked bottle of clear liquid from his coat pocket and gave it to Mr. French. "I just happen to have some sodium hypochlorite right here." He held the bottle aloft so all could see. Then he said to Judge Wilson, "Your Honor, if we might have another look at that bowl the State introduced into evidence."

"Mr. Shaw," said Judge Wilson.

"This is irregular," Mr. Shaw said, shaking his head. "Highly irregular."

Then the sheriff, Mr. Fyffe, produced the glass bowl. Judge Wilson told him to set it on the table in front of Mr. Linder.

"Dr. Kirkwood," Judge Wilson said, "if you'll kindly join Mr. French and Mr. Linder there."

Mr. French handed the doctor the bottle of sodium hypochlorite. "Doctor, if you please, could you use this as you would have the day of Leonard Reed's autopsy had you done everything you should have?"

Betsey could tell it didn't please the doctor at all, but he did as Mr. French requested. He poured the liquid down the sides of the glass bowl. The odor was sharp, and it prickled Betsey's nose. She started to cough. Mr. Linder had to hold his handkerchief to his nose. The liquid seemed to sizzle, and, when it was done, Mr. French picked up the bowl and carried it to the bench so Judge Wilson could see it. He then carried it to the jury box so the twelve men who would decide Betsey's fate could see it. Finally, he carried it back to the table, and now Betsey could see inside it. She could see the black stain still intact.

"Dr. Kirkwood," Mr. French said, "will you please announce the findings of our test?"

"The residue remains," Dr. Kirkwood said, "indicating the presence of antimony."

"The presence of antimony in Leonard Reed's stomach and intestines on the day of his death."

"Yes," said Dr. Kirkwood, and the courtroom erupted.

It took several minutes for Judge Wilson to call it back to order. Betsey thought the day was won.

Then Mr. Shaw said he had a few questions for Dr. Kirkwood.

"You are a man of science, yes?"

"I am."

"A man who believes in the laws of the universe."

"Indeed."

"Have you ever seen phenomena that you couldn't explain? Miracles, as they were? Outcomes that shouldn't have been possible?"

Dr. Kirkwood nodded. "I've seen a cancer disappear never to return. I've seen a man's heart start again after it stopped."

"Amazing. How do you explain those outcomes, doctor?"

"God works in mysterious ways."

"But you're a man of science."

"Yes," said Dr. Kirkwood, "but I'm also a man of faith."

"So you're saying that scientific explanation doesn't always hold up in a court of law."

"I'm saying, Mr. Shaw, that sometimes what happens shouldn't, but it does, and there it is, irrefutable."

Mr. Shaw paced back and forth in front of the jurors. "And what of witchcraft, doctor? Do you believe in witches as well?"

"The origins of medicine are closely linked to the supernatural. Witches were often thought of as being able to cause an illness or to cure it."

"Would a witch be able to influence the interaction of arsenic and hypochlorite?"

Dr. Kirkwood grinned. "If one believed in witches, then, yes, I suppose she could."

"And could a witch cause a milk cow to go dry the way Heinz Ernst said that Elizabeth Reed did?"

"I suppose a witch could do whatever she wanted to do."

Betsey saw the jurors turn almost as one and study her with their severe countenances. Mr. Shaw clapped his hands together, and the sound shook her.

"That's all I have," he said. "Thank you, Doctor. You've been most helpful."

The Verdict

THAT EVENING, MR. FRENCH AND Mr. Linder were in high spirits. They sat on chairs that Sheriff Fyffe had dragged into Betsey's cell and celebrated what they were sure would be an acquittal.

Mr. Linder even allowed himself a nip of bourbon from his pewter hip flask. "That is, Mrs. Reed, if you have no objections."

Betsey sat on her bed, her hands clasped in her lap. She felt as if she might just jump out of her skin. She knew the jury was deliberating her fate, and in spite of Mr. French's and Mr. Linder's optimism and good cheer, she couldn't forget the way those jurors looked at her at the end of Dr. Kirkwood's testimony. They looked at her as if they were seriously considering that she might be a witch, that she'd somehow worked a spell on the evidence—that black residue that remained after the hypochlorite had been added—and was now feeling pretty smug on account of it.

"No," she said to Mr. Linder. "I don't mind."

"Thank you, Mrs. Reed. I believe I'll have another." He tipped back the flask and took a longer draw. Then he said, "You worked the hocus-pocus, French, even if Shaw tried his best to undo it."

"You don't think he did, do you?" Mr. French started to get up from his chair as if he couldn't bear to sit still. Then he eased himself back down. "Tell me the truth, Linder. Do you think we've got this one?"

Mr. Linder returned his flask to his pocket and revisited Mr. French's closing argument, counting off the main points on his fingers. "No arsenic in the cupboard, a negligent autopsy, no arsenic found in Mr. Reed's body, only antimony from the stibnite that he ingested, an unreliable witness in Heinz Ernst. Shaw was grabbing at straws."

Mr. French relaxed then. He looked at Betsey, his eyes twinkly in the candlelight, his mouth stretched wide in a grin.

"We've done it, Betsey," he said. "By jingo, we have."

That night, as she tried to fall asleep, she kept going over what Mr. Shaw had told the jury during his own closing argument. He'd told them that she was a woman driven by lust and greed, an adulterous woman with a husband who displeased her, a husband she preferred to see gone, a woman with the means to make sure she got what she wanted, a witchy woman who could alter the laws of nature. Mr. Shaw argued that Eveline Deal was just as bad, a girl who consorted with Leonard Reed, a girl who had her own secrets to protect.

"What sad women," Mr. Shaw said. "What a sad tale."

Betsey couldn't disagree. A sad tale from the lovelorn. She and Eveline, not so different as she might have once believed. Two lonely women, anxious and desperate for love.

❦

Eveline hadn't left the courthouse lawn. She'd told Tom to please go back to the Musgroves' without her; she needed some time to be alone. "All right, Eveline," he told her. "Whatever you say."

Though it was dark, she sat on a wooden bench, and she did something she hadn't thought to do since her father's death. She prayed. She prayed to God that the jury would find Miss Betsey innocent.

"If anyone needs to be punished," she said, "it's me."

She'd led the coroner's jury to believe that Miss Betsey kept a paper of arsenic in the cupboard when she knew it wasn't true. All because

Miss Betsey had called her an ugly girl. Then she'd turned away from God, and now here she was, asking him to listen to her prayer. What else could she do but believe that God would forgive her, that he would bless the innocent and redeem the guilty, that he would forgive her sins, that he would make sure Miss Betsey went free.

"If she hangs, I'll never be able to go on," she said.

A man's voice came from behind her, and before she turned she knew who she'd find.

"Of course you vill," the voice said, and then she turned and saw Heinz Ernst stepping out of the shadow cast by a giant walnut tree. "You vill because you'll have no choice."

How odd, she thought, that at this time of her need, the man who killed her father would appear, the man who had damned her with his testimony.

"I don't want to see you," she said.

He sat down on the bench beside her. He stared straight ahead, and his voice was soft. "Try losing a son," he said. "Try going on den. May dat never happen to you."

"You killed my father."

"Ja." A skein of clouds was passing over the quarter moon. "Dat much is true, and I'll have to pay for dat."

"But you'll be alive."

"Sometimes I vish it vasn't so."

With that, he rose from the bench, and without another word, he walked away, leaving Eveline alone in the dark to think about the way things happened, often without reason.

Word that the jury had reached a verdict came at ten o'clock the next morning. It was a glorious spring day. Even Betsey could tell that in her cell. Sunlight came through the high window and slanted across the foot of her bed where she sat reading the Bible that the Reverend Seed had given her. She could hear birdsong from the trees on the courthouse lawn. The sunlight was warm on her hands.

She was reading the story of Job, a man of faith tested by God.

Then Sheriff Fyffe came, and he worked his key into the lock on the cell door. "Mrs. Reed," he said, "the jury's back. It's time."

Her heart quickened.

"Now?" she said.

"Yes, Missus," said the sheriff, "now."

She closed the Bible with care and sat a moment, rubbing her hand over its worn leather.

"I'd like to comb my hair," she said.

She recalled the sheriff's wife, Floss, and how she'd brought a comb and mirror when Betsey first arrived. How gentle Floss had been as she combed the tangles from her hair. A kind, cheerful soul, and Betsey felt a stab of sorrow rise in her anew over the memory of Floss's death from the cholera. Why was it that some who deserved to die didn't, while others like Floss, who should have had more time, got taken? Reverend Seed said it was because sometimes God needed his best servants in Heaven. If that were indeed the case, Betsey reasoned she might live a good bit more considering the fact that she had never been a good servant. As Mr. Shaw had made plain, she was, for the most part, a selfish lustful woman, who had dreamed of a life without her husband. Murdered him, she hadn't, but dreamed him dead? Yes, oh yes, too many times, yes.

"All right, then." Mr. Fyffe stood with his arms crossed. "Hurry along."

❧

Eveline and Tom approached the courthouse from the west, caught up in a throng of people who shared their destination.

"I'm surprised you're still here," Eveline had told him when she came back from the courthouse lawn and her odd encounter with Heinz Ernst. "I figured you'd be on your way back home by now."

Tom was sitting on the step at Lemuel Brookhart's sister's house. He stood up and said, "You don't understand. I'm not going anywhere. I love you."

Now she was glad to have him by her side, actually a bit in front of her, clearing a path for them through the crowd that had gathered on the courthouse lawn, unable to find a spot in the packed courtroom.

"That's her," she heard a man say.

Out of the corner of her eye, she saw fingers pointing in her direction.

"What a sweet puss, that one," a woman said in a cloying tone that told Eveline she was exaggerating that term of endearment until it turned into its opposite.

Another woman completed the transaction. "Ah, yes, a sweet pussy," she said with a savage voice. "The idea."

So this was to be her life now, she thought. The subject of gossip; the object of disgust. Lord help me, she thought. She put her head down. She grabbed onto Tom's hand and followed him into the courtroom.

∽◉◟

The jurors entered and took their seats. Mr. French reached over and patted Betsey's hand. Mr. Linder sat easily on her other side, his legs turned to the side, one over the other at the knee, as if he were enjoying the spring day from a veranda somewhere in his native Kentucky. Betsey could hear him humming under his breath. He was humming "Take Your Time, Miss Lucy." A comedic ballad about a mother telling her young daughter to take it slow when it comes to matters of the heart. *So take your time Miss Lucy, Miss Lucy, Lucy, oh!*

A bouncy melody. A carefree tune. What a song for a moment like this.

"Linder." Mr. French reached behind Betsey and poked Mr. Linder in his side. "Really, Linder. Won't you stop?"

"Relax, French," Mr. Linder said. "Nothing to worry about."

The jurors were solemn. Betsey noted that right away. These twelve men in their wrinkled black suits. Some of the men had gray beards that hung to their chests and backs humped from age and work. Others were younger and freshly shaved.

The foreman, Emsley Wright, carried a walking stick with an ebony shaft and an ornate head of sterling. He anchored it to the floor and pressed against it as he rose to his feet when Judge Wilson asked him for the jury's verdict.

A wasp was in the courtroom. Betsey could hear it buzzing as it bumped against the ceiling or the wall, frantic to find its way back to open air. She lifted her eyes to see if she might spot it, and while she was searching the ceiling, Emsley Wright read the verdict.

"We the jury find . . ." He paused, then, overcome with a fit of coughing. He reached into his coat pocket for a handkerchief. He held it to his mouth. His shoulders heaved once, twice. Then he gathered himself. He slipped the handkerchief back into his pocket. He said, "We the jury find the defendant guilty of the crime as charged."

The courtroom was so quiet, Betsey could still hear the wasp. She closed her eyes. "Oh, heavenly father," she said.

Judge Wilson asked each of the jurors to pronounce that the verdict was his own, and each of the jurors said yes, yes it was.

Mr. Linder muttered under his breath. "The dirty bastards."

Betsey heard a breath of air leave Mr. French, as if someone had given him a blow to the stomach. "Impossible," he said.

But apparently it wasn't. Just like that, in a snap, it was done.

The Sentence

AND NOW THIS DAY, COMES the prisoner and defendant in custody to receive the sentence of the court. The Judgment of the Law and the Court pronounces it is that you, Elizabeth Reed, be taken from hence to the place of your confinement and that on the twenty-third day of May you be taken from thence to some convenient place within one mile of this courthouse and there hanged by the neck until you are dead, and that the sheriff execute this sentence, and may the Lord have mercy on your soul.

Ugly Girl

THE REST OF HER LIFE, Eveline never forgot the summer the Mister died and all that followed. She lived a very long time, long enough to know two wars, to listen to a phonograph, to talk on the telephone, to ride in a motor car, to have the right to vote, to see a moving picture, to see people dance the Charleston, to read a new magazine called *Time*, to see Harry Houdini escape his water torture cell, to hear of Charles Lindberg and his solo flight across the Atlantic. She had children and grandchildren, and even a great-grandbaby, but all it took was the smell of coffee, or the taste of salt, or a roaring fire, or the way sunlight fell upon a glass vase, or the sight of a woman with her eyes lined with black to take her back to the girl she'd been, the one who'd been unwilling to tell the truth because Miss Betsey had said something to wound her. *Ugly girl*, Miss Betsey had said, and *ugly girl* she was.

Her mother had already heard the news of the verdict and the sentence by the time Eveline returned home. She'd heard, too, the particulars and all the secrets that had come out during the trial. The gossipmongers were busy at their work.

"They say you were with that man," she said to Eveline, the very first thing she said to her when she walked into the cabin. "Leonard Reed. They say you were his whore."

"Mother, please." Eveline set her carpetbag on the floor. She was so tired. After all the noise of the trial and the shock of the verdict, all she wanted was to sit somewhere for a very long time and not have to say a word to anyone. But now here was her mother, nettling her. "I really wouldn't think you'd want to talk about this," Eveline said.

"Well, I do want to talk about it, missy." Her mother reached out and took her by the arm, pinching her elbow so hard it hurt. "Is it true? Is that what you are?"

Eveline jerked her arm away. She started to answer and then stopped. "For you to even ask that question." Her mouth was trembling, and she tried very hard not to cry. "I guess it shows what you think about me."

"It's not what I think that counts." Her mother waved her arm wildly about, as if to indicate the neighbors and villagers outside the walls of the cabin. "It's all of them, every one of them. It's what they're saying, what they're thinking. Eveline, I'll never be able to hold my head up to meet their eyes."

"Would it make any difference if I said it wasn't true?"

"It's not, is it? Oh, Eveline, please tell me it's not."

All day, her coach had traveled under leaden skies, and, finally, she could hear thunder off in the distance. The muggy air was still and close, and she felt a trickle of sweat run down the inside of her arm. She wanted to tell the truth, but she didn't know what it was. She'd never done what all those gossips were thinking, but she knew how she'd felt making the walk from the village to her mother's cabin, passing groups of people who huddled together and spoke in low voices as she went by. Standing now before her mother, who waited for her answer, she knew in a way she hadn't quite before what Heinz Ernst had tried to tell her. When trouble came—even trouble of your own making—and people made up their minds about the sort of person you were, what could you do but keep putting one foot in front of the other? Only now, she knew the thing that Heinz Ernst hadn't spoken of, that feeling of being stuck, of always being the girl who'd got caught up in the drama between the Mister and Miss Betsey and, yes, Ethan Delz. The ugly girl who'd not told the whole truth until it was too late; now, no matter how long she lived, she'd always be that girl.

The longer she stood there, not speaking, the more her mother shrank from her—or maybe it was Eveline who was shrinking. She imagined herself receding, speeding back through time, getting younger and younger, and finally disappearing. Her mother and father were young and happy. The thought of her wasn't yet in their minds. A young glassmaker from Pittsburgh had just started showing his wares in the village. A pretty farm girl who wore veils on her bonnets caught his fancy. A merchant named Ethan Delz accepted a loan from his father and opened a dry goods store. Heinz Ernst was an immigrant boy who was trying hard to learn English. All of their lives were ahead of them.

"Eveline," her mother said in a whisper, coaxing her out of her fancy. "Won't you please tell me?"

The rain was coming down now in torrents. The noise was so loud that Eveline had to shout to make herself heard.

"Oh, Mother," she said, "of course it's not true." She turned away to watch the rain streak the window glass, and she whispered so her mother wouldn't hear, "But surely you've heard the rest of it. You must know that I'm a liar."

In the days that passed after the trial, Eveline stayed close to the cabin, glad that school was out for the year and she didn't have to face Mr. Brookhart.

Then, one day, as if she'd conjured him, he appeared at the door. He'd come, he said, to see about her.

"I've been worried about you," he said. "Eveline, you shouldn't let what people say harden your heart. You're a smart girl. You'll find a way to get beyond this."

He stood at the door, trying his best, she knew, to be her teacher. He looked down at her over the tops of his spectacles. He spoke in his teacher's voice, just a little stern, and he told her in essence what Heinz Ernst had told her, to keep moving on, to keep putting one foot in front of the other.

But how could she? "I let the coroner's jury believe that Miss Betsey poisoned the Mister," she said. "It should have got set right. After what came out at the trial, no one should have thought she was guilty. But they did, and now . . ." She couldn't go on. She couldn't bear to think of Miss Betsey hanging by her neck. "And that's my fault," she said. "How am I supposed to live with something like that?"

"Time will go on," Mr. Brookhart said. "It may not seem like it now, but just watch. It will. The days will go on, and so will you, and there'll come a day when it'll seem to you like someone else told that lie, someone you can barely recall."

"It's lovely to think so," Eveline said, and then she started to close the door.

"Wait." Mr. Brookhart placed his hand to the door and pushed it back. "We're all guilty in this in some way. We all believed what we wanted to believe about Elizabeth Reed."

Eveline stared at him for a very long time. The she said in a flat, direct voice, "I'm the one who lied."

"We have to forgive ourselves," Mr. Brookhart said. "Each one of us. We have to trust that there will be wonderful days ahead."

She pushed hard on the door, then, and he let her close it. She heard him on the other side saying, "I'm sorry, Eveline." She didn't know exactly what he regretted. The way he portrayed her on the witness stand? The fact that she was guilty of a sin no one could redeem? She decided it didn't really matter. She stood there, listening to him breathing on the other side of the door. "Eveline?" he said. "Please."

But she wouldn't answer, and soon she heard him going back up the path. She imagined him returning to his home, warming a bit of supper for himself, eating it alone at his table, reading a bit later before blowing out his candle and going off to bed. Such a spare life. Had his loneliness been enough to make him say what he did about her, all for the few minutes that everyone would be giving him their attention? Had she been longing for the same when she told the coroner's jury what she did? Was it then that lies began to feel like love?

She was still thinking on that in the evening when Tom came to call.

"It's time we settled this," he said.

They walked down the path together to the springhouse. Eveline thought of the evening last summer when Tom kissed her there and she told him it couldn't be her he wanted. But he persisted, and he persisted still on this evening in spring, another summer about to begin. Now she knew herself better than she ever had, and what she knew was this: she was lost, utterly and completely lost. So lost that she could go in any direction she chose, and it would take her somewhere better than where she was.

So when Tom said, "I mean it, Eveline. Either you're going to marry me or you're not," she said, "All right."

They were standing in the shadow of the springhouse. The air was cooler there. Eveline felt a chill come over her, and she stepped closer to Tom. Mr. French had said that the State must have cut a deal with Heinz Ernst. He'd been sent to the penitentiary, but in time he'd be back on his farm with his wife and his children. It had been three weeks since the trial, but already Eveline felt life going on. She was amazed that a girl like her, a girl who had started everything, could be here, free and clear on this beautiful evening in spring, and could lay her head on Tom McKinney's shoulder and say, again, "All right."

"All right?" he said.

"Yes," she told him. "I'll marry you."

The Baptism

BETSEY SPENT HER DAYS READING her Bible and talking with the Reverend Seed. He came each evening after his supper when there were still a few hours of light left, his Bible tucked under his arm, his head down as he strode across the courthouse lawn. Those who saw him were often heard to remark that he was a fool to spend his evenings with that woman, that evil woman, the one who poisoned her husband, but the Reverend Seed wasn't aware of what people thought; he was too busy trying to save Betsey's soul.

"God's forgiveness is without condition," he told her one evening. "All you have to do is ask for it."

She'd heard this from the Reverend Seed before. All she had to do was repent, ask God's forgiveness, and then be baptized to rise from the water a new person, without sin. She remembered the morning last summer when she heard Eveline singing while she drew water from the cistern, a hymn about the clouds breaking and the dawn soon to come. How silly Betsey had thought the girl then, moon-eyed over the Ascension. Betsey knew she'd been too much concerned with the here and now to make room for any thought about the hereafter. What would Eveline think of her now if she were to see her sitting in her cell, her Bible open on her lap, talking with the Reverend Seed about redemption?

Just that morning, Betsey had read a verse in Isaiah that made her think of Eveline at the cistern. *Then shall thy light break forth as the*

*morning, and thine health shall spring forth speedily: and thy righteousness
shall go before thee; the glory of the Lord shall be thy reward.*

Betsey wished she could see Eveline once more so she could tell
her she brooked no grudge against her. What was done was done, and
nothing could undo it. She wished Eveline a lifetime of happiness, one
lived long and well.

"There's no reason for bitterness," she told the Reverend Seed. "No
call for confession either. Nothing can change what's going to happen
to me."

With that, the Reverend Seed closed his Bible and stood up from
his chair. "The glory of God awaits you, Betsey, if you'll only repent."

"What have I done that's wrong?" she asked him.

He sighed. "We all know our sins," he said, and then he bid her
goodnight.

∽⦿∼

On occasion other visitors came to see her. Mr. French and Mr.
Linder came to express their dismay over the verdict and the sentence.

"It's not your fault," she told them.

"It's not right," said Mr. French.

"Maybe it is," she said. She'd been mulling over what the Reverend
Seed had told her about everyone knowing their sins.

"But goddamn it," said Mr. Linder, "you've committed no crime.
You didn't even have any arsenic in your cupboard. Eveline Deal made
sure of that."

Betsey looked at each man for a good, long while, before starting
to tell them the story of everything that had happened that August
morning when Leonard came up from the glasshouse telling her his
stomach felt like it was on fire.

She'd poured him a cup of coffee that morning before he went out
to blow the candlesticks he'd promised her. She'd poured the coffee,

and, yes, Eveline had been correct in saying that she saw her take a paper parcel from behind the tea plates in the step-back cupboard, untie the string that held the parcel closed, and put a pinch of white powder into Leonard's coffee. Betsey closed her eyes a moment and saw herself doing it. She saw herself stirring the coffee with a spoon while Eveline was carrying a pan of biscuits to the table, where Leonard was sitting. Just before the girl got to the table, she stopped. She stood there, her eyes fixed on Betsey and what she was doing. It was then that Eveline's arm began to tremble. She tried to go on to the table, but before she could get there, her arm gave way and the pan tipped and the biscuits slid to the floor.

"Eveline," Betsey said, snapping at the girl. "My word. Now what's Mr. Reed to do without his biscuits?"

"Oh, that's all right," said Leonard. "Accidents happen. Can't be helped."

"They shouldn't be spoilt." Eveline was on her knees, gathering up the biscuits into the fold of her apron. "I swept the floor just now before I started cooking."

"Don't be ridiculous," Betsey said. She carried Leonard's coffee to him. "I won't have my husband eating dirt. Throw those nasty biscuits out and bring him some of that corn mush, and for pity's sake, make sure you don't spill it."

It was then, while Eveline was busy at the fire, that Betsey realized what she'd done. She went back to the cupboard where she folded up the paper to tie it again. She saw the printing on it: *Tink and do*. The words Heinz Ernst had written. She'd grabbed the wrong parcel. Instead of the one that held the salt, she'd undone the one that held the white arsenic that Ethan meant for her to use to poison Leonard.

He was just then lifting the cup to his lips. She knew she could stop him. She knew she could say, "Leonard, wait." But if she did, she'd have to tell him why he couldn't drink that coffee. One thing would lead to another and the whole of the story would be known, the story of her love for Ethan, the story of a woman who almost murdered her husband.

A surprising calm fell over her. It was as if she were surrendering to what she'd wanted all along. *All right, then,* she thought. *I'll let him drink it.*

By the time she came to her senses and knew she should stop him, it was too late. She closed up the paper and tied it tight. She stuffed it back behind the tea plates.

It wasn't until Leonard had finished his breakfast and gone out to the glasshouse that she began to panic. What in the world had she done?

Eveline was trying to apologize to her for dropping the biscuits. "I'm so sorry. I just lost myself somehow."

Betsey told her she was clumsy. She said she was nearly useless. "I don't know why I pay you," she said. "I honestly don't. Now take those biscuits out and scatter them for the chickens."

"Yes, Miss Betsey."

As soon as Eveline stepped out into the dooryard, Betsey hurried to the cupboard and reached behind the tea plates. She glanced behind her to make sure that she was indeed alone. She closed her hand around the parcel and pulled it out of the cupboard.

At the fireplace, she untied the string again and emptied the powder into the fire. She touched the edge of the paper to the flame, and the words *Tink and do* burned away. Then a gust of wind blew through the house—the girl had left the door standing open—and snatched the scorched paper out of her fingers. A gust of wind come from out of nowhere on a day that was otherwise still and stifling. The paper flew across the floor, and Betsey went after it, but then Leonard was at the door, his hands on his stomach.

"Oh, Mrs. Reed," he said. "I'm quite discomforted."

She grabbed onto him as his knees buckled and he started to fall. She saw Eveline coming back to the house. Betsey held onto her husband, her heart pounding, and she helped him to his bed. She glanced around the house, but the scorched paper was nowhere to be seen, not to appear again until Eveline found it in the dooryard. At least Betsey had disposed of the arsenic. *At least*, she thought, *I've done that.*

Now in her jail cell, she said to Mr. French and Mr. Linder, "So you see that when I brought my husband his coffee that morning, I thought I'd accidentally put arsenic into it. I had no idea that Eveline had made that impossible. I brought Leonard that coffee and I did nothing to stop him from drinking it."

She closed her eyes. She heard Mr. French say, "We can file an appeal, Betsy. Surely, we must."

"No." She opened her eyes. None of this had been a dream—not Leonard's death, not the trial, not the sentence, none of it. Here at the end, she could do nothing but speak the truth. "I had evil in my heart," she said. "Surely, it's not wrong to hold me to account for that. I had no idea that I was just putting salt into that coffee, just the way Leonard liked it every day of his life."

That night, she heard a noise at her window, a faint tapping. She stood atop her bed and saw someone outside, crouched down near the window. A hand pressed to the glass. A man's hand, narrow with long slender fingers. A hand she recognized as the one she'd held in hers countless times. The beautiful hand of Ethan Delz.

Oh, how she'd once loved him. She remembered when he cut the length of purple wool for the dress she made, how he touched her wrist and told her the material flattered her, how she'd been able to imagine a life with him. She'd heard the sheriff, Mr. Fyffe, talking to someone only days before about how Ethan's dry goods store had burned. "You can bet that fire didn't start itself," Mr. Fyffe said. "People don't take kindly to the sort of business Delz was up to with another man's wife."

He was on the run now, Mr. Fyffe said. John Wynn up in Heathsville had a warrant for his arrest. The charge? Conspiracy to commit murder.

That was what hurt Betsey more than anything, the fact that she'd let things with Ethan go so far that his own life was now in jeopardy. If she'd only kept to herself, if she'd allowed no flirtation, if she'd only stayed with her husband, no matter the cost to her happiness. Where was that happiness now?

Here, one last time, she pressed her hand to the glass, spreading her fingers, trying to cover Ethan's with her own.

She could hear him weeping.

"Don't," she said.

He said something to her, something she couldn't quite make out, something about being sorry, something about love. Then a man's voice rang out from the other side of the courthouse lawn. "There he is, boys. That's him."

"Run," she said to Ethan. She knew this might be the last thing between them, but there was no time to say all she wanted to say. "Run," she said again.

And he did.

∽⟐∿

So it was that on the evening of May twenty-second, Betsey asked to speak with the Reverend Seed one more time.

"I suppose I'm ready," she said.

The Reverend Seed scratched his head. "Ready?"

"That's right," said Betsey. "I'm ready to have my sins washed away."

She went on to say that she wanted to be baptized. She wanted to rise from the water, unburdened, ready to meet God in his Heaven.

"Won't you do that for me?" she said. "Won't you baptize me in the river?"

"Do you repent of your sins?" the Reverend Seed asked her. "Do you ask the Lord God to forgive you, to take your sins from you? Do you wish to walk with Christ?"

It was dusk, but no candle had been lit inside Betsey's cell. The last of the dim light through the window was barely enough for her to make out the slender frame of the Reverend Seed. She knew he was leaning toward her, holding his Bible before him, waiting for her answer. Years before, she and Leonard had stood before a minister. They'd promised they'd love each other forever. Betsey could feel the tears coming now no matter how hard she tried to stop them. She thought of how young they'd both been, how the rest of their lives stretched out ahead of them with hope and promise.

"I do," she said in a whisper.

Then the Reverend Seed took her by her hand and helped her kneel on the floor with him, and he told her to bow her head, and she did, and she listened to Reverend Seed's prayer of thanksgiving for this soul, once lost, who now had been found.

❦

A little less than a mile from the courthouse at the east end of the village, a hillside looked out over the Embarras River. Tall maple trees, their limbs shadows in the moonlight, lined the riverbank. The wagon in which Betsey and the Reverend Seed were riding creaked along, Sheriff Fyffe managing the reins. The Reverend Seed had convinced him to allow the baptism. Atop the hill, Betsey could see the platform and the timbers of the gallows that awaited her come morning.

Sheriff Fyffe carried a pine knot torch and led Betsey and Reverend Seed down to the river. There, they removed their shoes and stockings. The Reverend Seed rolled his trouser legs up to his knees. Betsey gathered her skirts.

The Reverend Seed took her hand, and together they waded away from the bank until the muddy river water was up to Betsey's waist.

The Reverend Seed removed a bandana from his hip pocket and folded it into a tidy rectangle. He told Betsey to hold him by his wrist, and she did.

Then, in the glow from Sheriff Fyffe's torch, the Reverend Seed started to tip Betsey backward. She felt the mud of the riverbed between her naked toes. The Reverend Seed held his bandana over her nose and mouth.

"I baptize thee in the name of the Father and of the Son and of the Holy Spirit," he said.

Then Betsey was under the water, her body weightless for a delightful moment, before she felt the Reverend Seed pulling her back to the surface.

She came up with water streaming from her face and hair, with her dress and underthings clinging to her body. She came up with a shout.

"Hallelujah," said the Reverend Seed.

"Praise God," said Betsey.

And like that, it was done.

She slept a dreamless sleep that night, a sleep unlike any she'd had since she was a child. She slept and slept, her burden lifted, until just after dawn, when Sheriff Fyffe came to tell her it was time.

May 23, 1845

AT FIRST EVELINE SAID SHE wouldn't go—she couldn't, she just couldn't—but daybreak on the morning of May twenty-third found her and Tom on the courthouse lawn, her white Ascension gown in her arms, the gown she'd sewn along with her mother back in the fall when she'd sworn she was going up. Although she found it hard to believe in God now, at least for herself, she wondered if Miss Betsey might take some comfort from that gown if she could at least touch it and feel the stitches Eveline had made once upon a time when she was someone who believed in goodness.

"Do you think they'll let you see her?" Tom asked.

Eveline looked straight ahead at the courthouse door. "All I can do is try."

"I'll wait for you here," he said.

It turned out that Sheriff Fyffe felt sorry for her. "I shouldn't say this," he said, "and if you tell anyone I did, I'll deny it, but just between you and me, that woman doesn't deserve to be hung. Any fool should be able to see that much."

Eveline said in a very small voice, "I just want to give her this." She lifted the Ascension gown as if she were offering it to Sheriff Fyffe.

"Reverend Seed baptized her last night, you know." Sheriff Fyffe picked up the brass ring that held a long key. "Come along," the sheriff said. "Just a few minutes."

Miss Betsey was brushing her hair, and the bristles made a gentle ripping sound as if she were carding wool. The first of the sun was slanting through the window in the cell. It fell across Miss Betsey's hair and brought a luster to it, that glorious black hair that Eveline had always envied.

When Miss Betsey lifted her face and saw her there with the sheriff, she stopped with her brush held in midair, and she made a noise, *oh*, as if someone had taken her breath.

Then she gathered herself. "Oh," she said. "It's you."

Sheriff Fyffe unlocked the cell door and motioned for Eveline to enter. "I'll be back directly," he said. He swung the door closed and locked it again. "Be quick with what you've come to say."

And what had she come to say? That was the question swirling through Eveline's head. That she was sorry? That she never meant for something like this to happen? That, like Sheriff Fyffe said, Miss Betsey shouldn't be facing the gallows? It was her fault, Eveline's. She knew that, and she felt certain Miss Betsey knew it, too. What words could make any difference at all?

"Eveline," Miss Betsey said, and her voice was unlike any Eveline had ever heard from her. A light voice, an accepting voice, one Eveline could have listened to forever. "Eveline, dear, what have you brought me?"

All Eveline could do was to unfold the Ascension gown and hold it before her.

"It's your gown," Miss Betsey said. She reached out her left hand and then caught herself, letting the hand hover, her fingers trembling. That's when Eveline knew that beneath the voice of calm, the voice that accepted her fate, Miss Betsey was afraid. "I used to think you so silly when you said you were going up. Now I know what that must have meant to you."

Finally, Eveline found her voice. "That seems like so long ago."

"It does," said Miss Betsey. "Look at how time goes."

"The Mister . . ." Eveline started and then stopped.

Miss Betsey laid her brush down on her bed. She picked up a piece of black ribbon, pulled her hair back, and tied it.

"I know you thought well of him," she said. "I hope he knew that, too. He was a man who didn't believe he had a right to much. He was a hard man to love."

"He was making you those candlesticks."

"I can't believe you remember that." Miss Betsey took in a sharp breath and put her hand to her mouth. Her voice, when she spoke, quavered. "I'd give anything to have them now."

Eveline reached out, then, and drew Miss Betsey to her. The Ascension gown between them, they wrapped their arms around each other.

"You were a girl back then," Miss Betsey finally said. "I was the one who should have known not to get too close to trouble." Eveline was crying now. "You go on," Miss Betsey said. "You go live your life."

Sheriff Fyffe was back. He was opening the cell door. "We have to move along now," he said in a gentle voice. "Day's a wasting."

Eveline didn't want to let Miss Betsey go. She thought that if she kept holding on, time would come to a standstill, the way a clock pendulum froze in mid-swing, and what was going to happen wouldn't. She knew she was a fool. She'd always been a fool. A foolish girl, Miss Betsey had called her more than once, and she'd been right.

"You're not the only mooncalf," Miss Betsey said, as if reading her mind, and Eveline wondered if what people said about her being a witch might be true. "I've been fool enough for both of us."

Finally, Eveline said the words she'd been trying to get out since she stepped inside the cell. "I'm sorry."

"Me, too," said Miss Betsey. "Sorry for so much. Go along now. That's all we can do."

It was only after she was outside on the courthouse lawn with Tom that she remembered the Ascension gown and how she'd left it on the floor of the cell, where it'd dropped when she moved away from Miss Betsey.

"My gown," she said. She took a few steps back toward the courthouse. Then she felt Tom grab her arm.

"It's too late," he said.

The sun was full up, and streams of people were passing by, their voices bright and gay as they made their way to the river.

∽⌇∼

"Such a day," a woman in the crowd said. "Lord-a-mercy."

And it was, a magnificent day near to summer. A balmy day, the sun splintering through the limbs of the giant maples along the riverbank, where already boys sat, looking down on the gallows, having shinnied and climbed up to their perches. The breeze stirred the leaves. The air smelled of the muddy river water and the wild onions growing on the banks, horse dung and wood smoke from cooking fires, hot grease and coffee. A number of folks from away had camped there the night before; some had come from Indiana and Kentucky and Missouri, and one man playing a Jew's harp and dancing a jig claimed to have made the trip from Tennessee. The honeysuckle was just beginning to bloom along the edge of the woods, and its perfume was fragrant. Swallowtail butterflies, black and tiger and zebra and spicebush and pipevine, fed at the blossoms. Ruby-throated hummingbirds hovered and darted and dipped.

Music played—fiddles and concertinas and mouth harps. People called out to those they knew in the crowd. *Hey there, Burley! Did you ever think you'd see it? A woman strung up? What a show.*

Drummers sold miniature gallows, whittled from pine, with nooses wrapped from twine. "Get you one," a barker with a long neck and a big Adam's apple said. "Prove that you were here the day they hung the glassmaker's wife."

"Mercy," Eveline said to Tom, that one word. Mercy for the day and everything that seemed too noisy and big. Mercy for the people who'd come to bear witness. Mercy for the girl Eveline had been. Mercy, most of all, for Miss Betsey.

"Here she comes," said Tom, and soon others in the crowd were shouting and pointing, and the boys sitting on the limbs of the maple trees were hooting and waving their hats.

Eveline saw the wagon coming up the hill. Sheriff Fyffe was laying to the reins, urging the two draft horses on. The Reverend Seed sat beside him, his back straight, his chin lifted, his Bible in his lap. Behind the bench seat, in the wagon proper, Miss Betsey rode atop a pine coffin. Eveline's heart thumped when she realized that Miss Betsey was wearing her Ascension gown.

The crowd's noise died down, and the throng of people parted to let the wagon pass. Eveline could hear the wagon bed creak and the horses snort and the leather reins slap their backs as Sheriff Fyffe called out, "Get up. Get up now. Get up."

Such labor to get that wagon to the gallows at the top of the hill. And all the while, Miss Betsey was singing. Eveline nearly crumpled to the ground to hear her—if Tom weren't there to hold her up, she very well might have—because the song Miss Betsey was singing was the Second Advent hymn that Eveline had sung so often when drawing water from the Reeds' cistern. She recalled the earnest girl she'd been. She missed that girl and the joy she'd felt, a joy she feared would never come again.

But here was Miss Betsey, her voice growing stronger, singing, "Awake, awake from sleeping." Singing, "Attend the midnight cry." Eveline felt her lips moving, whispering the rest, "Ye saints, refrain from weeping. Your Great Deliverer's nigh." She sang along with Miss Betsey while the wagon made its way up the hill.

Then Sheriff Fyffe was leading Miss Betsey up the steps to the scaffold. She never stopped singing. She sang while the Reverend Seed prayed for her soul. She sang while the hangman tied her hands behind her, then tightened the noose around her neck and placed the black hood over her head.

And Eveline sang with her, sang every word of every hymn that Miss Betsey knew. The sun was up above the tree line now. Eveline shaded her eyes with her hand, but still everything splintered around her, broke apart. The gallows, Miss Betsey, the hangman, the gleaming blade of the ax he'd soon use to cut the rope and spring the trap. Eveline saw it all in pieces: the sun's rays through the maple leaves, the boot soles of the boys sitting on a limb, a corner of the black hood, the coiled noose, and then, so quick it took Eveline's breath away, the trap springing open, the violent drop of Miss Betsey's body, the way it turned round and round, twisting at the end of the rope.

Eveline told herself not to look away from this thing she'd wrought, to take it inside her, to feel the regret that would never be far from her all the rest of her days. Already she was beginning to forget what it felt like when the Mister painted her eyes, when he held her to him, when she ate the finely ground glass, or the way it made her swoon to sit with Miss Betsey and read the letters from the lovelorn in *Godey's Lady's Book*. The small pleasures—the pretty things, the Mister called his glassware—the fragile, beautiful charms of a life.

Finally, Tom said to her, "Are you ready?"

"Ready?" she said.

"To go home."

He took her hand, and together they came down from the hill. She was amazed to see her feet, one in front of the other as she moved over the grass and on through the day, a day that was full upon her now, bright and clear.